W0050155

PENGUIN BOOKS

A DAY IN THE LIFE

Anjum Hasan is the author of three novels—*The Cosmopolitans*, *Lunatic in my Head* (both shortlisted for the Crossword Book Award) and *Neti Neti* (shortlisted for the Hindu Literary Prize)—as well as a book of short stories, *Difficult Pleasures*, shortlisted for the Crossword Book Award and the Hindu Literary Prize, and a book of poems. She lives in Bangalore.

PRAISE FOR THIS BOOK

'Craftily written . . . The elegant, pondered and deep-reaching prose of this collection allows subversive humour to surface effortlessly . . . Hasan has honed the adroitness of the chameleon, blending in all corners of a contemporary India'—*The Hindu*

'Anjum Hasan's writing has never lacked craft or perspective. The fourteen stories in *A Day in the Life*, Hasan's sixth book, surpass her own exacting standards. The tenor might be meditative, but the prose is light-footed, spry, often droll, sometimes downright wicked . . . Whether the protagonists feel at home or (more often) out of place, the places themselves are evoked with detail and tenderness . . . At their heart, Hasan's tales are investigations of the question of belonging'—*India Today*

'Hasan's prose is introspective, carefully observed, and imbued with more than what is said. This is a slow, reflective prose of indirection, of startling and poetic images, of characters who are outsiders, standing at the margins, who look at the landscape from an angle, of narrators who have more to tell us than what they say . . . Hasan's gaze is clear-sighted and unflinching as she writes about urban life . . . A finely crafted collection'—*Indian Express*

'Placing characters from different classes, religions, and moral outlooks alongside each other, Hasan delicately puts different milieus in conversation . . . Often, the insights in *A Day In The Life* emerge from absurd encounters between very different people, and Hasan's subversiveness in creating quirky occurrences in routine lives is delightful'—*Mint*

'To read *A Day In the Life* is to experience the distinctive contentment that the form of the short story provides . . . These moving, subtly devastating and somehow impossibly humorous stories are meticulously crafted, but they succeed as they do only because they are shot throughout with an astounding degree of empathy. Hasan handles her characters with a dignity and affection that is infectious, as they try, with whatever tools they have at their disposal, simply to make sense of it all'—Scroll.in

'Anjum Hasan's short stories are to be savoured for their quiet sophistication and power . . . [A] remarkable, radiant collection of short fiction . . . *A Day in the Life* sets out to examine, interrogate and sometimes resolve the quotidian in the sparkling—sometimes funny . . . but *always* apt—prose Hasan is known for . . . Keep this book by your bedside, on the table, and during comings and goings, as the week waxes and wanes, taste it between meals, after dessert or on the run. The return of the short story has been almost perfectly timed for revenge'—*Open*

'*A Day in the Life*, set in varied locales across the country, offers a medley of characters, experiences and situations that are not only relatable but beautifully etched, realistic portrayals displaying different levels of inner angst in an extremely nuanced manner'—*New Indian Express*

'This collection of fourteen intricately-crafted short stories offer a happy and eminently readable blend of character, setting and style. These miniature portraits detail lives of ordinary people in today's impersonal, mechanical urban societies playing out to reveal fascinating insights'—*Deccan Herald*

'In *A Day In The Life*, author Anjum Hasan views life from close quarters and presents an extremely intelligent take on daily living. Dreams, achievements, foibles, misgivings, triumphs, compromises; her characters epitomise a wide spectrum of human emotions . . . Her stories are shining beads that together transmute into a breathtaking necklace'—*Tribune*

'Almost all the stories are stamped with Ms Hasan's unique style, which never hurries, is always in control . . . She [writes] with extraordinary skill. Her concerns might be quotidian, but they manage to capture something of the zeitgeist of our times'—*Business Standard*

'Remarkable and insightful . . . Engrossing . . . Elegant'—Hansda Sowvendra Shekhar, *National Herald*

'A special mix of storytelling and sly memoir. If literature's task is to describe what it means to be alive, Anjum Hasan is particularly good at capturing life during times of change. Whether writing about present-day Bangalore or Benares in an earlier century, Stockholm or Shillong, she is always an alert and thoughtful observer. And every few lines, there is a turn, a word, or a question, that makes the heart thud'—Amitava Kumar

PRAISE FOR *THE COSMOPOLITANS*

'*The Cosmopolitans* is leavened with enough wit and irony to make for an engaging, uplifting read. As intense and cerebral as the novel is and as relevant as the questions are, this is also possibly the most fun Hasan has had with a novel. There's a lightness of touch, bordering on the zany, that serves the core ideas well. Pick up *The Cosmopolitans* to read an author at the peak of her powers, long may they last'—*Mint*

'Fiercely intelligent . . . Hasan, who made us aware of her mastery of craft in her debut novel, *Lunatic in My Head*, now gives us a novel of ideas, one that is utterly necessary in an India where money is the only antibiotic that passes for both diagnosis and cure . . . *The Cosmopolitans* is a must-read'—*Indian Express*

'Anjum Hasan's new book is that rare thing: a novel of ideas, a novel that questions assumptions, a novel that celebrates woman outside the home . . . Qayenaat is a rootless woman, a failed artist. She is what a man has been in so many novels—and whom we accepted and applauded as the hero in search of himself . . . The remarkable thing about Hasan's novel is that it forces you to have a conversation with yourself: and it has been quite some time since a novel has been so intellectually provocative'—*India Today*

'Chock-full of irony . . . A tantalizing novel about art and artists . . . Hasan's precise, poetic voice soars . . . scrupulous and affectionate, and a joy to read . . . Lyrical'—*Open*

'Hasan covers a vast fictional and ideological terrain. Artistic freedom and its accompanying responsibilities, money, intellectual and artistic pretensions, sociocultural intolerance, the resurrection of brutal practices in the guise of "tradition"—all these find their way into her comédie humaine. The result is a novel that nudges the reader with familiar if uncomfortable questions and innuendoes . . . *The Cosmopolitans* is an unusual read in the ways it holds up a mirror to contemporary India . . . It reminds us of too many things we should address but would rather let alone'—*Hindustan Times*

'What is skillfully evoked in the novel is the precarious position of those Indians who do not fall into assigned gender roles, or rigid categories of caste and community. And yet they have to negotiate life among others who identify strongly with these man-made boundaries'—*Deccan Herald*

'Hasan effortlessly creates a mélange of complex characters . . . Just like her previous works, Hasan's poetic prose resonates with the reader the entire length of [*The Cosmopolitans*]'—*Tehelka*

'The reader seamlessly enters Qayenaat's stream of consciousness, aching with her as her old love for Baban erupts, biting nails as the romantic status continues to linger in a gray zone, worrying over Qayenaat's monetary hassles, wallowing blissfully in the angst of middle-class Bangalore while groaning over the fading of old traditions and arrival of the technological boom concentrated in the snazzy area of Whitefield . . . Hasan's mastery over the fiction form fuses both parts [of the novel] with exquisite craftsmanship. Hers is the innate magic with words and plots where delightful similes tumble around with gay abandon, and humour lights up even the darkest areas. The prose is rich, nuanced and riveting . . . A writer's writer, Hasan's prose can stimulate the average reader as well as the discerning one . . . *The Cosmopolitans* is a precious novel, to be read, shared, discussed and revisited every once in a while'
—*New Indian Express*

'Skilfully interweaving India's many separate and rapidly changing worlds, Anjum Hasan brings an ironic and subtle intelligence to a great novelistic theme: superfluous men and women lurching out of a decayed old order, exposed to the conflicts and tensions of an endless transition'
—Pankaj Mishra

'Perspicacious, funny, and at times profound, *The Cosmopolitans* gives us an unusual, compelling portrait of India today precisely because it shuns the well-worn formulations of the "state-of-the-nation novel". An ambitious and oddly tender book by a poised, highly intelligent writer'
—Amit Chaudhuri

'A book of constant surprises . . . Hasan's deceptively simple and elegant prose, her lush and graphic descriptions throw open arcane concepts'
—*DNA*

'*The Cosmopolitans* is an intellectual novel, and punctures with sophistication the eponymous quiet cosmopolitanism of its nature and structure, with several clever surprises'—Scroll.in

'This is a major novel, dense, rich, complex, especially raising questions about notions of love and the lives of women today . . . Anjum Hasan has joined the outstanding Indian writers, cosmopolitans of our time'
—*Journal of Post-Colonial Writing*

'Delicious collection of short stories . . . Hasan has done a masterly job placing these stories before us like delicate, translucent slivers of life'
—*India Today*

'The short stories are masterfully crafted, and examine people and their relationships through a lens that is at once thoughtful, critical and ironic'—*People*

'While many are brutally honest in admitting the fact that the short story is a genre struggling hard under the shadow of its mightier cousin, the novel, the arrival of a collection of short stories like *Difficult Pleasures* . . . busts all such myths'—*Telegraph*

'These are humane, unshowy tales that depend more on character than on plot for their effects, and the best of them . . . are moving and eloquent'
—*Indian Express*

'Each of the thirteen stories is a gem . . . Beautifully told and effortlessly written'—*Tribune*

'The lyrical style and intricate detailing of her characters' inner selves that was evident in her novels works even better in this collection of short stories'—*DNA*

'Think of the book as a collection of prose photographs, each deftly capturing some version of the urban Indian. You can look at them from a distance while still falling into their lives'—*Tehelka*

PRAISE FOR *NETI, NETI*

'Hasan is an assured writer . . . This is a novel that will speak to a generation'
—*Indian Express*

'One has heard of the Delhi novel and the Bombay novel, and finally, here's a Bangalore novel'—*DNA*

'Hasan is . . . an artist with her words. There is writerly accomplishment in every turn of phrase'—*Deccan Herald*

'*Neti, Neti* can legitimately claim to be the definitive "new Bangalore" novel'
—*Mint*

a
DAY IN THE
LIFE
STORIES

Anjum Hasan

PENGUIN

An imprint of Penguin Random House

PENGUIN BOOKS

USA | Canada | UK | Ireland | Australia
New Zealand | India | South Africa | China | Singapore

Penguin Books is part of the Penguin Random House group of companies
whose addresses can be found at global.penguinrandomhouse.com

Published by Penguin Random House India Pvt. Ltd
4th Floor, Capital Tower 1, MG Road,
Gurugram 122 002, Haryana, India

First published in Hamish Hamilton by Penguin Random House India 2018
This edition published 2019

ISBN 9780143447207

Typeset in Adobe Garamond Pro by Manipal Digital Systems, Manipal

Printed at Manipal Technologies Limited, India

www.penguin.co.in

This is a legitimate digitally printed version of the book and therefore might not
have certain extra finishing on the cover.

For Vijay Nambisan, who is missed.
And for Kavery.

CONTENTS

CONTENTS

1

THE STRANGER

There were no new ideas to be found in the city so I retired last year to this small town—an experiment to see if I could live in a house with a tiled roof that sometimes leaked and little storybook windows that muffled rather than let in light. Four months straight it rained with pounding urgency, bookended by two of drizzle. Sentences that I thought had no currency any more, not in the twenty-first century, still applied here, in this drenched hill town. *It was a dark and stormy night.* Or, *The wind howled in the trees and loudly rattled the windowpanes.*

One could imagine a very old place, a sparser and hardier monsoon existence hidden in the folds of the green valleys, even though they'd been killing off the vestiges in recent years—building hotels over the Christian graveyards and glassy shopping complexes where there'd been trees and empty space. Still, a few bungalows with compounds and driveways from a hundred years ago remained, and in the bazaar lots of those crooked little two-storey split-level shophouses with wooden casements, which too must have been here at least since the British were writing in their gazetteers about who was up to exactly what business in the district. With the rain and the daily power-cuts, the Gothic mist creeping over everything all the time in season and the silence that lay over the hedgerows in the lanes away from the town centre, this was still a place where you could play at being someone else.

I'd seemed to be coasting along like everyone else in the city but was really eyeing something deeper—a love affair or a glittering friendship. I was lonely and didn't see it. When this hit me, when I turned forty, then forty-five, and still felt unmade and unresolved, still chasing something just around the corner, I stopped. I had some money from two decades in the industry—if not scaling the heights of the corporate ladder, then not sliding down it either. Enough to ride on for a few years if I yielded all ambition, so that's what I decided to do. Become nobody or, at least, a sincerely regular man. Cease thinking I was going to get anywhere either in the realm of intellectual achievement or human relations.

What can better aid coming down to earth than a half-forgotten small town: that stained suburban air, the permanent emanations of open sewers and busy bakeries? A whole population's worth of people with reduced hopes, happy to cut their coats according to their cloth.

I've been here almost a year now, one monsoon to the next, and I have a house of three small rooms which is too big for me, a talkative cook in a burka and a target of getting through all the mouldy books in the back rows of the local library, which no one seems to have touched since circa Independence. I do try to give some kind of shape to my days—watching the blackbirds with my morning coffee; walking with the late afternoon sun when there is one; helping, because I was inveigled into it, the landlord's middle-school-going boy and girl with their homework; just sitting around reading in the evenings as I drink brandy with hot water, or bad wine, or whisky with ice on summer nights when it's really warm and I'm feeling like I might start to be sorry for myself. Who was it who said Proust's pinings and dissatisfaction represented the illness of the cultivated classes in a capitalistic society? I'm trying, with the benevolent aid of my neighbourhood liquor store, to undo my cultivation, and sometimes casting off these chains can hurt.

I wake up in the dark: it could be 4 a.m. or well past seven. The clacking rhythm of rain on the roof seems to be saying, I'm here to stay. *Okay*, I tell it. *I can live with you*. It's all right to wake up in an indeterminable darkness, not knowing what day of the week it is, and no longer needing to call up the thought of the project I'm working on or dwell on the inexorable nature of modern work. I stay in bed till Amina bangs on the door. The bell's stopped working.

'Is it Tuesday, Amina?'

'I don't know. I just fell.'

I look at her left hand, cradled in her right. 'You haven't broken it?'

She glares at me. There's a thick, determined moss everywhere, and layers of black mould and grey lichen on the compound paving, mushrooms growing from fallen branches, grass sprouting from gaps in the roof tiles—a whole rain-fed lushness trying to break out of the earth and swallow the town.

Amina's burka is soaked on one side and her kohl-lined eyes a little teary. I ask if she wants me to take her to a doctor. 'I'll go home and see. Can't move it just now but it might be better tomorrow.'

'Go by the pharmacy and get some painkillers at least.'

'Don't know if the shops are open. They burnt the Koran last evening, those bastards. Sons of bastards. I heard about it on my way here.'

'Again?' I ask, startled. But it was different in the winter—someone had stoned the mosque in a nearby taluk. The explanation in the bazaar was that it was all 'political', meaning that someone had been paid or instigated to do it. A riot was said to be brewing and protest marches were undertaken, the town shut down, then the pressure of the incident dissipated.

'They burn the Koran Sharif. Someone should die for this.'

But she says it in the voice of one who is expected to be outraged and in an idiom that is clichéd, borrowed. She is more upset about her hand. She abuses the rain with quaint curses in pidgin Urdu and takes the money and analgesics I give her.

'What will you eat?' she asks.

She knows I could easily walk down to town and have lunch in any of the small places lining the main road, but perhaps she's come to believe that I'll be wretched without her daily meat curries. More than the food, it's the liveliness of her talk that interests me—her ongoing account of her ladies'-tailor husband who has recently transformed himself into a chauffeur in Dubai, her persistently ailing mother-in-law and untameable teenage twin boys, her never-sedate life in the Muslim neighbourhood of squashed houses strung out along Ganapati Street. But there is also something haughty and inscrutable about her hooded face; she seems to, without saying it, disdain her job of cooking for me and two other families, while at the same time seeing herself as indispensable to us. Her eyes are too proud to be a servant's, and she cooks messily and talks loudly. She seems to be waiting for some chance to break out of her role, yet never mutes her tirade or pauses in her narrative, never gives the listener a chance. She has absolutely no curiosity about me even though she cannot have known too many layabouts in her life, grown men with nothing to do.

She goes away, planting slow, firm steps across the compound, and I watch the rain for a while, how it levels out the world.

Today, or a century ago, the same rain, falling on the same landscape, feeding the roots of the same deciduous hill forests, softening the clay of the same roof tiles. Yet a contemporary sordidness intrudes, the actions of men that deliver this place into the present. They're not interested in the eternal wind soughing through the wet palms and the old stone plaques strewn around that record the building of the town. They want to, however crudely, make an impression on the world right now. So something is always going on here—speeches, counter speeches, political factionalism, communal stirrings, debates on who owns the land and who came before whom. They burnt a Koran. I think of that word—*burn*, the crisp, dry flavour of it—and how unconvincing it seems in this sodden weather.

I drink some coffee, then return to bed. I don't have a reason to wake up just yet. In fact, I could spend all day huddled here, thinking of nothing in particular, dozing my life away. I know other people who've cut loose, but always in order to do something extravagant, Judgement Day–worthy, or at least Facebook-worthy—become missionary organic farmers or theatre actors or adamantine travellers. I wonder if the practice of indolence and the foregoing of expectation isn't also a freelance art—a forgotten one in this whirring age of profit-driven action, no matter if that hoped-for profit is in hard cash or personality development. As for me, I'm not looking to have my personality developed.

But living here, I am starting to become aware of another side to my existence, a richer pretence I am drawn to. I'm not grumpy, I realize, just unsuited to my era. I dropped into the wrong time; I can't shake off this sense of misplacement. I stay in bed all through the bone-chilling morning, and the world, despite what I know about the heated talk in town, is just a square patch of blurred rooftops on the hillside. *He was a man who spent a great many*

years in splendid isolation. I am like some old-time explorer who
has located the object of his search and, having found it, now
wants nothing more than to live among the natives, sending out
dispatches celebrating his discovery. What would those reports say?

I finally rise. The power's out; I warm bathwater in a cooking
pot, disturbed by a vague feeling of withdrawal. Having spent too
many years in the connected world, I can still sometimes feel haunted
by it—the cries of unanswered emails, phone calls, messages, all
faintly audible in the silence of my new life. The ghosts of habits
past. There are transmission towers poking out from among the
houses and trees in the watercolour view from my window, and
cybercafes in the bazaar. Of course I'm not in splendid isolation.
But there are not many people I've remained in touch with, and of
the few I know, none's birthday is today as far as I can remember.

It's good to get out in the small, friendly patch of rainlessness
the morning offers. I walk down the lanes and the steep, slippery
steps cut into winding slopes and go into Hajee Hotel, which
is packed with town-visiting farmhands, shop assistants and
rickshaw drivers having lunch. The waiter I know scratches his
stubble and salaams. He has worked here for exactly thirty years,
and the place itself is not much older than that. Yet he's never not
cheerful, consistently unbothered by sameness. That's the small
town for you. He takes my order, informing me, as if it's the day's
news, that it will rain for another two months. I ask him about the
trouble. He says it's a sham. Someone's been spreading stories. No
Koran was actually burnt.

I'm sharing a table with an old man who has curly white
eyebrows and wide, watery eyes—dignified, shabbily dressed—
and is eating his lunch with the slow-motion leisureliness of
someone disinterested in time. He stares at me as if I'm inanimate
and then abruptly stops chewing and starts to speak.

'Which place, your native?'

'This place for now.'

'Tourist?'

'No, I live here. House, furniture, cook . . . full arrangement.'

He finds this amusing. 'Retired?' he asks.

How did he guess? I must look greatly unburdened, if not prematurely old.

'Myself retired also,' he volunteers, then goes silent to eat.

When he finishes, he says, 'Second World War.'

I notice how his accent sharpens when he pronounces those words, the sudden inflection of pride.

'Burma,' he says. 'Three years. Myself.'

Can he really be that old? I have been dreaming this morning of belonging to another time and here is this man before me who actually does. The war is all Commando comics for me—Spitfires and Dakotas and the Allies in airmen goggles deploying their swagger in the skies. I've never encountered anything of the war first-hand and know nothing about its eastern front.

'What did you do?'

'I was a batman. Driving my officer. The captain. Cleaning his kit. Helping in the surgery. Stretcher-bearer. All kinds of work. Very hard fighting. So many died. My captain survived.'

He pulls at the front of his perhaps war-era grey sweater, as if tugging at another person. 'Myself veteran,' he says, laughing. 'Second World War.'

'What's your age, sir?'

'Ninety, ninety-five,' he says proudly.

'Will you have some tea?'

He is happy to have tea and continues talking as I eat. The English captain and the Indians under his command fought the Japanese and their friends—those other Indians of Netaji's army—and this man was there, helping to bring back the dead and the dying, holding up lanterns so the doctors could operate through the night, seeing bridges, roads and airfields laid out by the Allies and whole camps blown away by the enemy, keeping his captain's boots shiny no matter the circumstances, driving him through blizzards of fire, and waiting out days of monsoon inaction. Now he lives an apparently normal life in Pension Lane, up on that very hill I can see from my window.

He says he walks into town a couple of times a week to follow up about some payments due to him from the Solider Welfare and Resettlement Office on the main street. He has friends there, he says. They're working on his case. Then he tells of his life in the years following the war.

'When I come back, I work for the same captain, as before. Cook for him and his family. Gardening. He had a house here. After two years, he gone. Independence. But he was born here, you know. This town. His father also army man. Come here from Madras. Not go back. He's buried here—in Protestant cemetery.'

He asks me about my family. I shrug, tell him I'm not married. He finishes his tea and gets up, seeming to have recalled something, shaking my hand and walking off as if summoned by the past he's been reliving. I chat with my waiter, Ahmed, whose leading joy are his two children—because they go to the convent and have outsmarted him, with his own connivance. They will never wait tables like him.

If I miss anything from the city, it is hanging out weekends in that cafe at the corner of 80 Feet Road and Devasthana Road, with its shelf of thrillers and worn-out board games, stodgy cane furniture and sturdy espressos, run by a man called Shanmugan, who had missed, by a few years, belonging to the generation that called every business a start-up and every visit to a foreign country an off-site trip. That place must have had a spot of neighbourhood glamour once, but by the time I found it, the shisha bars and microbreweries had nearly snuffed it out; only college couples stretching their pocket money came there any more, and the waiters from Kalimpong and Siliguri slouched and strutted, with plenty of time to fix their hair and work the pool table. I would talk with Shanmugan, whom I grew to like. He had a slightly shady, nervous look, like he indulged in too much online porn, but he was a good, interested reader of the novels and analytical books of the day, and had cynical views on everything—the software industry was a con, the hipster restaurants were a bubble, the real-estate prices were a scandal sky-high. The friend or two of his who dropped by were exactly like him—happy with, yet not sorry to get away from, wives and children; not failures but on the wrong side of success. We'd hang out and I'd lose my usual estrangement. The tenor of this set of guys who were some years older to me suited mine perfectly—that underlying sense of one's present becoming past, the script starting to run out of one's hands.

Here in Hajee, the talk has a different drift or none at all. The working men don't waste time on conversation while they eat, and their eyes burn with the night's alcohol or the day's anxieties as they lock into the food. There is something about a hungry man eating—old hunger, remembered hunger. They may be earning enough to feed themselves but they still know all too well—one slip and down the hole you go. You can see that terror in the near-feverish haste with which they tear into their parathas and slurp their gravy. I have moved on from Shan's Cafe, I think. Having connected briefly with that man who fought in an ancient war and who doesn't and cannot know anything about me, and watching these others who eat with their almost shocking need clear on their faces, I am closer to the truth about something.

I leave Hajee and walk around without definite purpose in the shop-filled streets with their slowed-down monsoon commerce as the rain starts again, and near the town hall I run into my landlord, Sujay Gowda. We step away from the downpour and he asks me if I've given his proposition thought.

'I have, I have. Let me settle down and then we'll talk.'

Gowda is always trying to get me to become useful: buy a bit of land on the outskirts to cultivate or go into business and start a made-to-order furniture or agricultural implements shop with him. He is hugely industrious; he works in a bank but is also part-time farmer and real-estate agent—the link between the old ones with the land and status who want to sell and the new and newly prosperous ones reaching out from the much bigger town nearby who want to buy. Gowda always has a whiff of intrigue about him; one can practically hear in his easy, frequent guffaw the whisper of dirty business, black money, stashed secrets. But all on a Gowda scale, for there is nothing oversized about his operations. The same capitalist manoeuvres that in the city would bore with the extent of their bamboozling become interesting and accessible to me in Gowda's case. He is a small, fat, utterly canny fish in the big, infested pond. He confirms now that a Koran has been burnt and the town is to shut down.

'I thought it was a rumour.'

'No, no,' he replies contentedly. 'For sure it has happened. It is all political, you see.'

It is not clear to what extent the political enables or impedes him. In the end, what everyone wants, these interludes of engineered hatred notwithstanding, is to make money. The buildings that are starting to eat the slope of my hill proclaim this truth. Gowda doesn't need to spell it out. I tell him I met an old man who'd fought in the war.

'Mr Vincent C. Rodrigues. He remembers the *firang*s. Ask him and he'll tell you how they took over the Virabhadra Temple, built that church right over it. It's a museum now. And the life they led in the bungalows. Ask him. He's seen it all come up and go down.'

Gowda laughs, then advises me to fire Amina and have his wife send me my meals for less money. 'She is cooking anyway, you see, so no extra work. And what about the whisky?'

He has dispensed with the British history of the town in the most marvellously succinct way. Maybe that was all there was to it—arrival, takeover, a church, bungalows, the war, departure and a man who has some recollection of it all. I think of the historical filter through which Vincent C. Rodrigues probably sees this town—the phantom outlines of things that I've only read about in the library. Where we see the small bungalows of today, he sees that much grander one, now vanished, built by an early-nineteenth-century raja to house his European guests; where we see electronic-goods shops, he sees those selling tinned peaches and crocheting thread supplied from Madras; where the shopping arcades are now, he sees the regimental messes dating from when this became a British cantonment town; he sees the stone-marked boundaries of the several military stations that comprised it; he sees the church before it became a museum and hears the words of the Sunday sermon in it; he sees the emptiness of the hills, that original greenness I've been hankering for. He sees these things without awe or angst—they are simply the facts of his memories.

Gowda is on his phone, informing someone that he dislikes the talk they're giving him. Then asks me again about the whisky. We have a plan to drink together. I suggest that evening, and he says he will get his wife to fry some fish if I come over. He and his family live in a new concrete mansion they have raised next door, though they once, in some humbler time, occupied the old house I now do. I thank him, then change the subject so as not to bring up Amina again, but he is busy suddenly, on another call, rushing off without goodbyes. I remain standing there in the building's porch. Slowed by the rain's rhythm, I am dreaming again of having known another—more languid—time, despite the speed at which Gowda took off, the cars whizzing by and the hectic disco thump of the music coming from within the town-hall auditorium where schoolchildren seem to be practising for some Independence Day extravaganza.

On another rainy afternoon like this, in my early days here, I'd visited an elderly doctor with that most mundane of office-derived illnesses, a dysfunctional back. Examining it and declaring me to be, in pathological terms, spineless, he'd told me, as well, that from the time he was a child till circa 2005, everything about this town had been more or less the same. The place I saw before me was the result of a mere decade of upheaval. I was witnessing the remaking, in crazy haste, of what had been left unbothered over a lifetime. My back hurts at that thought, or at the memory of the doctor's diagnosis, and I plunge into the rain, heading to the pharmacy to replace the painkillers I've given Amina.

Vincent C. Rodrigues is there, buying masses of pills. The pharmacist nods at me without interrupting the conversation he is having about the burnt Koran. The Muslims want to stage a big protest—several hundred people strong—but have been denied permission to do it, he says. If they can't go ahead, they'll boycott the next election.

'All political,' he says.

Rodrigues doesn't respond to that. He blinks at me and says, 'Hello.'

He seems to have forgotten we just met but then he asks, 'So . . . your family . . . What happened?'

'Oh, I'm all right.'

He turns to the pharmacist and declares, 'Bachelor.' They both look at me, my thinning hair and thickening paunch, and seem from their expressions to be waiting for some accounting for the tragedy. No one is a bachelor by choice, it appears. There's never a story in marriage and children, that universally common fate, but always one expected from someone who has evaded or been denied these things.

I have long exhausted the subject, so just ask for my medicines, then say to Rodrigues, 'Is it still around? The house you worked in?'

But he is waving some papers he has with him, suddenly agitated. The pharmacist tells me about it in more coherent English than the old man can muster. Rodrigues needs new glasses. He thought he could get the soldier-welfare people to cover it but they've been taking for ever. He had to register to begin with, and it was trouble to organize any proof of address because everything is in the name of the son he lives with. Then he waited three months and the promised smart card came. He promptly lost it—it slipped from him on one of his walks into town—and he had to apply for another. When that came after another delay, he was told that he'd been misinformed—ex-servicemen are not automatically entitled to spectacles unless they've had cataract surgery. He can, however, apply for a Spectacle Grant, for which he must submit an eye-test report from an approved hospital and original medical receipts.

'They must be countersigned on reverse by attending doctor. We are trying to find out which hospital is the right one. I want to help him but it is complicated,' says the pharmacist ruefully. I realize Rodrigues was being optimistic when he called the men in the welfare office his friends.

'We go,' he says, happy that I am now fully apprised of his story. 'I show you the house.'

I am going for a walk with the man who sees the town through impossibly old eyes. He takes his time, stopping to greet people or being stopped by them. Everyone likes a bit of bonhomie. Urban speed has entered their lives but not yet taken it over altogether.

Then we are walking uphill, towards the stonewalled convent school, and the buzz of the street fades away in minutes. Rodrigues tells me about his family—the great-grandchildren, the granddaughters-in-law and two grandsons, the son who has spawned all this. I hope he doesn't ask me again about mine. I had admitted defeat years ago when I couldn't marry the girl I was meaning to. She decided she was better suited to a man who, on the face of it, was no different from me. Study our curriculum vitae and you won't be able to tell us apart. The same pragmatic educational path, the same sort of job profile and bank balance and leisure preferences, the same coming of age with the stink of newly minted middle-class wealth in our nostrils. And yet we had absolutely nothing in common—except the girl. She was friends with us both and tried to ally us, as if her own confusion about which one she wanted could only be resolved if we became buddies. We met a few times and discussed that at once most potent and most sterile of subjects: politics. He was an ordinary bigot—that by now familiar combination of right-wing loyalty, free-market compulsiveness, distaste for the poor and excitement at the economic ascendance of India. Like me, he holidayed in Europe and bragged online about it; like me, he had jumped four jobs in ten years only for the money. Yet I looked at him tongue-tied, unable to shape words out of my liberalism with which to condemn him. I condemned him to her and so, illogically, she chose him, while I decided to keep an eye out for someone vulnerable to twenty-first-century disquiet. No one turned up.

'This is where,' says Rodrigues. He smiles and opens his umbrella slowly, unperturbed by the fresh gusts of wet wind that have already drenched us both. The bungalow before us, made nebulous by the rain, standing in a wasted garden of overgrown grass and two stumpy trees, seems to be a trick of the imagination. How is it that in a town so intent on movement, so desperately forward-looking, there also exist such forgotten relics? Rodrigues seems to have conjured up the place with his talk of the war. I have covered this lane on my walks, seen an old, mossed-over well farther up, near one of those fading plaques from the previous century: *In grateful memory of the late Mrs Philips by whose generosity the municipality was enabled to build the neighbouring houses for poor cowlis and to lessen the congestion in the Cowli Bazaar.* But I'm quite sure I've never seen this Rodrigues bungalow before.

I think of my own house as an antiquity, its black-tarred outer walls and cracked floor, but this specimen before me is even more thrillingly ramshackle. The tiles, muddied by decades of monsoons, are drooping over the awnings, and the wooden posts holding the roof up over the veranda are bent and sagging like damp matchsticks. The walls are stark white, and the doors and window frames a colour no longer favoured by house painters—a sombre shade one could describe as dark leaf-green. There are two low storeys in front, with a higher pitched roof of the same tiles over the single floor at the back. Despite the spectral quality of the house, people live here. There are curtains in the windows, the disintegrating roof has been papered over with bits of corrugated tin, and the acacia trees have been trimmed of most of their branches.

Vincent C. Rodrigues shuffles up the dangerously slick mud track through the garden and bangs officiously on the door pane.

A hunched woman with a face that doesn't seem to match her aged frame appears at once and Rodrigues pulls the door wide open for me without looking at her, ordering her to make us some coffee.

'Owner outside,' he explains. 'Hotel business in Abu Dhabi. Big business.'

The lady retainer who smiles courteously at us and doesn't question our intrusion is, it turns out, also some kind of distant relative of the family; she lives here with her daughter, a student at the nursing college, and is just about able to keep the place together by the look—and smell—of it. The historical reek of mould comes off the wicker chair in which I'm invited to sit and from the damp carpet at our feet. On the shelves are colour holiday photos of the present houseowners, but on one wall is a portrait, black and grey, of Rodrigues's bewhiskered captain with his family, a time-worn picture in an oval frame, covered in spotty glass. It seems to have been left behind there rather than installed.

In broken bits of English, he tells me that his boss was a reasonable man, as was his wife, who took Rodrigues's wife into the household staff when they were married. The couple left them a bit of money when they decamped in 1947. But the Englishman up the road was a terror who kicked him.

'He kicked you?'

'Here,' he says, rubbing his shins.

'Big fat man, I small boy. I worked in his orchard when I was a child. He owner of many orchards. Richest man in town. But he much angry. If we don't collect fruit quickly, he kick us. If we lie down to rest, he kick us. He also had a whip. Some people got whipped. I kicked. Then war came and I told the captain I wanted job with him. He said war is going on. You can come with me to Burma. Be my batman.'

'And that was lucky for you?'

'I speak English, that's why. Other fellows not speaking much English.'

There was Empire and then there were the assorted individual actions of the people who created and ran it, and these two are very nearly but not exactly the same thing. Why am I so keen on the past, sitting in this fusty living-room and hearing these stories, happy in a way I never was in the city, not even in Shan's Cafe. It is not, I realize—as lukewarm coffee and soggy biscuits are served, and the lady tells Rodrigues with shy pride that her daughter will be a nurse by the end of the year—that I see the old as unqualifiedly better. But I know this to be true: despite all the hulking new constructions filling the air, it is actually memories that form a deeper permanency. Nothing is as vivid as the pain from a blow received eighty years ago. This crumbling house is made solid by the fact that he once worked here, took care of the people who filled its rooms. He learnt to cook English food, he tells me—roast and bake and stew.

'I can send my grandson. Cooking for you,' he says suddenly. 'Everything he know. South Indian, north Indian.

An uncalled-for profusion of cooks. I tell him I already have someone, while he tells me that the boy recently lost his job at a Bangalore hotel because he'd been hired short-term without guarantees and after a year the management got cheap and wanted to replace him.

'Contract labour,' says Rodrigues bitterly, then asks me, 'Can you give me eight thousand rupees? Just for a month. I pay you back.'

I struggle to sit up in the arched-back chair and try to guess what this enfeebled old man might need that exact sum of money for—not five or ten but eight. Is it that, having spent a couple of hours with me, he has decided I am the enfeebled one who can be hit for an easy loan? Is that why he brought me here, to put me in an awkward position?

'I want to give a party,' he explains. 'Seventy years since war finished. I live. My captain live. So many people die. I want to invite all the friends and relatives and tell them. Thirty–forty people. Feed them properly. Make a speech.'

He explains that young people in this town have not heard of the Second World War. He wants to mark the jubilee so he can impress on the public just what he represents. He is barely even a footnote to a footnote in that war and yet it is the great event that, I'm beginning to see, gives him the breath of life—the obdurate will to walk into town and chase his Spectacle Grant, struggle uphill and visit his old haunt, cook up a feast worth eight thousand rupees.

Having learnt the reason, I am magnanimous about the money. I envisage years of chatting with him in return, a lifetime's worth of memories of Empire and war, freely shared. 'Of course,' I tell him. 'You can repay it any time.'

'When you give it?'

'Let's go to an ATM and have it done right now.'

We thank and take leave of the nameless guardian lady of the wobbly green-and-white bungalow and head back to the main street, which is coloured by a strangely diffused glow, some wisp of the sun struggling to slip out through the leaden rain clouds. The spell is enhanced by the fact that there are few people around. We are halfway down the street when I get it—everything's closed. We've just gone past Hajee with its shutters down.

Rodrigues is too intent on his walking, one foot carefully succeeding the other on the drowning pavement, and he doesn't seem to notice that the town has emptied. The two ATMs are locked too. The old man starts to wheeze. He seems to have had enough. I decide to walk him home if there is no rickshaw soon. Standing for a moment on the empty, quietened street, in that light from the sky so pale it is like a memory of light, I think of how small this place is. One can look all the way down the main street to the very end of it, and that is the extent of the town's hub. There is something curiously diminutive too about everything that happens here—this shutdown, the event that caused it, the anger of the people whose book has been desecrated. I feel an affection for the life of this place—the whole imperfect mess of it.

'They are coming,' says Rodrigues. I hear the chants of *'Murdabad!'* and then the first glimpse of a procession of upset men at the head of the street. *How did they have the time to paint banners so quickly*, I wonder. Or are these left over from the previous protest, since they are—these men in skullcaps, their white pyjamas high above their ankles—essentially protesting the same thing? They cover the length of the street in a few minutes and suddenly there are policemen with lathis and helmets converging on them from our end, appearing wordlessly, grim-faced, from behind where we're standing. The procession keeps going and then, at the first sight of a raised lathi, the men break up and flee, some slinging stones they seem to have been hiding in their fists. Rodrigues looks on unmoved, as if watching fools fight. A sharp-edged pebble skims my nose and blood slowly trickles down to my lips.

'We can't just stand here!' I shout.

It is slow progress away from there and down the road perpendicular to where we are; when we get to the end of it, Rodrigues lumbers into a rickshaw at the stand, gives me his phone number and tells me I'm a good man. I walk back with a finger pressed to my nose. There is a mist now between me and everything else, and silence again. I cannot see farther than a few metres into the swirl that clothes the houses and the trees and fills the lane like a great cloud of billowing white flour. The bleeding stops soon enough—not a deep cut. I stick a plaster on it when I get home and then stand looking out of the window. *He was a man suddenly roused to action by a ghastly wound to his person.*

I envy those men in the procession their passion and I felt it for a moment too when the stone struck me. *Do something*, I'd thought. But it's already gone and I am back to this—the slow combustion rather than the blazing spark. Who was it who said sorrow is a harder emotion to bear than anger?

In the evening, the fish is one shade short of a burnt brown, and Gowda has opened a new bottle of Peter Scot. He is full of town gossip as usual. Dozens of men taken in after the lathi charge but they will most likely be freed the following day. The youth who burnt the Koran has been arrested too but his motive is not clear yet. A Public Works Department official was caught taking a bribe of four lakh rupees from a man he had contracted to repair the PWD quarters.

I start to get drunk and boast about how I'm going to fund Vincent C. Rodrigues's party.

'Yes-ah?' he asks, and tells me that Percy, Rodrigues's son, is a long-time crook who's lately been running a prostitution business that everyone knows about but no one has interfered with because he has political connections. He brokers black-money deals and organizes girls for interested tourists.

'His time will come. You see, the municipal council elections next month the Muslims will boycott because of today's events, and so these people in power will have to go and with it all of Percy Rodrigues's friends. Vincent himself is harmless. What can he do? But if you give him your money, that's it. They will never stop pestering you. You will get pulled into their activities.'

He refills our glasses, then exclaims with a start as if he's just heard: 'Eight thousand for a party? What are you saying, sir? My wife can feed thirty people—veg, non-veg, everything—for five thousand. She knows how to manage.'

His wife comes into the living room, as if she's been eavesdropping from the kitchen, waiting for this cue, another couple of massive over-fried mackerels on the platter in her hand. Gowda doesn't thank her nor suggest that we have had enough. She goes away without looking at him or saying anything to me, her glass bangles clanking. I realize I ought to be grateful to my landlord for warning me off that dodgy Rodrigues junior, as well as for other things—renting me his house, inviting me home on occasion to drink, keeping an eye out for me. But I don't feel obliged, just irritated. I had wanted to please the old man.

'That poor fellow,' I say. 'Even his Spectacle Grant . . .'

'His son has enough money to buy him ten spectacles and yet he sends Vincent into town every week to chase two hundred rupees!'

How does Gowda know all this? Who, in fact, is Gowda? I want to challenge him but I'm a stranger from the city without access to the backstory about anything. He has moved on to his favourite subject.

'You see, with the tourists coming into town, the absolute best sector to get into is hospitality. What do you say to us starting a canteen together? You just put in the money, I'll handle the rest. My wife will cook. Where is the need to hire anyone else? Daughter and son can also come in and help after school.'

The lights go out.

We sit passively in the dark till Mrs Gowda reappears, this time with lit candles in a saucer. The wind is picking up as it does every night.

'Gowda, I'm still thinking of the past. I am not ready yet for business.'

'You mean about your girlfriend?'

I had told him once, on another night of drinking like this one, about that particular failure.

'Not just her. But history. The old things. This town, for example. There are so many reminders.'

'Monuments,' says Gowda. 'Historical monuments. Have you been to the museum?' He's slurring whereas the drink is making me clear-headed and expansive. Why not think way bigger than Gowda, show up his paltry schemes for what they are?

'I want to find out about that old house down from where the big well is,' I say. 'Do you know it? Just as the road starts to slope up towards the convent, a green and white house. I visited there today with Rodrigues. It's a beauty but crumbling. The owners are away, maybe they come once a year and look things up. But I can't imagine that they feel much for the place, though they've let some of the old stuff be. There is still a photograph of the original owners on the wall. Soon enough they'll have it sold and torn down, they must already be considering offers.'

Gowda is actually silenced by this, wondering what I'm getting at. I can hear the wife in the kitchen, bangles rattling busily, probably frying more fish with a vengeance though we haven't touched the new batch. The candles flicker.

'I've been thinking about it all afternoon. If I have to spend, maybe it should be so as to save an old thing. I don't need to make money, but I could preserve an old thing. Not all these small-time ideas you're suggesting, please. They'll drain my savings and they'll bore me. But if you help me make a deal on that house . . .'

He murmurs something indistinct that sounds disapproving. The Gowdas' daughter comes in to ask if I'd like to stay for dinner. I say a polite no, ask her perfunctorily how her studies are going, then return to Gowda.

'You know what would thrill me? To keep it the way it is— patch it up but not rebuild it. I grow old and it grows even older around me.'

I look at him for a reaction and find that he is totally out, his usually mobile face and calculating eyes have yielded to the whisky-fuelled conciliations of sleep. In the dim light of the dancing candles, he looks like a giant moustached baby. He must have nodded off as soon as I started to talk, unused to the sound of anyone's voice but his own.

It was a dark and stormy night. The wind howled in the trees and loudly rattled the windowpanes. Walking back to my own place through the lashing rain, I think of Amina slipping on the moss but, enlivened by the whisky, I'm not afraid of falling. And my inspiration remains—why not stake everything on something, why not pluck a figment from the past and give it life? If I am to return to the world of projects, this is how they must look— superfluous, wild, only as tangible as the feel of rotting wood under my fingers.

In the morning, the first thing I do on waking is call Rodrigues and ask where I can meet him to hand over the eight thousand rupees.

2

SISTERS

The sick and the healthy have nothing in common, thinks Jaan. She's been dreaming of a solitary man testing nails against wood, but on waking knows there are dozens of men hammering the new world into shape outside, the air dense with the dust they have raised. There is nothing tentative about their rhythm—it is the most confident sound in the world, and it will not allow her to go back to sleep. These are the healthy: they are huge, they dominate the skyline, they eat up the bandwidth. The sick, huddled in bed, are small and particular; they are the punctuation marks in the prose of life. And life rushes forward, tripping over them in its impatience.

I must be sick, thinks Jaan. She glances at the clock. Only four. At least three hours to go before the husband returns from work and she can present herself to him, the whole frozen mass of her in socks and woollen jacket, her teeth chattering under the quilt, while outside the sun burns the small, brave leaves off the potted chrysanthemums and softens the tar in the cracked roads. She closes her eyes in order to find a point beyond pain, searches in the debris of her fever-racked mind for an easeful spot in which to rest her sore bones. But every corner has been ambushed by the same word. Sick.

She checks the time again, imagining half an hour has gone by, but it is only seven minutes past four, so she takes up a glass of water and swallows a pill from one of the aluminium strips by her bedside. On the nightstand is a sedimented history of her sickness: pills for her present condition, for the earlier one, and more underneath those for the one before that; medical reports and doctors' prescriptions; the cloudy-white streaks of chest X-rays and the jagged freehand of electrocardiograms; dark bottles with bright labels and even brighter capsules enclosing bitter promises. Right at the bottom of all this paraphernalia is a notebook in which she has recorded the following observation: *She does not know what is wrong with her.*

There have been times during the past months when she has woken with the blood singing in her veins and her body no longer talking in that language which only medicines are known to silence. She has leapt out of bed, washed her hair, reasserted authority over her maid, cooked breakfast, and then brought out the notebook and celebrated the vanquishing of suffering. But, inevitably, it has returned, this nameless condition, in a matter of hours or days, always before the body can properly fill up with hope again, pain returns and renders hope a silly myth.

This afternoon, trapped in the burning highs and arctic lows of her fever, she has drawn the curtains, but the sun filters through the thin cotton, softening the gloom. The furniture in the room is veneered chipboard. The floor tiles are a smooth egg-white, easy to clean and easy to dirty. Paperbacks cram the bookshelves and the suitcases under the bed still have airline luggage tags on them.

Her flat is on the fourth floor of Peaceville, a giant apartment complex of twenty featureless pink-and-cream towers, arrayed like silos in groups of five around small patches of lawn. Peaceville has the lustre of the new; the candy colours look good enough to eat, but the residents are all too familiar with the chipped mouldings, the cracks in the walls, the paint-spattered banisters. The building looms over the surrounding ones; it is distressing to imagine the extent of time and work, cement and sand and water, metal frames and plastic loops that went into its construction. Jaan often looks at it, staggered, and thinks: *It must have just appeared overnight.*

———

Across the road from Peaceville, Jamini comes out of her two-room hut, tying up her hair and stomping her feet before stepping into a pair of sequinned sandals.

She has worked barefoot on the earth all her life, helping her husband push reluctant bullocks over the soil, laying out rice saplings, walking through the slush of rain-irrigated fields and wielding the sickle during harvest time with those feet squarely planted on the ground.

When she left her village in Andhra Pradesh—and came to Bangalore on the promise of making more money than the pittance she earned wearing her back out on the fields every day— it was with a group of women who'd been contracted to work on construction sites: break into the ground with iron rods after the bulldozers have levelled it, dig up and cart away the soil so that the foundations can be laid. After they finish, the men take over, and later more women come to pass bricks to the bricklayers and carry panniers of wet cement up the ramps that lead to the scaffoldings. But these are small-built local women, fragile girl-women who leave their babies sleeping in the shade of their makeshift tents and work so slowly it makes Jamini curse and spit. She and her sisters from the village are big, dark and powerful, have huge arms and cropped hair, and are not bothered by the sun. They are used to its harshness on their skin and to the feel of the hot earth beneath their feet.

In the early days they were all right. She and her husband, who fed the concrete blenders and helped lay out the latticework for the foundations, could afford the rent on their two rooms. They had electricity for television and water gushing out once a day from the communal tap. The children did not go to school but were safe playing all day in the slum's lanes, a self-enclosed world that grew alongside the larger one outside. And then, inevitably, more and more women like Jamini turned up, pushing the daily wages down and making work scarce.

As Jamini laboured on the tall apartment being built along the stretch of road near the slum, as the wastelands filled up with more apartments, office blocks and shopping malls, as the rich came to live and work in spaces where there had, until recently, been nothing, that sense of nothing persisted. There were no trees lining this road, no faces on the pavements that had aged here and no old houses to contrast with the new ones—nothing to mark the passage of time.

When her heavily pregnant neighbour asked Jamini if she would like to fill in for her as a domestic help for a few months, she affected indifference. She was not about to let the neighbour feel she was doing her a favour. But neither did Jamini take too long to agree; she'd be a fool to pass up a chance to make some decent money. She knows nothing about working as a maid but is convinced that there is nothing to know except that this new job would allow her, for the first time in her life, to wear shoes. So she'd gone out and bought the snazziest pair of heels available for under a hundred rupees.

Jamini, tottering a little, is glad she is finally going into one of these buildings. She would like to see how the people she has glimpsed behind car windows live, what they do with the distinction of inhabiting these pristine heights. She crosses the road daintily, learning to balance her bulk on these small squares of sophistication, and enters the tall gates of Peaceville.

———

'Let's go see the doctor,' says Javed, his eyes on the screen of the laptop balanced on his knees. He is sitting in the easy chair by the bed and scrolling through his emails. Jaan thinks of the vast hospital a kilometre up Sarjapur Road, through whose drab corridors she and Javed have wandered so many times, from cashier to lab to waiting room to doctor's chamber, from one specialist to another and then back to the same crowded pharmacy for a new stack of medicines.

'No,' she says, closing her eyes. 'No.'

'What then? You can't lie here and suffer,' says Javed in an even voice, the same voice in which he speaks to his colleagues on conference call from Europe about incentives and quarterly targets, and the very one he uses with the corner joint when he orders takeaway. He pauses in his scrolling and starts to type.

'Do they still like you in the office?' she asks her husband. He's been taking frequent leave on her account and missing deadlines. He chuckles briefly, his fingers flying. He does this every evening, hanging on to his laptop and rooting endlessly in his inbox for God knows what, checking every few seconds for new mails and occasionally answering older ones.

Eventually, he glances at her and says in that calm, punctuation-less way of his, 'I'm off to Hyderabad for three days tomorrow so let's go to the doc so you don't get worse when I'm away, all right?'

Jaan is about to suggest that perhaps what she needs is a holiday in the hills or by the sea, remonstrate with him about his blind faith in doctors, when the doorbell rings. Javed, laptop clutched in one arm, goes to get it. He is gone for what seems like a long time and Jaan drifts off, sleep settling heavier on her weak limbs than the thick covers she is swaddled in.

'Why are you asleep so early in the evening?' asks a woman's voice. 'Are you sick?'

The lights haven't been switched on and she cannot clearly discern the woman's face, but her rough voice and the hand on the hip strike Jaan as imperious. For the first time that day, she makes an effort to swing her feet off the bed, fight the fuzz in her head.

'Who are you?' she asks.

'I just explained to your husband. I've come to work here.'

And so Jamini takes over as their help, turning up at eight thirty every morning, leaving her new sandals by the door and starting the day by inquiring into the details of Jaan's health. Shakti, their previous maid, zipped through her tasks with an air of deadly efficiency but inevitably left grease on the dinner plates and curls of hair in the corners. Jamini never seems to be in any hurry. She has a lot to say—about the poor quality of the restaurant food that the couple often rely on, the ineffectiveness of their washing machine and the sad state of their potted plants. She starts cooking for them. She decides that the ironing man who comes for their clothes overcharges, so she takes on that too. Then she starts to find fault with the vegetable and fruit that Javed picks up on his way back from work and she is soon bringing in the groceries as well.

Jaan's fever abates but is replaced by a long spell of vertigo. She watches from her bed the room tilt and spin around her, as Jamini takes over her life. Jaan used to, even if sporadically and half-heartedly, boss over Shakti—point out her shortcomings and threaten to slash her pay if she didn't shape up. Shakti would just mumble her assent and carry on as before. With Jamini, there is nothing to find fault with.

'What's the date, sister?' she asks Jaan one morning.

Jaan is not sure, a sign of grave degeneration, she thinks, not being able to tell how far into the month they are. She is getting worse.

'Whatever the date, you've been in bed for too long. Get up,' says Jamini.

Jaan pretends to be asleep but the maid bullies her till she drags herself out of the room and her bedclothes can be soaked in a tub of foamy warm water. Jamini lugs the mattress and blankets out to the balcony to sun them. She gives Jaan some peas to shell and goes off into the kitchen saying something about onions and masalas; the grinder howls and then a faint aroma, familiar yet elusive, starts to fill the house.

Jaan sits at the dining table with the peas, trying to ignore her dizziness and focus on the question of what distinguishes people from one another. All the flats in Peaceville are of exactly the same size and design. The people living in them work similar jobs, their kids go to the same schools, they shop in the same supermarkets and their TVs spew the same stuff night after night. Could their headaches be identical too? And the smells of their kitchens and the contents of their dreams?

She'd always assumed this was so. But since Jamini's arrival something has shifted in the atmosphere of her own home and she knows now that people, no matter how alike, are always different, and that each family has its own secret recipe for existence.

Jamini comes to get the peas and asks if Jaan plans to leave the house. She wants to dust the furniture and needs her out of the way.

'There's nowhere I want to go,' says Jaan. 'I'm dizzy.'

'You don't have work?' asks Jamini sternly.

Jaan thinks of her job—as a statistical analyst for a marketing-research firm—from which she is on indefinite leave. It worsens her dizziness.

'I could take a walk around the building,' suggests Jaan, although that is the last thing she wants to do. Looking at Jamini's beefy frame and her hard black eyes, she realizes she is a little afraid of this woman. But it's just a game—the bossy servant and the timid boss. If she wanted to, she could fire Jamini without notice.

Jaan goes down in the lift, aghast at her callousness. Jamini is not a gift she can throw away. She is obliged to her. *What could I offer her*, she wonders, making her way gingerly around the walkway by the lawn, calibrating her vertigo with every step. Everyone is away this early in the afternoon except the toddlers just back from preschool, expending the energy they still have left by running around in circles, out of the clutches of their nannies. Jaan looks at the kids and their chaperones and wonders if she knows them, like she wonders about everyone else here, the people she and Javed sometimes nod to in the elevators. She smiles tentatively at the children, then moves away from them.

When Jaan returns, the house is agleam and lunch ready. After they have eaten, Jamini begins to talk.

———

'You know about Shakti, don't you?' she asks.

'Has she had her baby yet?'

'Where is your memory, sister? The baby is already a month old. She's started to talk of taking her job back.'

'Well, it *is* her job.'

'I want to stay,' says Jamini, the words spoken with her usual forthrightness but in a tone that is also subdued, pleading. This show of vulnerability makes Jaan nervous. She goes back to bed and shuts her eyes. Jamini follows her to the bedroom.

'There's a new family in 409. I saw them move in day before yesterday. They'll need help, they have two boys. I can send Shakti to them instead.'

Jaan is impressed at her resourcefulness. Where did she develop it, in what kind of life lived amid what kind of desolation? With Jaan's assent, Jamini rushes off to talk to the lady in 409 and convince her to hire the maid she's recommending.

She returns, beaming and successful, and settles on the floor near Jaan's bed. Jaan can feel the heat of Jamini's happiness; she opens her eyes sleepily and closes them again. The car horns on the busy road outside make an incessant symphony about the pleasures of speed. *The world does not need me*, she thinks. She is spun around slowly and then faster and faster on the pivot of her vertigo. She tries to yell but the honking feels louder.

Jaan is brought awake by the sound of Jamini's voice. She sits up in terror and looks at her.

'You have to get better,' Jamini says. 'Maybe a massage will help.' She goes to heat up some oil in the kitchen and starts with Jaan's feet. A shock goes through her body. Jamini's grip is so powerful, Jaan is certain that the little life she has left is going to be knocked out of her by this woman's inhuman strength. She has big, calloused hands and seems to know nothing about massage.

'Tell me if it's too hard, I'll do it gentler,' she instructs, but it seems that she can massage only one way—brutally. She starts to sing as she rubs oil into Jaan's back, her voice rough and off-key, but the song's rhythm works its way into her hands and they relax without losing their grip. Jaan starts to breathe more evenly; her distress slowly fades. Jamini explains to Jaan the meaning of the words—a folk song about two birds who build a swing over a well with a piece of thread. Then the swing breaks but the birds don't fall into the well, they fly away. The song seems no less absurd to Jaan than Jamini's friendliness or the odour of sesame oil and chewed betel leaf suffusing her room.

The massages and the songs—prayers for a good harvest or paeans to ancestors—become a daily affair, as do Jaan's walks in the grounds. Jaan half listens to the singing—dozing or, as her dizziness slowly recedes, trying to make sense of the newspapers. At other times she chats with Jamini about her life back in the village, a life that revolved around growing, nurturing, storing and cooking food, pouring work into the land, worshipping it, singing to it, loving it through the turning of the seasons. And all this despite the fact that the land always belonged to someone else, and that in their upland village, where no river reached and the rains could be erratic, the land was as much a curse as a boon.

Unlike the other maids Jaan has known, who write themselves off but are desperate for their children to get somewhere, Jamini seems to have no ambitions for hers. Send them to school, urges Jaan, and Jamini says she'll see. She feeds her children ragi and the cheapest greens in the market, and they seem, from her description, to be growing strong and capable. The boy works as an assistant at a scrap dealer's, sorting through the piles of broken electronic goods that come through these new apartments, learning to assess the value of seemingly valueless things. Her eight-year-old daughter dreams of being a salesgirl: tapping her painted nails on the glass counter of a cosmetics shop and speaking rapid-fire English. For the time being she helps a neighbour package fried snacks to sell in the small shops lining the slum.

Jaan and Jamini go shopping together. When they walk out on the roads around Peaceville, Jaan sees the great and general agitation of the city, while Jamini sees a lone woman selling guavas that are ripening fast in the sun, and so liable to be bargained for. She notices the glint of a goddess's nose ring in a small wayside shrine before which she must close her eyes and fold her hands; she points out the man standing by a cigarette-and-tea kiosk with sawdust on his pants, looking new to the city—a carpenter from Bihar?—who could perhaps, for a reasonable price, make the bookshelves Jaan wants. She sees the policeman extorting the chaat-stand owners so that they can ply their open-air trade in over-spiced snacks every evening, and she whispers to Jaan about the driver who is cheating on his Peaceville employers by taking their spare car out in the afternoons to pursue a sideline as a house broker.

Gradually, Jaan becomes well enough to consider going back to work. She lies awake at night, feeling like she has used up a lifetime's quota of sleep, and thinks of Jamini. She asks Javed one morning if they should give her another raise. In between his perpetual email-scrolling, his absent-minded eating of his breakfast, his fleeting goodbye kiss, Javed says that a pay hike is a good idea. So Jaan tells Jamini. Jamini smiles and says, 'I will stay with you people. I'm not going anywhere,' and Jaan feels foolish, as if she were trying to bribe her.

Later that week, Jaan returns to work and the days slowly start to acquire the shape they once had. She submits to the breathless rush of the morning, feeling the press of deadlines in the small of the back when switching on her computer, the jokes and small talk, the gossip and innuendo over lunch, the slowness of the afternoons when troubling questions about the meaning of it all make their daily appearance. A reviving cup of coffee at four o'clock, some scrambling around to complete the work she had hoped to finish much earlier in the day and, an hour or so later, the release. When Jaan returns, Jamini is there, waiting for her. She does not know a thing about statistics. This alone makes Jaan love her.

———

One ordinary midweek morning, after Javed has left, Jaan becomes preoccupied with a conundrum as she puts on her shoes. She noticed, the previous day, in one of their worksheets, an error in the data samples that she and her team have been basing their mathematical model on. Bringing up the error now is undoing two weeks of work. Ignoring it means giving a misleading report to the client. What is the right thing to do? She sits staring at the clock and then realizes that this worry has been replaced by another. She's running late for work and Jamini hasn't turned up yet. Jaan gives it another five minutes, then rushes through the door. There's no sign of her maid in the evening, and when she doesn't turn up the following morning either, Jaan realizes that Jamini does not have a phone. So she calls Shakti.

'She died,' Shakti says.

'Jamini?'

'She died,' repeats Shakti, in an altered tone, as if imparting fresh information. Jaan, astounded, disconnects the call and waits for something to happen—for her maid to turn the key in the door or Shakti to call back and explain. How could Jamini die? Who or what could kill her? She's never taken sick leave or discussed mortality.

Jaan has to call again.

'Shakti, I don't want to know what happened,' she blurts before the girl can speak. 'Please just tell me where she lives.'

Shakti doesn't say anything, then says, 'What's the use of your going there? I'm finishing at 409 now, do you want me to come over and do the dishes?'

Jaan says no, gets directions and puts away the phone. She searches deep in her lungs for the next breath. *It's okay, she was only your maid. She isn't dead, it's a misunderstanding. She was killed by overwork, you're responsible. She can't be dead, I need her. Please, please, please, not her.*

She is chewing hard on her lip as she stands by the four-lane road near Peaceville, waiting for motorists to notice her panic and allow her to cut through. When she finally enters the thoroughfare of the slum, the traffic is different in kind but equally ferocious; she takes a few timid steps in and then retreats in the face of the crazy tempos loaded with bundles of mattresses or crates of soft drinks, cows and motorbikes and blaring cars.

She makes it into the by-lanes and then there are no further obstacles; here life proceeds without shoving itself in her face. People live half indoors and half out; everywhere are pushcarts of wilting vegetables, water pitchers and bicycles, women in nightgowns and children with screechy, commanding voices. Jaan finds Jamini's house; she sees through its open door a teenage boy sitting on the floor, playing with a toddler. A TV stands muted on a shelf. A shaky-looking bed takes up most of the space and has a big mess of clothes piled on it. There is nothing funereal about the scene but as soon as Jaan says, 'Jamini?' the boy, in a man's voice, replies, 'She's dead.'

'How?' Jaan says, softly, so that her voice doesn't break. She is still standing at the threshold; he hasn't asked her to come in. A couple of women gather around Jaan and peer into the room as she is doing, apparently in search of an answer to the same question. When the boy doesn't speak, they heckle him.

'How did she die?' he finally says. 'How do people die? She fell ill, she died.'

'She used to come to me. She was never sick,' counters Jaan.

'She had a headache. Then she died.'

Jaan can now see the exhaustion in his face and the grief he has already exhausted. He puts the baby aside and goes into the inner room. Jaan waits for him to come back, then realizes he's started cooking. The reek of the kerosene stove he has just lit fills the windowless interior. Around the stove, on the floor, are a small collection of battered pots and plastic spice jars. The baby bangs a toy down and speaks out in a private tongue.

Jaan steps inside and calls out, 'What happened to her? She's always had good health.'

Again the boy takes his time answering her, and when he does, it's with his face still turned.

'Every second woman in this colony is looking for work. Go talk to them if you want a new maid.'

Jaan finds herself speechless with anger. For so long, she could see nothing beyond sickness; then Jamini came and taught her a certain selfless grace by example. But she's gone now and it's absurd for Jaan to be in this smelly room—a room almost cinematic to her in its poverty and crumminess—and be insulted by a stranger. She thinks of the hour that has gone by and the office work that the tragedy of the day has rendered impossible. Rage flares in her again.

'Come back here. I need to know what happened,' Jaan shouts at the boy.

She frightens the baby but not him. He leaves off his vegetable-frying and comes close to her. 'Madam, I don't have time to answer your questions. I have to feed this child.'

'Who killed her?' says Jaan, trembling.

They stare at each other, and the curious female onlookers still standing by the door murmur something. Unexpectedly, the boy laughs. He takes up the squalling baby and shakes his head.

'You heard?' he asks his neighbours. 'My mother died, and before we can find a picture of her to hang on the wall, some fancy lady comes to our house and says we killed her.'

'You got the wrong house,' says one woman.

'She didn't wake up yesterday morning, no matter what we did. You should have come then if you cared,' says the other.

Jaan looks at the hostile faces. How could her wise, loving sister belong to this mean place? She is turning to leave when she notices the glitzy sandals peeking out from under the bed. They look cheap and ridiculous. Jaan stares at them in horror. She saw them every day. Yet she'd never noticed them before.

She finds herself sinking to the bed, felled by sudden tears. The neighbours come into the room now to study Jaan at closer quarters; someone gives her a glass of water. They confer over her head in a language she doesn't understand and in a tone that seems to suggest she's largely irrelevant to them.

'She was my maid,' says Jaan, blowing her nose. 'She took care of me . . . I liked her.'

The women nod, but look disbelieving.

The boy completes his cooking and then relents, talking to Jaan as he forces fistfuls of rice into the goggle-eyed baby's mouth. His name is Shankar. Two evenings ago, says Shankar, as his mother was returning from work, she was knocked down by a speeding car jumping the lights just as they turned red. The driver had stopped and helped her up. Before a crowd could gather or the police get wind, he had urged her into his car and they were off. She was dazed but otherwise fine, and there was only a small gash on her forehead. She told him she didn't need to see a doctor. He left her outside St John's with a five-hundred-rupee note in her hand. She had walked back, bought two portions of chicken biryani from Royal Biryani Corner, got home, told the family what happened. They were happy about the biryani. But Jamini couldn't eat it. She started vomiting, then had a headache. Soon after, she went to sleep and never woke up. They cremated her the following afternoon.

Shankar's father is back at work and Shankar does not know where his sister is. She's been acting strange since their mother died.

The baby is his cousin. Jamini's younger brother and his wife, daily-wage labourers like her, had turned up from the other end of town when they got news of her death. Early this morning, they heard about a call going around for a spot of digging required in the neighbourhood so left their baby with him.

Jaan's face is wet again. She wants to be there, ensuring Jamini goes to hospital, cursing the bastard who ploughed into her.

'What can we say when Devi herself wanted it,' says Shankar, raising his tired, old-man eyes to a small garlanded picture of the goddess in an alcove in the wall.

So then there is nothing left to say.

'Your mother was . . . a good person. Did she ever talk about me? I live in Peaceville, those big apartments nearby . . .'

'I don't know,' says Shankar. 'I'm at work most of the day. We need money.'

Jaan remembers and digs into her wallet.

'I owed her this,' she says, handing the notes to him. He smiles at her for the first time, and his teeth resemble his mother's, teeth so remarkably white and solid they seem like a form of wealth he carries around in his mouth. But he has no money. She gives him more, emptying out the wallet blindly and feeling the weightlessness of the notes between her fingers. He thanks her and shakes her hand and asks her to stay for tea.

Later, back home, Jaan sits down with her notebook and looks over the half-finished entries about her broken health and her fear of extinction. Then she goes to bed and waits for it to come, the tremor or flush or twinge. The string has broken and she waits to see if she will drown or fly away.

3

THE QUESTION OF STYLE

The word for it was 'stylish'. Stylish girls had Lady Diana haircuts, wore low wedge heels from Bata and chocolate corduroy bell-bottoms. Some wore midis and some wore maxis and some wore minis. Ribbed skivvies in single colours were in. Flared, high-waisted jeans and Keds. Or tight churidars with lots of *churis* around the calf, matching kurtas in satin that reached just above the knees and chunnis wound around the throat but not covering the breasts. Dark leather moccasins with coloured beadwork on the front. Chunky sweaters. Chiffon saris patterned with gardens.

The stylish were a tribe of their own—they either had cascades of hair, sometimes plaited, like the gorgeous dungarees-wearing pop star Nazia Hassan's, or that layered, feathery bob copied from the Princess of Wales. She had just got married and everyone seemed to know her. She was stylish for sure.

'*Ish*, so stylish,' the older girls said to each other. It meant you looked fine, or it meant you were attempting to look fine and could thus be mocked.

My younger sister, Daisy, and I were less than ten years old and not yet stylish. Perhaps we'd never be. We could not aspire to stylishness, being skinny, awkward, myopic and unwealthy.

We didn't have what it took. The right clothes were crucial to stylish but not just the right clothes either. A worrying mystery was part of it too—something ineffable about the way a sleeve caressed your wrist or a collar enclosed your throat, how you walked, tossed your head, put your hands in your pockets. Leaning on the garden wall towards the half-busy main road, we looked out for the stylish every evening. Meanwhile, I knitted panties for my dolls and let my hair grow till my waist, while Daisy's was too long to be short but too short to be long.

She could have entrusted herself to our left-hand-side neighbour who'd trained with Shahnaz Husain and even looked a little like her—smooth and plump and confident. The lady had recently set up a beauty parlour in her front room, where a poster of her big-haired, bug-eyed heroine hung and on the shelves were jars of pink and black and green beauty products. We had been in there to shyly confer with her. She could give Lady Diana haircuts for fifty rupees. Her husband was out in the compound of their bungalow, where his long, big-snouted, copper-coloured antique car was parked, calling out for their Pomeranian. 'Pom-Pom!' We heard him yelling this name so often that that was what we called him. Pom-Pom! But we didn't have fifty rupees to spare for Shahnaz.

So one Sunday when I was nine, I took up our grandfather's scissors, the heavy iron ones he used for his tailoring, and said to Daisy, 'Let me give you a haircut.' At this point in my life, I was forever running towards or away from something, every game involved flight or hiding under dusty beds, flinging the basketball far and away, climbing a ladder to the roof for the badminton shuttle. I would trip and fall, twist an ankle or wrist, then be swathed for weeks in Relaxyl and stretch bandages. But I'd also pick myself up and carry on. I could not turn perfect cartwheels like our right-hand-side neighbour but I taught her to skip. This neighbour and Daisy were the same age and friends. I taught them skipping, single and doubles, how to twist the rope in mid-air. I could outrun everyone and deftly bring down oranges with the clefted bamboo stick, but I was accident-prone. I had a history of crashing into glass doors. At two, I had managed to knock into a pot of bubbling porridge and burn the skin right off the back of one hand. At five, I dropped deep into a forest stream and almost drowned.

That winter morning, I snipped a little of my sister's hair and it came away so easily between my fingers. I was restless, eager to bring some novelty into our lives—even though we had Lyril soap to bathe with and Cuticura talcum powder, a couple of nice dresses each, made by our grandfather, and slip-ons flecked with gold. These shoes were downright *telu*, which, in the lexicon, was the very opposite of stylish. They were loud and so they were telu, a word we had made up to brand unstylishness, describe those who were outcasts in the house of style, who cared nothing for the oil dripping from their plaits and the missing garters in their school socks. They were telu, others stylish, and we two girls hung on desperately somewhere in between. We put on our slip-ons reluctantly and perused old copies of *Seventeen* magazine at the right-hand-side neighbour's, brought in by her foreign relatives—agape at the pristine-faced models, feeling ourselves aglow with the possibilities of stylishness.

We were sitting on the outside steps—Daisy with a towel around her shoulders, compliant, trusting, and I with those big scissors I could barely handle. I cut off Daisy's rat-tails and cleared her neck. I took up tufts and let them fall away. The hair on the back of her head started to thin out. I combed and snipped, urging my sister to sit still. Then I aimed at her fringe.

Grandfather was not yet missing his scissors. He wasn't tailoring this morning but he was often at it. For birthdays and festivals, he stitched clothes for us out of small squares of ordinary cloth and thin air. He would consider an expensive frock worn by the right-hand-side neighbour and turn out a perfect imitation in a couple of days, down to the ruffled sleeves, smocked front and lacy frills. He stitched all the clothes he wore—the warm, buttoned woollen vests and the sharp-edged trousers. He stitched quilt covers and shopping bags and kurta-pyjamas. It was him and his old, black, hand-cranked Pfaff, well-oiled and singing; the pockmarked silver thimble that went on to his forefinger when he took up hemming and putting in the buttons; the faded British-era biscuit tin in which he kept his spools of threads and bobbins.

Grandfather was an artist but he was not stylish. He saw to it that the grandchildren were clothed, and to supplement what he made us he'd go to the footbridge in the town's market square, where the sellers of second-hand clothes had their stalls, and buy us trackpants and winter jackets. They had labels from abroad and looked crumpled. Rumour had it that they were meant for the poor in Bangladesh, not for the sellers on the footbridge and certainly not for us. I would listen to George Harrison's song for Bangladesh and feel guilty about those clothes.

Meanwhile, the thrill of taking matters into my own hands. My first attempt at tidying the fringe was hesitant and led to uneven results. I gave it another go and the lopsided look improved. Strands poked down from one side, which I then took away. I combed Daisy's hair sideways. 'Show me,' I said, and it looked all right. I had given her a haircut in the sense that I had cut her hair. But there was nothing stylish about it. Where were the perfectly set waves that crowned the princess's head? Where was the glamour of that golden crop? I pulled down the hair over my sister's forehead and started snipping again.

'Careful,' said our mother from somewhere inside the house, but she was distant. I imagined she trusted me because she let me make tea and handle knives, clean out the rice and sweep out the rooms. In any case, I couldn't confide in her about our lack of stylishness because my mother was stylish herself, impossibly so. She wore silk saris in thick colours, with matching lipstick, and had her hair done at Jenny's, which was the oldest stylish place in town. She owned fascinating shoes—brown suede and blue leather and a pair of handcrafted, burgundy, crocodile-skin high heels, made to order by a Chinese shoemaker. She used only Yardley and Max Factor, and wore pure-wool cardigans. So when she said *careful*, both Daisy and I knew it was to be taken only half seriously. If I fell off the ladder to the roof and broke my neck, if the open wound on my knee from falling on the right-hand-side neighbour's tar-and-chip compound turned septic, if a Diwali cracker burst in my hand or if Pom-Pom escaped from the left-hand-side neighbour's and bit me, then my mother would rouse herself. For the rest of the time, she merely scolded absent-mindedly.

The hunt for stylish continued despite her. Daisy and I cut out pictures of luxurious clothes and lip-glossed women from the magazines and pasted them at odd angles into old notebooks. We would get a TV in some years and watch Shabana Azmi and Zeenat Aman, who were stylish, and the Doordarshan newscasters, who were not.

Daisy's fringe was now shorter but uneven. I cut some more. Now it was straighter. I cut a tiny bit more. Now it was uneven again. And so on till her forehead was revealed and then the top of her scalp began to show. And still that line of hair wouldn't fall straight. Suddenly Daisy demanded to see a mirror. 'What have you done?' she screamed. She looked like the victim of an illness that had selectively eaten up her hair. Our mother came out and Daisy finally began to cry.

Some moments of mixed emotions followed: our mother's great exasperation at my stupidity, even though she had originally acceded to my do-it-yourself plan; my own conviction that I had missed stylishness by a whisper, that a few snips more or less would have done it; Daisy's sense of adventure dissolving into a feeling of betrayal. 'Cover her head and take her to the barber,' said our mother. So the two of us went, ignominiously, down the street—me, disgraced, and Daisy with a woollen cap concealing her disfigurement. There was the grocery shop where we bought our atta and soap, the typing school, the pakori-wallah who doubled as an electrician, the mithai shop, the paan-wallah, the gentle man in a dark suit who sold toffees and hard-boiled sweets out of huge glass jars along with pencils and exercise books and then the barber in his dirty white pyjamas. He was the one who usually dealt with our hair and he had no truck with style and Lady Diana. I had to explain the problem to him, while my sister sat scowling on a wooden plank reserved for children that was balanced on the arms of the barber's chair.

Was it then, on that shameful morning, that this unattainable word started to fall away from us? The barber did what he could with the mess, and in a few weeks Daisy's hair grew out and the accident was forgotten. But the dream of stylish loosened its hold on us. There would be moments in the years to come when we'd be touched by it again—the time my mother took me to town and bought me shoes with the elegant word 'Henry' printed on the soles, for instance, or when my sister went across to the left-hand-side neighbour and finally got herself that Lady Di haircut. But on the whole, we seemed to have given up the fight. I gradually stopped falling down, lost interest in hide-and-seek, no longer took up the cord of the electric kettle and sang into it like Nazia Hassan.

We remained children for a little longer, still yearning for the sophistications of an adult world, till that too passed and we became, for better or worse, the people we were meant to be, no more those we hoped to become.

4

THE LEGEND OF LUTFAN MIAN

One sharp-edged January day in 1872, Lutfan Mian sets out for Benares with his friend Gopal Singh. They are both nineteen and each has woken in the nocturnal winter dawn in their adjoining homes in the Panchmandir mohalla of the town of Rasra. The copper bell in the temple is resounding through the neighbourhood. Elsewhere in town too, morning has been rung in by the devotional clanging of metal on metal, and before that by the muezzin, a man never heard to have sleep in his voice. People stirring under their quilts could swear they were roused just a moment ago by the nightwatchman knocking his cane on the ground and his calls urging wakefulness on himself. And now already, slowly seeping into the darkness, that first gentle infusion of light. In midwinter this light is the colour of water running off the top of boiling rice and always accompanied by that clear voice mellifluously proclaiming *'Ash-hadu an' la ilaha'* from the mosque.

The women, whose waking is stealthy and invisible, who rise between the muezzin's call and daybreak, have already returned from the fields with their spouted brass *badna*s of water. They are settling down in the courtyard open to the sky, where they spend most of their day; they knead flour and push lit logs into the brick hearth to begin roasting semolina in large, open pans for halwa.

Lutfan is impatient. It is too early to go out to the pond so he throws a rusty bucket down the well behind the house and draws up icy water, ignoring the serrated leaves of neem floating in it. He takes off his kurta and unties, lifts up and refastens the coarse cotton lungi around his waist, then pours the water over himself. Despite the shock of the cold and the shadowy dawn, his thin, dark frame is poised, sure-footed, on the stone platform. He dries himself with a ragged towel hanging from a nail in the neem tree, ties it around his middle and pulls down his wet lungi, thinking of Benares and worrying, already talking to his friend Gopal in his mind. *I am not sure the money is enough.* And Gopal says as he has said so many times before, *I will give you the money. I will win it and give it to you.*

'Is breakfast ready?' asks Lutfan, passing through the courtyard. 'Not yet but almost,' mumbles one of the women, and he doesn't know which one, there are so many: his grandmother, mother and sister, his two aunts and a young cousin, while two other sisters are somewhere around in the large house, absorbed in some other daily task: winnowing dal, stuffing red chillies for a pickle, learning their Arabic and Persian alphabets. The women don't look up from the floor, where they are rolling out parathas and chopping a handful of cashew nuts to garnish the steaming halwa with. Others are already on to lunch. A giant pumpkin is being sliced on the sharp crescent blade of a *hasua*.

Lutfan grumbles about their slowness but doesn't stride through the courtyard as usual. He stands there staring for a moment and thinks of his wife-to-be cooking with them, her eyes downcast, the end of her sari pulled low over her head. He'd be ashamed to look in on her, he cannot do it. Then he imagines himself alone with her in the tiny, low-roofed *kotha* on the upper floor of the house where he sleeps with his grandfather, the room cluttered with hoes and ploughs, sacks of grain, cane baskets. And this thought too agitates him greatly, bringing the taste of something like shame into his mouth. He isn't hungry and cannot wait to leave.

'Why are you in such a hurry today, where are you going?' asks his mother, raising her eyes to his.

He doesn't answer her, but on the other hand saying nothing will give him away so he remarks, casually, 'I'm going out with Gopal.'

She waits for more; her youngest son is usually full of talk. It happens to children born into a household of adults and much older siblings; they pick words too large for their small mouths and they chatter all day to keep the attention on themselves. But he is quiet today and Lutfan knows from her expression that she has noticed his anxiety although not its exact cause.

'You're getting married,' she says, her rough voice modulated by a small edge of pleasure. His cousin, diligently stirring semolina, suddenly giggles at him, her eyes flashing briefly in the glow from the hearth. His mother ignores this small misdemeanour; her son is getting married in two days, so no matter now if other girls rib him.

'Who says you have to do all the running around yourself?' she scolds Lutfan. 'Send the boys, get Amir to go hurry the tailor. And Babua to rent three of the largest cooking pots.'

But Lutfan is intent on avoiding his nephews, and the job he has in mind is a delicate one, complicated and clandestine. He goes up to his room, dresses and returns to swallow down his breakfast.

And then they are off, he and Gopal Singh, walking through the streets of Rasra, this small country-town that is Lutfan's universe. Today, its early-morning tranquillity seems too lethargic for him; he is impatient of the whitewashed stone dargah whose keeper, watering the dust of his compound, spots Lutfan and, smiling, calls to him to ask if he is running off to Benares this early in the morning, without realizing that the joke is fact. Lutfan returns his greeting and hurries on, past the shuttered mission school, whose insides he has never seen, and the empty madrasa, where he has grappled with the Koran, and whose threadbare carpets and jagged brick walls he knows only too well. They pass the town market, the municipal office, the Nathji temple. In minutes they have left it all behind and are going through the orchards owned by Lutfan's father. The litchi is in flower and the mango trees, all leaves and shadows at the moment, will follow soon. Only the guava trees bear winter fruit, the pale sunlight-coloured skins revealing nothing of the luscious pink inside. They will be plucked and sold over the season, in the market of the *qasba* and also outside, in the larger towns of Mau and Ballia. As children, early in the season, Lutfan and Gopal would shake down the delightfully chewy, hard, fledgling fruit, but Lutfan is no longer in the mood to be a boy. He is going to Benares for the first time as a man, with Gopal Singh, who goes there every week.

Gopal's a big shot. He is a *dak harkara*, a foot-runner with the imperial government's postal service. He delivers post from the zilla headquarters at Ballia to the much bigger city of Benares and brings post back to Ballia. He wears a red-and-yellow tunic and calf-hugging pants, bells strapped on to his arms and ankles to forewarn snakes, a spear to fight off dacoits and tigers and a bugle to herald his approach to humankind. He is paid by the weight of the letter he carries and the distance he runs. Gopal has a reputation, for he can cover the hundred and forty kilometres to Benares in a day; no other runner in these parts can beat that. But today he's in a dhoti, a *dushala* of grey wool flung across one shoulder against the cold; he saunters, swinging a stick at the ribbed, old mango trunks and singing, in anticipation of the harvest festival the following week, a Sankranti song about the pleasures of kite-flying. He is not on duty today; Wednesdays and Sundays he returns home to Rasra and fills Lutfan's ears with tales of the big city.

'I am going to win,' he calls out to Lutfan, who is walking way ahead, for Gopal is as well known a wrestler as a runner and is confident that his opponent today will go down the way the others usually do.

'Walk faster then,' replies Lutfan. 'What kind of harkara are you?'

'The fastest one around. But even I'm not as fast as the telegraph lines.'

'What lines?'

'Arré, *touke samajh mey na aayi*,' mocks Gopal lightly in lilting Bhojpuri, and Lutfan is sore and keeps his face turned. Gopal continues to sing and does not mind. But Lutfan knows his friend is concerned about that telegraph.

'You won't remain ignorant of it for long, my friend,' says Gopal. 'I've met runners in Benares who lost their jobs because of it, this marvel that the government has been building for years. Soon, it is said, the telegraph will take over the country, relaying messages faster than men can, much faster than a horse courier even.'

'So how does it work? Do letters travel on the wind?'

Gopal explains how those wires that run high, straight lines against the sky enable messages tapped in one place to turn up, miraculously intact, long distances away.

'It's all a miracle of electricity,' he says. He knows that Lutfan, a child of Rasra's lantern-lit darkness, is in awe of this invention too. There are so many ideas that separate them.

But Lutfan and Gopal have been friends from before they had ideas—about closeness or distance. Their friendship has remained that way, a solid yet ordinary thing between boys growing up within shouting distance of each other's homes. The differences between them, the words in which their families pray or how their women dress, are too obvious to make a difference to them. Lutfan is the son of a small-time market farmer and Gopal the son of a rich, landowning thakur. At five, Lutfan clung to the doorpost of the Singh house, refusing to return to his own, convinced that the milk from its dairy tastes superior to the one in their canisters, which is delivered fresh every morning from the very same dairy. At ten, both boys saw, for the first time, the British collector ride through town on a high brown horse and followed his entourage as far as the police station. They looked for cruelty in his face, having been told for years about the extraordinary *rob*, the arrogance, of the man, and instead saw such vividly florid skin they've never forgotten the colour since. At fifteen, Gopal Singh went into government service and became a runner, even as he grew into the darling of the local *akhara* and, indisputably, its strongest wrestler. Lutfan began supervising the packing of fruit to dispatch, while his elder brothers oversaw the orchards and his father devoted himself to his other line—importing bales of printed calico and colourless khadi from Calcutta and Benares and supplying it to the handful of retailers in Rasra.

Next week Lutfan is marrying his cousin Mumtaz, his mother's brother's daughter. He has known her as a child in a red satin gharara, visiting their home at Eid, stuffing herself with gosht pulao, then wandering through the upstairs kothas without shyness, clearly impressed with the domestic set-up of the richer relative. And then she drops out of his memory; perhaps she took on the suitably inhibited mien of an older girl and sat quietly in the courtyard with the women on those subsequent Eid visits, well out of the men's way. Lutfan had never thought of her till the previous month, when an aunt brought up the subject. And now it is fixed.

Mumtaz lives in a village only an hour's walk from where the boys are now, having left the fruit trees behind and striding through the fields. This is the thakur's land, fields that start with the smaller beds of tomatoes and peas and then merge into the lush expanses of sugar cane and great stubbled plains from which the kharif crop of paddy has just been harvested. Somewhere on the blank horizon, beyond the small jheel they can see shimmering before the slowly rising sun—the waterbody to which this cultivation owes its greenness—is where Mumtaz lives. She will leave it for good next week. Again Lutfan feels a tenderness so searing it makes his heart lurch and he marches even faster, Gopal calling to him to wait as he plucks a shaggy length of green gram to chew on as they walk. He would like sugar cane but they don't have a sickle to cut it with and the rock-hard sticks are too strong even for this brazenly strong boy whose biceps are already twitching in anticipation, more than a hundred kilometres away from Benares and the big gymnasium where the wrestling competition is to be held.

They are walking south towards the great cities of the Gangetic plains. They might rest for an hour in Kasimabad, eat puri-aloo at Gopal's favourite wayside stall, then continue towards Ghazipur. It will take them all day to get there, and after spending the night in a dharamshala they will become part of the urban traffic between Ghazipur and Benares, hiring a horse-drawn *tanga* like everyone else in lieu of the rural walking of the previous day. Their cloth bundles, the ends tied together to make shoulder straps, each contain a change of clothes and a twig of neem to clean their teeth with, while small stashes of silver coins are secure in the inner pocket of their kurtas. The icy feel of the metal through their vests reminds them that they have a purpose. They are on their way to Benares: Lutfan to buy one of the city's famed and expensive silk saris in order to impress his bride-to-be, and Gopal to win a wrestling competition.

'It'll take two whole days,' says Gopal, but there is no complaint in his tone. To amble in the soft winter sun knowing the road is long and the destination not urgent is a form of freedom for him. This stopping and starting, the conversations and tea breaks en route, the chance to take the longer but more civilized path through a settlement instead of the treacherous shortcut through the jungle—all this is luxury for Gopal, the runner, whose nickname is 'Bijli', lightning, but who, even so, must worry about those rival telegraph lines. His worry does not cut into him, however, unlike Lutfan's. They walk side by side now and talk about it.

'This is folly,' says Lutfan, not because he entirely believes it but just to feel again the weight of what he is doing. 'Abba will scream when he hears. Money wasted on a silk sari when a muslin one would do.'

And there is more than just money involved but he wouldn't know how to express it. It is something to do with women and men, the unspoken idea that men don't go out of their way for women, that women don't deserve the exceptional attention of men. Lutfan has heard of these magical Benarsi silks from his father, who speaks of them as business, whereas in Lutfan's mind they have acquired the sheen of love. He feels love for them and a tortured, anxious love for the almost unknown woman he is going to marry. The two loves have fused into this resolution to sneak off to Benares with Gopal Singh and bring back something that will make Mumtaz sit up and the other women envious.

Gopal, to whom all things and not just money come more easily, confirms that Lutfan is doing the right thing.

'Why not?' he asks. 'It's time you went to Benares and saw what is what. And next time maybe we'll be able to take the train.'

If the British can draw lines across the whole country, then perhaps one day there will be a train through Rasra too. The rail line between Benares and Howrah was opened ten years ago and Gopal describes to his friend, as he has done before, how much he enjoys standing at the station in Benares and watching the trains roll in, delighting in their sound and fury.

'A thing that makes so much noise cannot but be effective.'

Lutfan is unusually silent again.

'Don't worry. I will show you the train,' says Gopal. 'I'll show you everything.'

———

Lutfan remembers nothing of his journey from Rasra to Benares as a child of four or five, but can still hear the ekka-wallah clicking his tongue to spur on his pony while Lutfan and his father bumped behind him on the cart through the narrow alleys of Jaitpura, searching for the house of the family elder who had just died of cholera. Later, he was given a chamcham to eat in a small clay dish and has never forgotten the stunning sweetness of that spongy brown sphere through the crunch of the poppy seeds coating it. Out on the ghats he saw a woman so ancient he wondered if she was Hav'vah, wife of Adam, the first woman on earth in the tales he'd heard all his infant life. But his father was furious at the blasphemy and had got even angrier when Lutfan, on their way back home, urinated against a tamarind tree. To his father, trees have always been sacred, fire holy, monkeys incarnations of Hanuman and not to be messed with.

These beliefs have seeped into Lutfan over the years. Yet as he and Gopal, after their two-day sun-filled, heart-gladdening, foot-numbing sojourn, now come down to Benares's mighty river, its far horizon still smothered in fog, Lutfan misses noticing its expanse, the multitude of morning bathers despite the cold and the priests under their bamboo *chattri*s already ready to receive them. He is looking for Hav'vah again, huddled by herself in one corner of the ghat steps and staring out across the water with the far-sighted eyes of the old. They have just reached the city and Lutfan still sees it as the setting of his one prior unforgotten experience, not a place with a life of its own.

Slowly, however, Benares starts to impinge on him. The two boys dip in the shallows, wipe themselves dry with their cast-off clothes, then climb the ghats and enter the tenor of the city. Lutfan is sure he can smell kachoris frying but Gopal says one does not fight on a full stomach. Before they can argue, there is a *tazia* procession in their path. Lutfan is arrested by the joy on the faces of the men. They sing and chant, while those at the head solemnly bear the replica of the tomb of that beloved martyr, the Prophet's grandson. Lutfan has never seen a tazia from this close—another thing inculcated in him since childhood is to stay away from those crazed Shias. Here it doesn't matter; he doesn't know them and they don't know him, and so, paradoxically, he can be familiar, leisurely examine the decorations and nod at the howling men in appreciation. A cow—the string of fresh marigolds dangling from her horns giving her a look of feminine insouciance—appears to be following the men but then halts abruptly, in the middle of the flow of people, to ruminate. Men in starched dhotis and women with the pulled ends of their saris swaying before their eyes continue walking without breaking their stride, touching the cow's side and then putting their fingers to their hearts, a passing gesture of devotion.

Gopal suddenly realizes that he must visit the Hanuman temple before the wrestling match.

'But you're going to win,' says Lutfan. 'You've always won.'

Gopal laughs and says, 'And I've always laid a coin at his feet, before every match.'

'Put a word in his ear for me too. About my marriage . . .'

'What about it?' asks Gopal, not smiling any more, being grave as a way of poking fun. He is married with a child and another on its way, and Lutfan's bachelorhood amuses him—one more sign of his friend's lack of worldliness.

But Lutfan is already full of Benares and for a moment cannot recall what preoccupies him about Mumtaz. He is distracted by the unmistakable feel of Sankranti festivity in the air: the thrilling crispness of new paper kites piled in shops, heaps of beaten rice, the smell of crunchy sesame and jaggery sweets and a man pouring out discs of bubbling sugar syrup on to a tray to make batasha. Children run between the open doors of houses facing each other in the sunless alleys. A toy seller hawks his finely carved wooden specimens from a hole in the wall, and from right behind Lutfan comes the smell of a pony's leathery sweat and the same marvellous notes from the ekka-wallah's mouth that he has saved up from childhood. Here, in the great city, Lutfan is both smaller and larger than the man he was when he set out from home two mornings ago. How can one person's desires stand out in Benares, where there are seemingly a hundred temples with the gilded feet of multitudes of gods to lay every possible prayer at? Yet how much more important he will seem to himself when he has returned to Rasra, in his bag the sari that is the object of his secret trip, the thing already distinct in his mind even though he is not sure he has enough money.

They make their way through the lanes to the southernmost ghat and the temple near it. Lutfan stops at a small square around

a rambling banyan tree, while Gopal works his way into the crowd
heading for a glimpse of the idol of Hanumanji. Back home,
Lutfan knows the neighbourhood temple; he has looked into the
eyes of its gods and slept summer nights sprawled on its cool
stone floor. But here, seeing the hordes of strangers flitting in
and out, he holds himself back. He does as Gopal says. Gopal had
promised that he would let Lutfan into everything but Lutfan
realizes that his friend is experienced and he is not, and there
is no way around this incompatibility. He wishes he'd learnt
to wrestle as a child instead of spending his mornings tracing
with one finger the letters of the Koran. Then he is guilty and
breathes a word of pardon to God. He thinks again of Mumtaz
and worries. There seems to be nothing to marriage. Men acquire
women and then these women become like things of the home
dulled by use—recognizable shapes, familiar presences. Will this
happen in his case too, or is there something he has missed, an
unknown vocabulary, a private knowledge, that will change her
from stranger to wife?

In the open veranda of a two-storeyed house by the square, a
recitation is in progress and, sitting there, Lutfan is slowly drawn
into the story, which he knows well. Lakshman is tracing the magic
circle for Sita outside their forest home, reminding her not to step
out of it. She promises her brother-in-law she won't. The reciter
has a printed book open before him, Tulsidas's Ramcharitmanas.
Now and again he turns the pages with a delicate concentration
but then seems to forget about the book as he performs the story
with flourish, now playing Sita's part, now Lakshman's. Lutfan
starts to experience not the evocation of a remote forest in a
distant time but its closeness to him. The square has dissolved
into that forest made vivid by the danger that Sita is about to face.

Gopal hands him a banana he's brought back from the temple.

'He's been at it a long time,' he says about the reciter. 'At least a year. Every afternoon you'll find him here. At this pace, it'll take him another year to finish.'

'It's not a child's lullaby, the Ramayana,' says Lutfan, marvelling at the man's patience and wanting his job. To sit like this every day for years at a time and charm audiences with stories and then be free to roam the streets, eat what one will from the wayside spreads, stop to rest on the plinth of any temple. And in the evening take a boat down the river and listen to the boatman's songs.

'Who pays him?' he asks, peeling and eating the banana whole.

'The city of Benares is full of rich merchants wanting to improve their karma.'

'Doesn't the raja provide for everyone?' asks Lutfan.

'Arré nahi,' says Gopal, dismissing his naivety. 'Such men could buy out the raja any day.'

He pulls off his dushala, gives it to Lutfan together with his bundle of things and then he is off; Lutfan gets up and runs after him. When they reach the akhara he is amazed again. Rasra's akhara is a small, packed mud enclosure, where the paan-chewing master sits in one corner having his limbs forever rubbed down with warm mustard oil, a model of decadence in a job that demands vigour. This man before them is a frightfully large wrestler, his eyes ringed with kohl and his head shaven to a copper gleam. He walks around barking at his boys who keep their faces averted from him as they swing huge wooden clubs or wrestle in a sandpit, intent on getting a grip on each other's waists or shoulders.

Gopal's arrival causes no frisson at all. At home he's a star but here he just tightens his loincloth and joins the row of boys doing squats. This bothers Lutfan, the casual way his friend Gopal, a man of great distinction, has become one with the greasy throng of bodies. Surely they're aware of who he is. These people—no matter that they live in Benares and see wondrous things every day—are not runners entrusted with the profound task of carrying letters to and from the high officials of the land as well as parcels of books and documents in English, the language in which, to Lutfan's mind, only matters of utmost gravity are expressed. Lutfan walks back and forth before the exercising boys, trying to catch his friend's eye, but Gopal is completely absorbed in the rhythm of the movement, swinging his arms, standing and squatting repeatedly without the least display of effort.

'Enough!' shouts the guru suddenly. Everyone gathers around him. Strung on a pole is a painting, on cloth, of Hanuman, his bare muscles gleaming golden, and they all join hands before him. The boys touch the master's feet in turn and he puts streaks of red on each of their foreheads and urges victory upon them. Then they all troop out into the streets, ready to compete in the *dangal*, the competition in honour of the Sankranti festival.

The rival gymnasium is identical except that it's decorated with coloured leaves and its pennant is green and blue unlike the scarlet of Gopal's akhara. Everyone is welcomed with a drink of sweet, warm milk mixed with crushed almonds and filaments of saffron. Lutfan is taken for one of the wrestlers and gets a clay cup too. He downs it quickly, the flavour as exotic to him as every second thing in this city, and then calls to Gopal.

'*Dikhai de,*' he says, urging him on.

'*Aur ka?*' answers Gopal confidently.

An announcement is made; men going about their business on the street start to troop in, happy to abandon their tasks and settle down to watch.

The first boy from Gopal's team is matched with a combatant twice his size. The boys throw a handful of dirt on each other to inaugurate the proceedings, and then, astonishingly, the larger boy's limbs are folded into each other like a length of stiff rope and he is put down without fuss. It is over in moments and the watching men cheer delightedly. The winner is handed a small velvet bag of coins by the leader of the organizing akhara. Gopal comes on next, smiling at his opponent like he smiles at everyone. His chubby rival seems equally happy. They lower their heads and take hold of each other but it soon turns out that neither can break into the other's strength, a strength which binds their feet firmly to the ground, an iron strength that must not, cannot, be overcome as much as cleverly tripped up.

Gopal tries time and again to fasten himself to his opponent's knee, fell the man by disabling his legs. But the man catches on to it and responds by hugging Gopal around the waist, almost lovingly, though Lutfan can feel in his own body, having watched wrestling bouts for years, the unyielding hardness of this grip. Gopal, he realizes with a surge of pride, is finally up against someone made of comparable stuff. His winning over this man is going to be a triumph. The other spectators are riveted too. Gopal's guru thumps the large bamboo cane he carries and growls incoherent words of encouragement at him. It goes on for several minutes; just as one wrestler seems to have found the pivot that will bring the other down, the other fobs him off through a calculated lunge of his own.

In the end Gopal has the baby-faced man crouched on the mud and is bending over him, preparing to force him on to his back and straddle him, pin him to the ground, win the bout. Lutfan has been creeping closer and closer to the pair in his excitement and is now near enough to see the perspiration on their faces and the mud streaking their hair.

'Arré *peeche hat*!' someone shouts at Lutfan, ordering him out of the way; he withdraws, startled, and in that instant the tables turn. Gopal is suddenly flat out, Lutfan cannot tell how. His enemy has his hands pressed to Gopal's shoulders, teeth bared in concentration, and the fight is over.

'What?' asks Lutfan, bewildered.

But the next bout is already starting and no one there knows Gopal well enough to try and analyse the upset or challenge it.

'You have to fight again,' says Lutfan.

'Let's go,' says Gopal, wiping himself hurriedly with a towel.

'Gopal harkara, you run?' demands his guru, coming up to him. 'When you run, do you use up all your energy by sprinting very fast or pace it out?'

Gopal says nothing as he pleats his dhoti. He keeps his eyes down and shrugs.

'It's the same when you fight. You were so sure in the end because you had him on the ground. That's why he could come back. Because he saw how sure you were. The sureness made you weak.'

'Start the fight again, that *dugla* was cheating,' cries Lutfan.

'*Abbé*!' shouts the guru, beating his stick on the ground. 'Who are you? Clear out of here. This is a proper Sankranti dangal, not cheap entertainment for *launda*s without muscles.'

'Let's go,' says Gopal again.

'But why did you let him beat you?' says Lutfan, his voice shrill with grievance. It suddenly comes to him that this is part of the nature of Benares too—the mammoth city is indifferent to the minor injustices being perpetrated in its alleys.

'It's the money that's bothering you,' says Gopal, suddenly annoyed. 'What's my winning or losing got to do with it?'

'No,' says Lutfan. 'When did I say anything about money?'

'So why are you grumbling then?'

'*Toukey apan ijjat ka kauno khayal huh ki naahi?*'

At this mention of wounded pride, Gopal stalks out; Lutfan looks at the glowering guru and then has no choice but to follow.

———

Again the river, open and without end, planted there as if to contrast with the crowded city. Lutfan watches as Gopal's torso is enveloped in the murky water flecked with flower petals, then his shoulders, then his face. He has disappeared and Lutfan is alone in Benares. Every turn he takes will lead him deeper into the confusion of lanes; he'll ask repeatedly for directions that the sprawl of the city will make impossible to follow. He'll wander aimlessly, like a mendicant, beg for food when his money runs out, then find a mosque to sleep in at night. Someday, maybe, chancing upon a party also heading to Ballia, perhaps even to Rasra, he'll find his way back home. But if not, if the distance between there and here proves too great and his friend has vanished for good, Lutfan will merge into this vast city watched over by vultures and gods.

The winter afternoon is mellow and already the sun has lost its short-lived noontime sting. A man farther up the ghats has started a small wood fire and is thrusting sprigs of green gram into it. When he sees Lutfan coming he prises the shells of the pods open, adds a smear of garlic chutney and hands a full leaf cup to the boy without saying a word. Lutfan gives him a coin, takes the snack and sits down to eat it with pleasure. He has no thoughts except of the moment.

'Buy me some too,' says Gopal.

Lutfan turns to see his friend standing behind him, his hair wet, his face glowing.

'So this is why you came to Benares, to take a bath?' asks Lutfan.

'I'm hungry,' says Gopal, grabbing a handful of Lutfan's gram.

'You're the fastest runner in the service but no one knows that here. Some fat boy fights you to the ground and you take it quietly instead of showing them who you are,' says Lutfan bitterly.

Gopal chews and doesn't answer.

'I came with you because I thought you knew the ways of this city,' continues Lutfan. 'How are we going to find a proper meal and then make our way back on the few coins we have?'

The ghats are enveloped in an afternoon lull. The priests seem to be dozing under their bamboo parasols. There are no vendors around except the man patiently fanning his flames, so Gopal buys himself a cup too and proceeds to eat it.

'We should go home,' says Lutfan. 'I'm sitting here killing flies while work piles up. Someone has to go out and buy a goat and a bag of rice, or will people eat grass at my wedding?'

He gets up, returns Gopal's bundle to him and lifts his own on to his shoulders. He wants to tell his friend that it isn't only a question of money but he already did that and repeating it will not undo Gopal's accusation. He kicks at the sand of the riverbank, strewn with the mouldering leavings of pilgrims, and is angry—at Gopal, at the lost opportunity, at this confounding city. Despite his annoyance, he has to wait for Gopal to take the lead. When he turns back to glance at him, he sees that Gopal, framed as beautifully as one of God's angels against the river lit by the sinking sun, is laughing at him.

Lutfan had hoped his friend's silence hid some small measure of contrition but there is no trace of it in his voice. He is laughing out loud and calls Lutfan a fool as a way of mollifying him.

'Arré *bhaiya, kahe ko khissiya gaye ho*? You want to go and look for hot kachoris?'

'No,' says Lutfan. 'You're a loser and I'm a fool.'

'Okay. Don't eat anything. Starve. But isn't there something you've been eating my head about for weeks? Some place called Jaitpura?'

Lutfan says, 'I'll go myself.'

'Very good. I'm sure you can make your own way there. Benares is your playground, isn't it?'

'What does it matter? You're no use to me, anyway. You don't have the money.'

Gopal smiles at Lutfan's answering sarcasm. This is new between them, the spectre of money. Lutfan has never needed it before nor depended on Gopal to loan it to him. And now everything is infected with it, even his regret at his friend's defeat.

'No money. But I'm still Bijli, the fastest runner. And let Holi come, there'll be lots of wrestling competitions then. I'm going to learn a few new tricks in the meanwhile.'

'Let's forget this sari. I don't want it. I've seen the wonders of Benares and that's enough,' says Lutfan.

'But this is a wonder even I haven't seen. And who knows, we might get one on credit. Aren't those sari-wallahs your relatives?'

And with that, suddenly, Gopal is off again and Lutfan must accept that everything is all right. Again the city starts winking its mysteries at him—an arm covered with bright bangles flashing in an upper window, the almost human voice of an astrologer's parrot at a street corner. In twenty minutes they are at the Eidgah, asking for directions to Jaitpura; once there, they search for the house of Lutfan's relative, the same family he and his father once visited. It was his father's cousin who had died then and the man they are looking for now is his son. His name is Benarsi Mian and he is a master weaver.

They find the house, pass through a dark entranceway and come into the courtyard, where two men are talking over saris of the most brilliant silk spread out on a rope bed. From the rooms on the left comes the loud clatter of handlooms.

One of the men rises and greets Gopal and Lutfan politely without asking who they are; he calls to one of the weavers, who comes out and pulls down a standing rope-bed for them. Only after they have been seated and given a drink of water from the clay surahi in the corner are they asked for their business. Lutfan explains and the man stands up again and clasps Lutfan to his chest. This is Benarsi Mian, a gaunt adolescent at the time of his father's funeral fifteen years ago, but now a clearly prosperous man of middle age, with rolls of fat under his soft, white muslin kurta and yards of expensive silk before him, which he is negotiating the price of. The boys wait till the transaction is done and the trader or middleman has carefully folded and bundled up the saris into a clean sheet, paid Benarsi Mian and taken off.

'How is Abba?' asks Benarsi.

'He's busy with the cloth business. I look after the agriculture,' says Lutfan, exaggerating a little.

Benarsi Mian smiles and says, 'We are small people. It's our good fortune that you've come to meet us.' Then he asks what they would like to eat and, in the face of his obviously false modesty, the boys demur, saying, despite the hunger tautening their stomachs, that they've already eaten.

Lutfan tries to think of a way of broaching the subject of his wedding, the possible sari, the absurdly small knot of coins inside his clothes. The weavers start leaving off their work one after another and gather around them, curious about the visitors. To Lutfan's surprise, Benarsi does not seem to mind. The place has a fraternal air; Benarsi Mian is the master of this workshop and yet the men are easy around him. This is new to Lutfan. The servile men and women who work on his farm back home would never think to mingle so freely with their employer, even less with their employer's guests. He puts the camaraderie down to the city of Benares; it is a place, he is starting to see, that takes each thing he is used to and turns it upside down. Even Gopal's defeat was the result of this: the sorcery of this city.

When the small talk about his family peters out, Lutfan asks how long they have been weaving. They laugh and say, 'Oh, for centuries.' One of them declares, 'It's the evening of our art. You should have seen us in the Mughal years. The kind of brocade we wove then, the magical patterns that came out of these workshops . . .'

'What's the use of crying over the Mughals?' says Benarsi. 'Zafar is dead, fifteen years gone since the war that routed him and more than fifty since there was an emperor on the throne with any wealth to speak of. There's nothing left of them.'

'True, true,' says another weaver. 'It's the English who are kings now.'

'Not kings—robbers,' cuts in Benarsi. 'Everyone can see how they're bringing piece goods into the city to undercut the prices of our silk.'

'Those who know the difference know,' says another, older, weaver wearily. 'Where is an ordinary scrap of factory-made cloth and where a yard of silk the texture of a butterfly's wing?'

'So would you like to buy a sari for your woman, big man?' Benarsi Mian asks Gopal, who, uncharacteristically, blushes and nods vaguely.

Lutfan steps in. His friend knows nothing of saris. 'Yes,' he says. 'We'd like to see your best.'

The weavers drift back to their work, apparently losing interest when the talk turns to business. Benarsi brings out saris and Lutfan is dazzled again. He knows the value of the sack-covered bales of cotton cloth that his father brings home to resell but this fabric being spun out before him, each colour glowing more fiercely than the last, seems beyond the measure of money. He is a beggar here, he suddenly realizes, and panic makes him voluble. He praises the incandescent silk and the more he admires, the more Benarsi brings out to unfold and shake before his astonished eyes.

Gopal finally opens his mouth but he seems to be speaking in Lutfan's voice, not his own ever-sure one.

'It's time we started out.'

But Lutfan has suddenly spotted it, a sari the colour of a ravishing sunset on a winter's evening. Its rosiness is of a magnificence that just does not seem man-made, and its border is sky-coloured too—a heavy blue brocade intricately patterned with silver. Lutfan stares at the sari in dismay, afraid to touch it, already lusting for it.

Benarsi immediately notices his expression and says, 'Very good, mian. This is a new piece. I can calender it if you wait half an hour.'

He does not bring up the cost and Lutfan is rigid with embarrassment now.

Gopal intervenes. 'Brother, won't you tell us the price?'

'I'm a small man,' says Benarsi Mian. 'What I need to keep this roof over my head and my workers going is what I take for my goods. But Lutfan Mian is a different matter. He's my brother. Let him pay me what he likes.'

Lutfan wants to run—out into the cheerful clatter of the street, to the river, to the road that will take him home. But he cannot take his eyes off the sari and he has no idea what his cousin is talking about. *Pay him what I like? Does he mean that I can toss him a coin like I did to the gram vendor? On the other hand, we could*

give him all our money and even that might fall staggeringly short.
Gopal and I will be laughed out of this house.

He looks to his friend for help. Gopal is right, he is a fool. He
came to the city on faith—that Gopal would win, that the sari
would be his.

'What do you do, big man?' Benarsi is asking Gopal, and
before Gopal can answer, Lutfan says, to inflate his own standing,
'He is, really, a very big man.'

But would a runner qualify as great in Benarsi Mian's scheme
of things? Lutfan starts to embroider his statement. 'It's his great
generosity that he accompanied me here today. He's always
so busy.'

Benarsi smiles and nods.

'Naturally you don't recognize him but you must have heard
all the many stories about him. I have to tell you that you're very
lucky to be spending so much time in his company, the famous
Gopal Singh.'

'Who?' asks Benarsi.

'Gopal Singh of Benares. Surely you've heard of him?'

Gopal is silent and expressionless, as befits a celebrity.

'Of course, of course,' says Benarsi hurriedly and Lutfan
knows he's got him. He glances at his friend—the friend with
whom he grew up playing so many small, conspiratorial games
against the world—and the pact between them is instant: we're
taking him for a ride.

'So I said to Gopal Singhji, don't even consider it. How can
you take the whole evening off and come with me to Jaitpura. Can
the lord sahibs be kept waiting just because I, a poor boy from the
qasba, wants to get a sari? And he says, "If the lord sahibs ask, I
will tell them friendship comes before duty. Besides, I have heard
so much about Benarsi Mian's work. I must see for myself."'

'It's God's bounty that you graced my house.'

Gopal smiles thinly and Lutfan hurries on with his story. He has been quietened by Benares and the journey and the idea of marriage but now he is his mother's loquacious boy again, the story pouring out of his mouth fully formed.

'You should hear his English. Forget speaking, he can read and write it so well, even the lord sahibs are put to shame. He usually wears English clothes too, it's only to come to your house that he put on these ordinary clothes so people on the street wouldn't gape.'

'Can I get you some lassi?' asks Benarsi. 'Aloo tikiya? Chai?'

'Nothing, nothing. We have to go. The lord sahibs are waiting.'

Gopal finally opens his mouth.

'I must tell the sahibs about your good work. Their *mem*s will send for you, I'm sure. They go on chattering about their love for the silks of Benares so I'll let it drop in conversation that your workshop is the finest.'

Benarsi's great paan-stained smile won't leave his face.

'Lutfan is right, you're a good and gracious man. Please don't leave my house without taking something with you. Didn't you say you liked this sari?'

Lutfan and Gopal go silent, awed by the prospect of their gambit paying off.

'I don't want to disappoint you,' says Gopal loftily. 'But I insist we pay for it.'

'Never,' declares Benarsi. 'How can you insult me like this?'

Lutfan interjects, 'He's not saying we'll pay you the market rate. But allow us to show our appreciation too. We'll give you a small token, that's all.'

He brings out his coins, as does Gopal. With many salaams and protestations and declarations of mutual respect, Benarsi is persuaded to take the money. He orders his weavers to get working on the fabric, press and polish it to bring out the sheen. While this is being done Lutfan and Gopal eat the fresh, syrupy jalebis that Benarsi has insisted on sending for. Business out of the way, he becomes expansive again and talks of everything, from the greatness of the raja to the laziness of his workers.

Then Lutfan rinses his hands and is presented with the sari. He can immediately feel the heat from the calendered silk seeping into his fingers. He thanks Benarsi on behalf of Gopal, the big man.

Benarsi says, 'This is nothing, brother. You came without telling me. Come on the first of next month, I'll save the most beautiful brocades for you.'

The boys say they will return but know they won't. Then, holding the sari to himself, forgetting, in that moment of possession, the great things still left to see, trains and telegraph lines and lord sahibs in the flesh, Lutfan tells Gopal, 'Show me the road home.'

So Gopal, humming a song about following a kite into the heavens, leads the way, and the boys are slowly obliterated by the cold evening mist.

And that is how it starts, the legend of Lutfan Mian. In the beginning, this momentous journey, whose story he narrates individually to every member of his family, is recollected as a slow and lengthy one. But over the decades his children and grandchildren, out of love for their illustrious parent and under the influence of tales of Gopal Singh's famous lightning speed, whittle the distance down, in their own telling, as taking a day in either direction. By the time Anjum hears it, her great-great-grandfather, Lutfan Mian, is known as the man who could walk to Benares and back in a single day.

5

YELLOW ROSE

Gulfam disliked going out. Every day, week by week, she saw a little less of the outdoor world of heat and dust that did not respond to a click or a swipe, that was composed everywhere of odd angles and misshapen silhouettes, that followed no clear laws, certainly not the magnificently simple binary ones that she lived by.

She had reluctantly inhabited that messy and messed-up world for the first twenty-three years of her life but had withdrawn from it in the last two, since she quit her job and decided to employ herself. She rarely looked out at the view. In fact, having moved house so many times, she had more or less forgotten what the prospect from living-room balcony or kitchen window was like. Something would bother Gulfam—a landlord suddenly dictating unreasonable terms from his penthouse somewhere in America; a neighbour in the course of an unwelcome chat, wanting to know the identity of the man who sometimes visited her; the maid inquiring once too often about why she lived alone—and she would give notice, call one of the half-a-dozen brokers she knew, impatiently urge on the movers encasing her meagre belongings with blundering care in bubble wrap and cartons, and leave.

She had hopped all over Bangalore with her minimalist ensemble of futon, sparse kitchenware, a couple of boxes of clothes and her laptop. She did not read, except blog posts and newsfeeds, so there were no books to lug around; she hardly ever went for parties any more and had let go of the fusty heirloom saris and last year's dresses. She made sure she always had just three pairs of shoes, two wine glasses, one ballpoint pen. Much of everything else she threw away. She was a determined discarder. She promptly got rid of birthday gifts of perfume or filmy scarves, clothes barely worn, any hand-drawn or dog-eared relic of her childhood, the creaky collections of photo albums and spiritual guidebooks her grandparents had left her and the useless decorative mementoes her mother always brought her and urged her to put on display so that she, Gulfam's mother, could find her bearings and feel marginally at home in the many un-homelike, bare-walled, hollow-shelved, empty-balconied flats that Gulfam lived in.

Gulfam dreamed of world happiness bred by a universal conversion to in-the-moment functionalism, played out in a perfectly controlled indoor existence. She loved futuristic movies awash with jargon and sleek gadgetry in which neither human nor physical nature intruded—no erratic clouds moving across the sky, no sudden moods altering the state of one's existence. Her favourite YouTube video at the moment featured the wedding ceremony of a man and a robot. Her favourite TED talk was by the world's neatest woman. Her favourite podcast was about how Mars would eventually be colonized by the very smart and the uberwealthy. Her favourite new technology was the flying car. She wished she had been attributed, at birth, a string of numbers instead of a name, that she lived in a post-apocalyptic society of humans with short-term memories and dreamless sleep, housed in prefabricated intelligent homes and needing nothing to live life and enjoy it except their handsets.

Instead she was in Bangalore, a city she could not discard—much as she wanted to—her association with. This was where she belonged: her parents had been born and were still stuck here, she still saw updates from her three school friends who had long alienated her with their enthusiasm for marriage and children, she had been pushed around in this city's buses to and from office and had had crushes, in retrospect mortifying for their juvenility and misdirected passion, on male colleagues. But she was about as old as the Internet was to Bangalore, and as a preadolescent, engrossed for hours in her father's laptop, she was already living almost entirely, even if she would not have understood the word then, vicariously. Those days it was GTalk, world-building games and gushy WordPress journals. Now it was online shopping, meme philosophizing and virtual consultations with therapists and accountants, when she needed them.

'You have the soul of a cyborg,' Mathew said to her one afternoon as they sat on her futon with their laptops warm from daylong use and their tepid cups of green tea. Gulfam and Mathew were working on an app for urban home-gardeners. On Greenfingers you could do: the usual. Order products, get advice from professionals, network with other gardeners, sell your produce. They had, just the previous week, successfully finished with an app that enabled you to compare the fees, ratings and curricula of colleges across the country and apply to the one that suited you. Every week, perhaps every day, all over Bangalore, someone in the course of a deadening office meeting or a coffee-shop conversation came up with the one application they believed was unique enough to reshape twenty-first-century existence, or at least make it perfectly simple to order in organic cow-dung cakes.

Gulfam and Mathew's fledgling company received commissions to bring to life a few of those multitudes of banal ideas.

Gulfam took his remark seriously. 'If I were rich I would emigrate to where they're fitting office workers with microchips in their wrists so they just have to wave their hands to open doors or pay bills.'

Mathew sighed. He wouldn't mind being rich too. 'I'll do this,' he said to the strings of code that filled his screen, 'till I am thirty and then you wait and see.'

'If I could get five crore somehow, I'd retire and live on the interest. And spend all my time volunteering for experiments in cloning and artificial intelligence,' said Gulfam.

'Even if you died or got brain damage?'

Gulfam nodded solemnly. 'Or even if I became another person. In fact, I would like to become another person.'

'You might go schizoid.'

'I could be. It already feels like it's not coming together. I need to do something about it *right now*.'

'You know that farm my parents have—the hundred-acre rubber plantation? I plan to take it over, put in some rocks, grow a forest, get a serious adventure tourism thing going.'

'Okay,' said Gulfam, bored by talk of farms and bored even of Greenfingers.

'Do you want to invest with me? We could move to Kerala.'

Gulfam got off the futon in surprise, clicked her laptop shut, lit a cigarette. Mathew had quit the office job at the same time as her and they'd drifted into a partnership together—another of those cafe chats that sounded casual and provisional but became the basis, surprisingly, to their parents and everyone else of that generation, of hard cash. He had a girlfriend but wasn't reporting to Gulfam this past month, as he used to, on her emotional instability and permanent office blues. Perhaps there was no such fact as the girlfriend any more, but Gulfam didn't want Mathew to hit on her instead. She had no interest in Mathew except for his computing skills, and she hoped that all this talk of Kerala and adventure tourism wasn't his idea of a come-on.

'Um,' she said, opening the living-room window just a crack and aiming her exhalations at it. 'I can't move to anywhere hot.' Bangalore smelt of sewers and other people's cooking. She shut the window with a bang.

'Where do you want to go, then?' he asked, flashing his jagged teeth. He didn't seem offended at her rebuttal. He was always good-humoured, Gulfam realized, and never earnest.

'To the moon, Mathew,' said Gulfam. 'As you very well know. Let's get back to work.'

Mathew was known as Mallu Madhew in office, to distinguish him from the other Mathew, a blue-eyed American from downturn-afflicted Detroit. His grandfather called him Saint Mathew. His friends called him Maths. Gulfam had always thought of him as just plain Mathew, and appreciated his view, because it matched hers, that one ought to think big or not bother at all. She didn't know very many people with the same outlook. Her own father had written her off for her lack of realism. His realism had led him to nothing but a well-paid, and apparently dull, career in international finance and a divorce from Gulfam's mother. He nevertheless held on to the view that the middle path was the golden one, even though to Gulfam it looked more like grey. She either wanted to be super-rich and undertake space travel, or live alone in a shack on a mountaintop with just an ambient light-powered game console for company.

'Margherita and/or marinara,' said Mathew, temporarily losing interest in home gardening, scrolling through the menus

on a food home-delivery app, his favourite for the reason that it
allowed you to compare pizzas across the city not just by topping,
size or price but also cheesiness, crunch and speed of delivery.

'I have some ideas regarding that five crore,' he said, having
ordered far too much food. His primary suggestion was antiques;
the ones in Indian museums were worth shitloads abroad, he
declared, and suggested Gulfam make friends with a low-ranking
museum official in order to do the smuggling. Mathew would
then scuba-dive with the antiques from India to wherever.
Gulfam looked at him and thought about the shallowness of her
love life so far. But however difficult it had been for her to find
anyone who cared about the search for extraterrestrial intelligence
as much as she did, it would be pitiable indeed if it came down to
this—a man with nothing but a bunch of rubber trees to his name
and jokey schemes in his head.

Yet, because he had spoken those words—what exactly were
those words, again?—because there was the suggestion of an
imagined future in them—and what is love except the promise of
such a future?—she was already, without even really wanting to,
seeing Mathew in an entirely new light. He had correctly identified
the nature of her soul. They had a successful business together. His
moustache was not unattractive. Maybe she could tame his hilarity.
Maybe she could interest him in building a state-of-the-art cyber-
forensics lab once the rubber trees had been dispensed with.

Mathew was on a call to some buddy or the other, discussing
some bike ride across the country they were planning or
planning to plan. His capacity for extended conversation never
failed to put off Gulfam, who generally shrank from human
contact. She would have liked to stop talking altogether, to
keep her cigarette in her mouth, her words in shorthand and
her feelings in emojis. Phone calls were better than meeting

in person and instant messaging was better than phone calls. She had even wanted to run their company over Skype, but Mathew had laughed and told her she needed to see a better therapist for her sociopathic tendencies.

How could she be capable of human love if she really was a cyborg? They'd both just be unhappy. And if Mathew was meant to be the one, oughtn't she have zoned into him earlier? Why the prelude of these two long years when all she'd seen in him was a friend and collaborator? On the other hand, wasn't that how relationships went? You spent your youth pining for the gorgeously inappropriate ones, not recognizing that the ideal—if plain-faced and wisecracking—chap had been under your nose all the time. How plebeian and commonsensical that sounded, how much like her father. And, yet, what was she to do with Mathew now that there was a distinct note of awkwardness in the air? Or maybe it was just her imagining it, as she continued to stand there and smoke a second cigarette, pretending to browse her phone, while Mathew paid for the pizza and was actually smiling at it lovingly before he proceeded to chomp it down. Suddenly, though, he broke off to say, 'Would you mind if I made an observation about you?' And then, without waiting for Gulfam to give him the go-ahead, 'You would be cute if you didn't smoke.'

Gulfam snapped the cigarette out of her mouth, then put it back in immediately. She was saved from replying by her phone ringing. It was her mother, Nusrat, who was due to drop in later that day for one of her weekly intrusions, a visit for Nusrat, but for Gulfam more of a visitation, a haunting from another sphere where eating balanced meals was of more consequence than job satisfaction and a verse of poetry more moving than the thought of life in the far reaches of the solar system.

'I am stuck in a situation,' said Nusrat. 'I parked in an inappropriate place for two minutes to buy you a flowerpot and the car was towed away before my eyes and now I'm marooned in the middle of the highway without a taxi or rickshaw at hand and my phone battery's on its deathbed. Plus I stubbed my toe trying to run after the tow truck.'

'It's okay, Ma. I wasn't expecting you till much later.'

'I'm on the wrong side of the road, everything's moving in the other direction, and I have a half-kilo sodden plant in my hand and the afternoon sun beating down on my head. I'm not complaining, but still. Can you come and get me?'

'How?' cried Gulfam. She aimed to be always cool, in keeping with her idealization of automatons, but Mathew's so-called observation, made with a smile from a mouth distended with marinara, had thrown her, and now her mother was appealing to her for help, which she almost never did. Nusrat wrote books, reared pets, kept house and took off, without warning, on self-appointed holidays. It was not like her to end up helpless in the middle of nowhere, and that she had managed to do so on a day when Mathew was being personal was plain ridiculous.

'Just get a cab and come. I'm texting you the location.'

'But Mathew's still here,' said Gulfam.

'Mathew! That lovely American boy you wanted to . . .' and Gulfam slapped her hand over her phone and glanced at Mathew. He was miming greed for a slice of her pizza; she smiled weakly and gave him a thumbs up.

'Ma,' she whispered. 'Don't waste your damn phone battery on inessentials. I am working and in any case you know I never step out before dark. My skin is allergic to vitamin D. I'll send you a cab.'

'I need to retrieve my car and I need a Band-Aid. I just had to get something alive for you to take care of and I know you might mistakenly murder a kitten if I left one with you so that's how I ended up like this.' She laughed but sounded weepy. What could have happened to Nusrat? Had the traffic exhaust that she blithely sucked in by the lungful on her daily walks and exploratory drives finally turned to kryptonite?

'Stay where you are then,' said Gulfam, haughty but worried.

She explained the situation to Mathew and ten minutes later they were in a taxi, she blinking painfully in the unwholesome four-o'-clock light of May and unable to remember the last time she had been out so early in the day. She shut her eyes despite the sunglasses on her nose, trying and failing to describe to Mathew the kind of creature her mother was, to forewarn him about her difference from her daughter, not an ordinary motherly incompatibility but a dangerously alien otherness.

Mathew seemed unaffected and said, 'She sounds like my mother except, of course, that my mother could never drive a car or speak English or step into an ATM.'

Gulfam wondered if he was joking and laughed weakly though she was actually horror-struck. She wasn't prepared for such antiquities in close proximity to her world—those men and women one sometimes came upon, punching their decade-old cell phones with exaggerated force and care and then pressing them tight to their ears and hollering into them as if communicating with spirits from outer space. How could she ever consider moving to Kerala if Mathew's mother was one such imbecile?

She was jumping the gun again. A whole hour had gone by since he'd coolly presented his proposal and she had in that time done nothing but dither. She was unused to hesitation, time-wasting doubt, the ambivalence of the weak-minded. She made snap decisions and swiftly discarded the detritus. She attempted to compile a quiz—the critical questions she ought to be putting to Mathew—but instead found herself opening her eyes, staring into his and saying, with less forcefulness than she ought to, 'I smoke, Mathew. I cannot quit just because you say so.'

He chuckled, either in sympathy or mockery, and then squeezed her hand as if they were lovers. Gulfam looked out of the window without really wanting to—the boarded-up construction sites, the dug-up pavements, the hard-up workers, the always provisional, always in-progress city—and she felt that, for once, it reflected her state of mind, that she was actually full of the imperfections of the present. She was no more than the daughter of her mother, on the verge of yielding to the, possibly, wrong person. Additionally—and this gave her a rush of vertigo despite Mathew's being a man of the world and giving the driver GPS-overriding directions—she had no idea where the hell they were.

When they reached Nusrat, she looked less distraught than she had sounded on the phone, and Gulfam was briefly annoyed. She was chatting with a haggard, smiling man, the seller of a pushcart full of white chrysanthemums, pink begonias, red impatiens and the single, yellow, limp-necked rose in a mud-streaked pot that her mother thrust at Gulfam. Nusrat's toe had bled all over the pavement, her face was lustrous with sweat and her hair a proper windblown, frizzled mess.

'He's from Uttar Pradesh,' she told her daughter with regard to the flower seller. 'Says he's been working here for two years but still doesn't know the language well. I told him not to worry. He's out on the streets all day—what else will he pick up but experience and tongues?'

'Meet Mathew,' mumbled Gulfam, as her mother sat down on the grubby pavement and caressed her injured toe. Mathew handed her the medicated plasters he had stopped the cab to buy.

Nusrat thanked him but she continued to display more interest in the flower seller. 'I asked him why he's here, so far from home, and he just laughed. What an absurd question to ask of a hungry man!'

Mathew suggested they walk to the nearest traffic police station; it wasn't far. Also, he had a friend there who might help with the retrieval of her car. So, with the Band-Aid sticking out inelegantly from her toe, Nusrat stood up and exchanged phone numbers with the flower seller—she always did this with the random pedestrians she met in the city—asking him to call if he was ever in any trouble or happened to be in her neighbourhood. Gulfam avoided looking at him, just as she kept her face averted from pizza-delivery boys, nosy neighbours, taxi drivers. People made her nervous.

'What a delicate marvel!' Nusrat exclaimed, and Mathew smoothed down his moustache and tried to look modest. But it was the rose she was talking about, apparently, not her daughter's friend. Gulfam didn't want it—it was already shedding leaves all over her T-shirt, and the shy yellow buds, wrapped up in themselves, looked too unsubstantial to last the journey to her flat. Nusrat pretended not to notice that her daughter had no use for her offerings, and she always brought her something as if it were the first time, as if the history of Gulfam's indifference could be undone by the gifting of yet another tea-light holder or pair of bookends.

'I've been driving only for the past year and this is my first run-in with them,' Nusrat was telling Mathew, speaking to him at last regarding the traffic police.

Mathew claimed to have no experience with the cops. 'Drunk driving, jumping lights, parking in all kinds of holes—and still nothing. My mates have had to cough up hundreds of rupees just because their helmet straps are undone or their headlights dented.

It's because I always give a fifty to the traffic swami. He keeps them off my back.'

'I don't mind them taking my car,' said Nusrat. 'They could have just said hello and goodbye while they did it.'

'Where is it?' exclaimed Gulfam to her stoically limping mother and her unflappable friend, trying to cough out the Bangalore dust she felt fastening its claws deep inside her throat. They had walked for several minutes and she wanted to be home or at least inside a cab going home. The arrogant whoosh of passing vehicles, the hideously inflammatory sun, the high gates of apartment complexes. She tried to call forth her superior android self, her still-fictional, all-purpose app, her winged, airborne machine, but instead found herself noticing, in her desperation, the figures they passed. It was unbearable how an old man in clean but frayed clothes walked with slow, arthritic dignity as if he had somewhere to go; how a woman ironed shirts with care under a makeshift shelter with film songs tinkling out of her Palaeolithic phone; how a small, sooty-faced boy dragged a plastic sack full of garbage and beat on the road with a stick as if prospecting for riches, singing and winking at Gulfam when she caught his eye.

'I'm from Kerala,' Mathew was telling Nusrat. 'My parents have a rubber plantation . . .'

'Oh, we're all from somewhere. I don't mean that. I mean we usually live in Bangalore but right now we're heading . . .' she paused before the police-station gate, 'to Bengaluru.'

The entrance to the station was overtaken by a small temple, featuring on its low, flat roof a chariot pulled by seven pink and white horses with a smiling sun god holding the reins. This unexpected monument could imply a connection between the sun god and the traffic police, or it may just have been one of those curious and meaningless juxtapositions that the city abounded in. In any case, Nusrat took a photo and the bald and overly well-fed pandit who sat guard over the enthroned and garlanded deities of black stone inside raised his chin in self-importance in response to her raising her phone. Mathew went up to the temple and joined his hands before the traffic swami, praying, it seemed, more to him and less to the gods. Then he pulled out his wallet and handed over a benediction fee. Gulfam could not tell how seriously he took his performance but it was apparent that this was not the first time he was propitiating traffic swami.

The station, which Gulfam had expected to have the murderous character of a 6-p.m. traffic jam, seemed quiet and orderly, clerks moving between rooms with files and cops in uniform visible through open doorways, chatting affably with each other about what did not, in the least, seem like the subject of the incorrigibly unruly drivers of Bangalore. They were asked to sit down and wait, and Gulfam—taking in the indifferent expression via which the cop on duty signified his importance, the many civilians who hung around looking unsure if they were in the right place and the groaning desktop computer whose bulk obscured the minion in plain clothes who sat typing at it—wanted to go home.

'Can we give them a bribe and get your car out quickly?' she asked.

'We are in Bengaluru,' repeated Nusrat. 'We must observe and we must wait.'

She was developing her interested look, the one that would lead her to stop dead in the middle of pavements to take photos of massively insignificant things such as street dogs, shopfronts or blossoming trees, back when Gulfam was little and still depended on her mother to ferry her around. It was the look that meant Nusrat was no longer treating the project at hand as being of fundamental importance, that the details were occupying her now—the actors involved and their lives, the ambience of the setting, the reactions of the audience.

'And what else are you, apart from being from Kerala?' she turned back to Mathew.

'An engineer. We're working on this app . . .'

Gulfam broke in to say, 'She doesn't have a smartphone.'

He shrugged. 'But she does have a brain.' And Gulfam remembered that his own mother was practically illiterate.

So Mathew patiently took Nusrat through Greenfingers.

'What would you say is the vision behind a thing like that?' asked Nusrat.

'It's a business. We're making a living, you see,' Gulfam interjected.

She wanted to protect Mathew from her mother, to distance her mother from Mathew. Nusrat was going to ask too many questions, or that one simple, devastating one that might show up the boy's absolute goofiness—just in her mother's view, of course, but her mother's view had a way of piercing Gulfam's heart despite her best efforts at imperviousness.

She was still unsettled by the memory of Mathew's hand in hers, or perhaps her anxiousness was the outcome of their short but traumatic walk. Whatever it was, all she wanted was to be back home, think over the day, try to gauge if Mathew's light-hearted style concealed any genuineness of purpose. Yet how would she do that? She couldn't ask him. She couldn't check online either—he had a multitude of identities spread over various social-networking sites, all of them in his own name, or the various versions of his name, but none of them quite him. Gulfam's worry deepened. She didn't know Mathew and she didn't know how to know him.

'What is your heart's one desire?' asked Nusrat, looking from her daughter to Mathew and then back to Gulfam.

Gulfam turned away and scratched her burning cheeks, wondering if they would fall off now after this solar assault. It was just like her mother to embark on philosophical discussions in the middle of a crisis.

'Getting rich,' Mathew answered.

Nusrat nodded sadly. 'He's a lot like you,' she said to her daughter.

'Give me a cigarette,' begged Gulfam.

'I don't smoke any more.'

Gulfam raised her eyebrows in disbelief and couldn't decide whether to head out into the battering world and look for smokes, or stay where she was, on the uncomfortable screw-down metal seat, pinched between Mathew's irony and her mother's sincerity. She stuck her earplugs in, got up and walked in circles, listening to some EDM, then pulled them out and said, 'I'm going.'

A policeman came up to Nusrat right then and said, 'Show me your RC, madam.'

He was sombre, his uniform looked pristine and he didn't seem to have time to waste.

Nusrat didn't understand the acronym.

'Registration card. You must prove that the car is yours.'

He went away to attend to other matters, just as Nusrat started to ask him something—if he had eaten his lunch or if he was having a good day. But, clearly, policemen, or at least this one, were not susceptible to her charms.

'I don't have it with me. Have been meaning for ages to stick a copy into the glove compartment. Got to go home then.' She stood up and then sat down again, wincing through her smile.

'This toe's being a bloody pain,' she said.

'We can go and get it,' said Mathew. And Gulfam, already at the door, groaned.

'My heart's one desire is to never come out of my house again,' she said.

'Can making money be an ambition? Wealth could be the outcome of what you want to do, the by-product. But the thing itself?'

Gulfam had no idea what her mother was taking about.

'Dream,' Nusrat suddenly said, as if handing out an order. 'Dream, you misled youth! Give yourself a chance to see things from the perspective of eternity. You could alter the fate of mankind and all you're doing is making shopping software?'

'And what have *you* done for humanity?' asked Gulfam, still at the entrance, as if talking from afar to a distant stranger. 'What did you do when you were young?'

'My father was twenty-eight in the year of the peasant rebellion in Bengal. He didn't go off with the students and intellectuals who joined the revolting farmers even though he might have wanted to. My mother was pregnant with me and he stayed. My grandmother's friend questioned a British officer visiting her college about the people dying in jails during the Quit India Movement, for which she had to tender a written apology. My grandmother herself said nothing but she talked about her friend's bravery for the rest of her life. And I . . . I memorize poems about the apocalypse. "I smelt the attack,/ I saw the rose-trees burning,/ But the garden never had rose trees."'

'Ah,' said Mathew with a piously enlightened look, as if he too was a purveyor of poetry. 'That's why this flower for Gulfam.'

They regarded the pot she had practically flung to the floor.

Nusrat nodded. 'She is my rose but she pricks too much.'

'Do you want to sit here all day or do you want that car out?' asked the prickly rose.

'Will you pick up the registration card for me since you're getting cigarettes?' asked Nusrat with great politeness.

Gulfam couldn't think of a reason to say no again. She waited for Mathew to stop talking and head out with her but Mathew was telling Nusrat about his antique-smuggling plan. And Nusrat was aiming her phone at a poster on the wall that said, 'You are Drunk and Caught. What Next? Don't Panic.' And another that proclaimed 'Drink + Drive = Die. Who is Your Next Victim?'

'So with regard to your question of what have I done, the answer is nothing. I don't have a record of intervention or a family history of heroism. But we all certainly knew what dreams to latch on to,' Nusrat said to her daughter.

Gulfam marched back to them, pulled out her mother's house-keys from her handbag and marched out through the door.

A cop passing by with his empty tiffin-carrier swinging from a strap in his hand asked Nusrat, 'These photos you are taking, madam. What for?'

Nusrat smiled as if she had been waiting for just this question, as if she had parked her car wrong only so she could come here and converse with this very cop—not fat but verging on portly, not rude but with just the faintest touch of menace to his smile.

'I am writing a story,' said Nusrat. 'I am always writing a story.'

'You're a journalist?'

'No, just a story,' she said.

'Okay, okay,' he said, waving at her but also waving her away, as if a story was the remotest irrelevancy he could think of.

'We too are trying a little to improve the world,' Mathew told Nusrat. 'We made an app for free for an NGO last month, connecting people who want to give things away in charity to organizations that need them. Suppose you have a bicycle you

want to donate and someone in an orphanage needs one. The app
will connect you.'

Nusrat nodded. 'But will it save you?'

'Save from what?' He frowned at her like she was slightly
erroneous code.

'From the fact that we don't want to come out of our houses.
We don't want to breathe the same air as them.' She pointed
vaguely in the direction of the typing lady, now vanished from her
desk, perhaps on lunch break. 'We don't want to look them in the
eye, forget getting to know them. There is only one earth but how
we've divided it up. What matters then if the garden is devastated,
if everyone has their faces turned the other way?'

'The garden . . . ?'

'In this burnt garden/ I recall/ gardens of remembrance,/
gardens of martyrs,/ a garden of graves with no bodies in them.'

Mathew looked sad. If Gulfam had seen him right then,
perhaps she'd have believed that he was himself for once, the thus-
far-unknown, real Mathew.

Nusrat took a photo of another poster with a traffic policeman
sticking an alcometer in a morose-faced motorist's mouth, the one
not looking the least bit drunk and the other insufficiently stern.

'I am fifty years old and I have never seen anything stranger
than this,' she said in a voice of hushed wonder.

'My first time inside this station too,' said Mathew. 'I usually
pay my dues in advance outside.'

'Gulfam, I mean,' said Nusrat. 'She is the weirdest experience
of my life.'

Mathew smiled. 'I like your daughter. She's cool.'

'You know what my problem is, Mathew? I can't imagine the
future. Gulfam tells me, "By the time I'm your age, Ma, people will
be eating only lab-grown food and communicating with each other

without opening their mouths—through Wi-Fi-enabled brain plug-ins." And I look her and think, *I don't know what she means.* I understand her words, I realize what she's describing might even be possible, but I just don't get the point. What is it for?'

'Maybe you should sign up for a tech blog. That way you'll get the latest analysis . . .'

'Humankind will fade out or crack up if we're unable to feel. We are nothing if we don't care.'

Mathew went back to looking humbled but also slightly distracted, like he wanted to check his WhatsApp messages.

A woman burst into the station saying, 'My car has been towed!'

No one paid her any attention. A group of boys in their early twenties, their helmets looped around their wrists and their jeans low on their waists, walked in and stood silently in a corner, waiting for something to happen, looking too fearful to approach anyone.

Finally the clerk with the files appeared and asked the distraught woman for her car number. In a few minutes, the same cop who had spoken to Nusrat came in and said to the woman in the same tone he had used with Nusrat, 'Show me your RC, madam.'

She already had it out; she appeared to be used to having her car towed.

He walked out of the station with the woman following him.

'They were so rough. They must have scratched my car,' she complained. 'I'm not paying a penny of the fine if the paintwork is spoiled.'

'See,' said Nusrat.

Mathew looked around him and saw nothing.

'That woman. She was upset. When the cop refuses to compensate her for the damages, she will be incensed. When she gets home and tells her husband what happened, he will be critical. When she talks to her children, she will be impatient. When she goes to bed, she will be disappointed. And that is how her day will go. Squandered on living.'

'Is that your story?'

Nusrat narrowed her eyes at him. 'You are cleverer than you look.'

'Can I ask you the question you asked us?'

Nusrat nodded in the negative. 'Ask me about fears, not desires. I am afraid, for instance, of running out of stories.'

Mathew said, 'If we could develop an app that . . .'

'Dream,' urged Nusrat again, in a tone much more desperate than the one she had used earlier, and the boy was forced to stop talking, look away from his phone.

'No more information, Mathew. Dream something with beginnings, middles and ends.'

'I will try,' said Mathew, sitting up and screwing his eyes shut as if he were going into prayer.

'All I see are many rubber trees,' he reported in a few seconds.

Nusrat looked for a moment like her face would crumple but instead she took up the flowerpot her daughter had discarded and sat it down on the seat between them. When Gulfam returned she found her mother singing a song, under her breath and out of tune. 'Won't you shed a tear / For my yellow rose / My yellow rose / In her bloodstained clothes.'

Mathew said to Gulfam in a whisper, as the clerk studied Nusrat's RC, 'Your mother, I think, doesn't have the soul of a cyborg.'

Then they all went down the road to the bus bay that also functioned as a dumping ground for the towed cars, and Nusrat, of course, interrogated the clerk as she hobbled, asked her about the nature of her work, the composition of her family and the fantasies in her head.

The clerk smiled. Her name was Lakshmi and she chatted back freely.

'How much money is enough?' Nusrat asked her.

Lakshmi said her husband painted houses; he earned a couple of thousand a week when there was work but there wasn't work every week. They had two schoolgoing daughters.

'All put together, it isn't enough,' said Lakshmi. 'Right now the blanket is so small, if you pull it up to your chin, your feet grow cold. And if you cover your feet, your shoulders are bare. Ten thousand a month would be good.'

'You heard that,' Nusrat asked Gulfam and Mathew, and they stood there watching as Lakshmi laughingly shook Nusrat's hand. Nusrat requested her to kindly share her phone number.

Back home, Gulfam left the plant outside her door for the garbage collector to pick up the following morning. Mathew followed her inside, then went back out, retrieved the dishevelled rose and, stroking its frayed leaves and wilting petals, brought it back in.

6

GODSEND

'Give me . . . more!'

Her kid refuses to eat, mine eats all the time. We stand on our balconies, both of us spontaneously outdoors at mealtimes, as if feeding were theatre for the trees and the traffic—me in the floppy tracksuit I've possibly been wearing since Alu was born, my neighbour in her cotton nightie till it's time for her to head out to temple or shop. Her three-year-old son stands beside her, tightly clutching the bars of the balcony like a prisoner in a film pondering his tragic fate, his gaze fixed on us. When Kalpana advances her daily ragi mush towards his mouth he turns his face away politely, as if from an affront to his delicate sensibilities.

'What's that?' I ask Kalpana.

'What's that?' repeats Alu with her hands on her hips, her imitation so perfectly adult that it becomes, unwittingly, a cruel parody.

I point at the banana leaf laid out on a stool. It has a mound of rice on it, a bright splash of sambar, a small vada, some greens, chutney, something that looks like payasam.

'For my grandfather, all his favourite things . . .' Kalpana says.

She turns her face to the sky and emits a high-pitched two-note call that sounds shockingly avian, then looks at me with an expression suggesting she has a hidden side. This nightie-loving housewife harbours a Mowgli in her heart perhaps, some secret second sense that I have yet to discover.

'Where are the crows?' she asks her son.

I glance at Monu to see if this interests him but he remains unmoved. He is a wispy toddler with rich, oily curls of hair and eyes that seem always on the verge of astonishing discovery. He could be just about to burst into eloquence but, in fact, does not speak at all. He might make the occasional juvenile sound, pleasure or pain sometimes break out as inarticulate noise, but he does not know, or need, words. This, combined with his resolute indifference to food, qualifies him to be a three-year-old invalid but Kalpana and her husband haven't sought medical advice. They've recently taken him to see a nameless saintly figure associated with the temple in Tirupati who has promised the boy will both speak and eat in good time.

I am about to ask how come grandad's favourite grub isn't special, why it's the ordinary fare Kalpana and her family eat, but I stop myself in time. This is yet another of my new propensities, inexplicably brought on by motherhood. It's like when you're stoned and keep getting tripped up by some small, suddenly marvellous, detail—a perfectly geometrical flower printed on a bed sheet, the resounding bassline in a pop song. I seem to be thinking sideways. Instead of focusing on the grown-up questions, my tired brain keeps straying towards minute nonsense. I try to look interested.

'Could it be a festival today?'

'Yes, the day we feed our ancestors,' says Kalpana. 'Mahalaya Amavasya. A special new-moon night.'

Then I understand about the crows: of course I know. I'm not that far gone yet into postnatal confusion. They're the bearers of the souls of the dead. We peer into the branches of the mango tree, which is growing out of the empty plot next door, but which seems to belong, in the open-armed welcome of its branches, to both of us. There are no crows camouflaged by the rustle of its long, tapering leaves.

Kalpana calls again and Alu echoes her call through the half-chewed rice in her mouth, which promptly falls out in a clump. She turns to me for more without even a second's hesitation at the accident. I go inside to refill her bowl, hungry myself, I realize, but in a foggy way, as if my own hunger, as much as my other needs, had become un-urgent, third person. I come back with warm rice and dal for her, and still no crows. They usually fill this small shared space of tree and balcony with their fat black squawks and squabbles. But today, when there's good, fresh Brahmin food to be had, no crows.

'Give . . . me . . . more!' Alu urges. As she snaps up the heaped spoon I proffer, she's a chicken; she spreads her arms and screeches, intent on deriving amusement even from empty air. A year ago she was flinging her toys over the railing one by one, so they have long been prohibited, but I still have to wrestle her every afternoon over the other distractions out here—the outdoor tap, the rice-paper lampshade, the terracotta animals, all of which she can wreak determined havoc on, not angrily but just as a form of infantile expression, a way of making room for herself. She growls at Monu, challenging him to say or do something, but he just stands there calmly observing Alu eat and play and fight. She interests him but not enough to respond in kind. I keep glancing at him in amazement—his serenity, his indifference—while Kalpana watches my daughter, who is the same age as Monu.

She often comments with open envy on Alu's chubby arms and flushed cheeks, the words and sentences that fall out of her mouth fully formed, as if she had stored them from some previous life of linguistic aptitude, not gleaned them all from this one.

I can see my daughter expanding before my eyes, yet things have run in a loop since she was born: the numbing monotony of putting together three healthy meals a day, the grey tracks I always seem to be wearing, the difficulty of remembering when I last washed my hair, a soreness in my joints I especially notice when it's time to get Alu from playschool. She will emerge engrossed in a companion, demonstrating to him or her a new way to torture her mauled Barbie. She doesn't look out for me, assuming I'll be there. She's confident that the world works. Her joy in things and people is so consuming that she never wastes time on disappointment. Tell her to stop, scold her, and she'll retreat for a few seconds and then start up again.

As I empty the last of the food into her perpetually open mouth, Alu, who knows how crows are usually shooed away from anything edible, asks, 'Why crow must eat?'

'It's the crow's birthday,' I say. 'Aunty is waiting for crow to come to the party.'

At this Monu gives out a small, cautious giggle, and Alu looks at me in delight at the reaction I've produced in the boy. She imitates his laugh to see if he'll laugh again, but he's retreated back into silence.

I glance at Kalpana who, tight-lipped, is still scanning the sky for her grandfather.

'He has to come all the way from Mysore. First he'll go to my sister's place in south Bangalore. Only then he'll come here.'

Nevertheless, at a sudden flutter in the tree, she lets out that same jungle sound and claps her hands encouragingly.

'No crow,' says Alu in disapproval, then shouts as both a form of address and identification, 'Squirrel!'

The creature, flurried and jerky as squirrels tend to be, stops halfway up the trunk at her command, then scampers with its tail erect into the branches. In the summer, mangoes of a uniform green smoothness will hang from this tree, as beautifully alien to it as Christmas decorations, and then disappear before their colour mellows, maybe monitored and collected by the children who live in the slum nearby. But the squirrels are always here. The tree is not just ours despite it leaning in that almost endearing way towards us.

Only, the squirrels don't count today. Kalpana is not in her usual mood, one of a pained, almost livid, buoyancy, and she makes no attempt to lure her son to his uneaten lunch with a story—how the squirrels are conspiring with the parrots who sometimes come to peck at the green pods on the peacock flowers in the front lane, how the sparrows are twittering the news through the electricity wires and the upstairs neighbours' cats talking about it—how all the animals know that somewhere in this house is a boy who doesn't eat, and they're making a plan to spirit him away.

'The bandicoots might get it later.'

Even before the sentence is out of my mouth I know I've been stupid. Bandicoots are beside the point. What made me think of them? This is about her grandfather, not the lower reaches of the animal world. Yet I'm bothered by that full leaf-plate: Will the food turn and smell, will it mobilize the red ants or those frightening, swollen creatures on powered feet I sometimes see at night slipping into the storm-water drains around the house? I should be reflecting on the dead and the many forms they take in the human imagination. I'm supposed to be drawing on my sociological ideas—for that's what I was preparing to be before Alu arrived. A scholar of sociology.

'Bandicoots?' Kalpana asks me.

'Sorry. There are just so many around these days.'

'Bandicoots aah?

Alu doesn't repeat Kalpana's repetition. Perhaps she too can hear the hurt and annoyance in her voice. Besides, food done, she is on the floor of the living room immersed in the next thing, which is her picture book about a girl lost in the forest. She peruses it daily like a bible, making sure to check everything is in place: the sagging striped socks on the lost girl's tired feet, the question mark of cooking-fire smoke hanging over the sky which might suggest to her a way out of the wooded maze.

'You don't observe this festival?' Kalpana asks me.

She's upset with me now but won't cut me off. We need each other as we live our exhausting, parallel, matching lives on these facing balconies. I wish I could say I do—an admission of me being no better than her, or her being as good as me—but all I can come up with is an apologetic 'The crows are sure to come.'

She knows I'm not a believer, whereas she is always agog over the rituals and the gods. She looks out for datura flowers in the hedges when she goes shopping, for those are Shiva's favourite and she has singled him out for herself in that vaguely erotic way in which gods are made personal. Every morning after her bath, her hair wet and her nightie crisp, she expertly draws an auspicious rangoli pattern, Monu standing to one side with a supervisatory air. The white rice-flour pours steadily and without a break from her clenched fingers as she traces on to the floor outside her front door one among the many interlocking, unbroken patterns catalogued in her memory.

And then there are the big days she is busy with the year round—each so different and yet all so predictable. She fasts on Tulsi Puja, then undertakes an evening celebration, like all the housewives around us do, of the wedding of her tulsi plant with Lord Vishnu, fanning her hands over the giant flowerpot, careful not to touch the leaves that women might water from a distance but only men can pluck. On Varamahalakshmi day, also dedicated to the bride of Vishnu, this time in her avatar as Lakshmi, Kalpana installs a little pink-lipped idol of the goddess in her living-room shrine, and wears one of her gloriously gaudy silk saris, plain magenta or royal blue, intruded on only by that dark border of pyramidal gopurams, for the evening affair before the much more serious shrine in the neighbourhood temple. She cooks pongal with rice and jaggery on a little wood-fire outdoors every year for the winter harvest festival of Pongal. On Ugadi she plucks leaves off the mango tree and goes out to buy sheaves of neem—the first she festoons her lintel with to welcome good things into the house in the new year, and the neem is eaten with jaggery. In the evening she will come over to my house with a plate of home-made holige, dripping with ghee. On all three days of Diwali her balcony is pretty with oil lamps, and on Ayudha Puja, the day of obeisance to the tools of one's trade, she applies the white stripe of *vibhuti* and red and yellow smears of kumkum and haldi not just on her husband's PC and car but also on her own pressure cookers and mixer–grinder. All those lifeless means of production become, for a day, touched with divinity, bedecked minor gods of steel and aluminium taking their place in the crazily crowded pantheon of the religion.

'So what about the dead people in your family?' asks Kalpana.

I've told her about my grimly atheistic parents. She knows how I came of age feeling neither the need to be avowedly anti-God like them nor deeply devotional like almost everyone else. We've even laughed about it—my parents' absurd antipathy to the name of God. But today Kalpana's beliefs are being tested:

I've mentioned bandicoots, insultingly, and grandad isn't flying out of the sky to eat the food she's cooked him.

'My dead are dead, Kalpana,' I say. 'They don't come back.' I know this is not good enough for her. I could put them to sleep and she will resurrect them with her fierce Hindu conviction. One's saying goodbye to the dead is not confirmation of their departure.

I think of the one grandfather I knew and can't remember much except that he wore a ring with a green stone. When he dipped into the pockets of his trousers, I'd imagine he was going to bring out masses of sweets but it was only a handkerchief to blow his nose with or a bit of paper he would fold into a bird or a boat for me. He died when I was three—Alu's age, I suddenly realize.

'You don't celebrate Deepavali even? Or the day of Krishna's birth?'

I nod in the negative, with apparent sadness, to keep up the charade. I don't mind the inquisition because it won't produce the least smidgen of religious guilt, and she knows this, so she can be insistent.

'What about your daughter? She might need some of this.'

'I'll ask her when she's a little older. Right now we'll just let it be about the crows, too complicated to also bring in the dead.'

'If you haven't had them since childhood, they're not beliefs,' says Kalpana, sounding more sociological than me.

I'm meant to be working on a PhD on the lives of local factory-workers—men and women who come from either very nearby, the villages adjoining Bangalore, or thousands of kilometres away, the blurred, desperate edges of the country, in order to bottle soft drinks, stitch garments, package electronics. It was going to be classic ethnography in the tradition of those old-timers—

Friedrich Engels, who wrote about the wretched condition of the working class in England in the middle of the nineteenth century, or M.N. Srinivas, who devoted himself to one village not far from here and illuminated it. I don't know when I can return to my respondents but in the meanwhile the project itself—in the snatches of magically still, late-morning time, when Alu is at playschool and I am before my computer, trying to hit on the pattern in the stories of cheap labour I have gathered—seems both unyielding and pointless. What new thing can I establish by recording that Mithun Bordoloi, from Sibsagar district in Assam, inspected the seals of jam, ketchup and pickle bottles on the assembly line for eight years, quit out of boredom, and in the hope of earning more elsewhere, annoyed his supervisor only because he wanted out, and now, three years later, is a hospital orderly on an equally lowly income and has still not been paid out his leaving benefits by the factory, though he calls that intractable supervisor every day and sometimes grows downright weepy pleading with him. Or that N. Madhu from Mandya district, who did buttons and zippers for an international clothing company, also for eight years, hanged herself to death from a noose deftly created out of the very string she used in her job, which she'd tied securely to an exhaust fan in the ladies' loo. She had never known anything in the factory but buttons and zippers, and she wanted more. What I earn is not even half enough for the family, she'd told me. I see now that I'd started to grow too interested in them as people to generalize about them as specimens. Besides, Karl Marx already provided us with the conclusion—work in an industrial, capitalist society is alienating.

Kalpana will not leave me to my strangeness today. 'I know your parents didn't care, but what about *their* parents?'

I quickly make up a tale. 'They were birthday grandparents. Always called on my birthday and something was sure to turn up in the post but I never spent much time with them. They passed away so long ago I grew up knowing them as dead. What about yours? Was this grandfather . . .' I incline my head at the sky and Kalpana looks up in hope again, 'someone you were close to?'

'Oh *verrry*,' she says, and tells me how disbelieving she was when, one day, just a couple of years ago, he took off to stay in an ashram in Tiruvannamalai, no longer around to instruct her on the Vedas—which one to turn to when a relative dies, which one gave you the low-down on married life. Or to interpret the Panchanga for her, that almanac that ruled daily action—told you, based on the position of the sun, moon, planets and constellations, the best day and time to start on a new project, travel, have your hair cut or even make love.

'His soul must be very much there somewhere—on the Tiruvannamalai hill. He was so happy there. But today he's expected here, for Mahalaya Amavasya. It's more important than even the ceremony performed on the thirteenth day after a person's death. You could skip that but you can't skip this,' she says, then considers the still-full bowl in her hand and her silent martyr of a son. We smile at each other because there's nothing more to say, our afternoon interlude is done.

I go back inside and find my daughter at my desk. She has poured herself a glass of juice from the fridge and spilt it on *The Girl in the Forest*, on my papers, the laptop keyboard, the floor. I stare at her, my throat painfully constricting, as she wipes her book on the already-grubby front of her pinafore.

'Alu,' I whisper.

She looks up at me. I cannot go to her, I have to lock my fingers behind my back to stop from hurting her or from bawling.

'What did you do, Alu?'

'Juice fall,' she says.

'What did you do?'

'Juice fall,' she shouts as if addressing a moron.

'I've told you the story of why this is not for Alu. You can grab and destroy everything in the house but not this. This is mine. Papa has office, Aunty Kalpana has her gods, Alu has her toys and books, and I have this little, little corner.'

'I know,' she says but isn't sorry. She's a three-year-old blob of ego, and for a moment I wonder if she's special in her baby selfishness. Are all kids so unfeeling?

'Go,' I say.

She slides down from the chair and her bare feet land in a puddle of juice. 'All gone,' I say, still at the door, unable to stir, still wanting to make her cry or, failing that, cry myself. 'It was already mostly gone and now you've taken care of the rest. Do you understand? You've wiped out Ma.'

Alu points to a picture on the leaking page. 'Girl found house,' she explains.

'Go.'

I hand her the empty glass, push her out of the room and lock the door. I feel like throwing everything—laptop, papers, the squelchy rug under the table—over the balcony. I feel like sleeping for a year; I feel like being reborn as a creature from a species that doesn't produce children. I wet a towel at the bathroom sink and start cleaning. It takes time and I take my time. I shake out orange drops from the keyboard. I wipe a sticky book and set it to dry before the room cooler. The papers I scrunch and find a plastic bag to stuff into, feeling that I am discarding Mithun and Madhu's fate as well.

I'm annoyed at Kalpana too, fed up of her endlessly fussy religiosity. We never discuss the human condition, only—apart from our domestic dailiness—this constant commerce with the gods.

In our vicinity—this tree-lined grid of small, new apartment buildings, older double-storeyed bungalows, the last of the empty plots, two temples, a couple of grocery shops—the human condition takes the form of the slum on the fringes, from which men and women come to work on the construction sites, couples whose infants spend their days rocking in improvised swings of old saris strung on the beams of the houses being raised or, if they're a little older, running wild, heaving around bags with refuse they might be able to sell some bits of, playing cricket with planks of discarded wood, stealing a little.

I'm struck by that familiar freeze I know many like me feel—apathy, shame and disinterest in equal parts—when I see these children hanging out in the lanes. I might chat with them in passing, buy them cupcakes from a bakery, turn my face away when they take down a neighbour's lovely display of frangipani, but I cannot do anything for them, really. The disaster they stand for is bigger than them and bigger than me, and all I have to offer are a few coins—metaphorical and real—of sympathy. Those coins are not to alleviate. They are a way of saying—let's definitely not look this problem in the eye.

Kalpana takes another view. She will shout them away from the mango tree, she'll shout them away from everything. Just their being around is a problem. They can't be up to any good. Poverty is not an embarrassment to her; it is, apparently, a failing on the part of the poor.

Of course, I could be coolly analytical about all this. She is merely one among millions who wants to maintain the status quo and believes in social stratification—who would argue that those on top are there because they're smarter and so deserve it. I want to research the unacknowledged power of housewives. The thought comes to me as I'm taking a shower, standing still and letting the water, too hot for comfort, scour me, cool my anger. Perhaps it's time to investigate the work that housewives do—not the cooking and cleaning alone, that old hat—but the even older hat, the work of keeping the gods happy and the family secure in their patronage, teaching the young ones the rangoli patterns and the Vedic laws. The women in their innocuous nighties, sweetly feeding crows and watering tulsi plants—actually powerful enforcers of conformity.

I lie down and let my exhaustion take over. I'm too tired to boil another portion of rice for my lunch. Instead I think of the dozens of housewives in the colony, keeping the reinforced concrete foundation of the middle-class nation in place. The husbands go to work with their multi-tier lunch boxes of home-cooked food snug in zippered cases, entrusting the job of sustaining—not just family values but the family as a value—to their wives. And for the women, fending off vagrants is as crucial to the role as shopping for the lushest plantain leaves on Ganesh Chaturthi. I imagine interviewing Kalpana and her friends and then going farther afield, taking in the whole neighbourhood, fanning out into all of north Bangalore, talking to every single stay-at-home wife whose husband's decent salaried job can pay for insurance and mortgage, whose children go to English-language schools. I might discover they are all in secret concurrence with each other—every religious ritual must be flintily adhered to, the children properly socialized and the irreligious neighbours challenged. It starts to seem like a tremendous discovery—perhaps the very institution of modern Hinduism is sustained by these women who, if they went to work instead, would be too preoccupied by flow charts and balance sheets to imagine Vishnu and Shiva as needing their constant attention. I fall asleep holding fast to the fragile thread of this new idea.

When I wake I go into the kitchen to make myself some tea. Alu is sprawled on the carpet, her face held up at a reverential angle to Chhota Bheem flexing his cartoon muscles on TV. Nothing new there. I sit on the sofa with my cup and the newspaper. I answer a text message from my husband. I put out the damp towels to dry on the balcony. The food on the leaf is still there, caking in the late-afternoon sun, undisturbed by crows or anything else. I should give Alu a bath, change her into cleaner clothes. Instead I do the dishes and then—standing there gazing through the kitchen window, working my way through a chocolate bar—I sense the city winding down. The traffic gets heavier in the streets below as the heat seeps out of the day. Kalpana isn't around. She's probably in the park, keeping an eye on Monu as he swings and see-saws with silent exuberance. Or she'll be jostling with other shoppers for vegetables to put into her evening meal, like I ought to be doing soon. I realize that the crows could land up now, encouraged by our temporary abandonment of the balconies.

'Alu,' I call out. 'Quieter.' But she doesn't lower the volume so I have to go over and do it myself.

I haphazardly pour flour into a bowl, splash water into it and start pummelling the dough. I could hardly say to Kalpana—*I want to study you, you interest me as a type.* I must stock up my questions, tell her it's a survey, something I'm doing for the university where I'm a student. A research project, not just my own fantasy about her contribution to social cohesion.

The light is fading by the time I'm done with the dough and Alu hasn't stirred from Cartoon Network. I put some milk on the stove.

'Come on,' I say to her.

I mix sugar into the milk and take it out to the balcony. She gets up and follows me.

'What happened?' I ask her. 'Was Chhota Bheem bad today? But he's always good.'

She doesn't look at me, turning her face away as she slowly slurps from the mug in my hand.

'Alu?'

'Sweet potato?'

'Little miss chippie?'

Nothing at all. Monu appears, his mother holding his cup of milk. He is sweaty and excited from his park visit but this, of course, has not changed his attitude to eating and drinking.

'Take a sip, *magu* . . . Drink, *kanna*.' Kalpana starts out loving him, but very quickly impatience starts to burn her up.

'Yow,' says Monu, or something to that effect. He's calling out to Alu. He's surprised to see her meditative. She looks, stony-eyed, into the distance.

'Alu is not talking any more,' I say.

Kalpana laughs.

'Alu not talking? That means the sun will rise in the west and fishes live on land.'

'You heard that, Alu? From tomorrow the world's going to be upside down.'

Alu remains unimpressed. Monu lowers his head in her direction and barks softly like a sad puppy.

'God will be happy because Alu is quiet,' says Kalpana. 'Finally he can hear all the other people's voices.'

Why must she drag God into everything? I glare at her.

'Encourage her,' I say. 'Don't make her feel worse.'

'What did you tell her to shut her up?'

I shrug.

'She's naughty, I know. But it's not her fault,' says Kalpana.

I know there's some criticism of me coming, and it does.

'Maybe you have to show her—the right and the wrong.'

She has brought this up before, my negligence of my child's moral education.

I look at my grumpy toddler scarfing down milk from her big Ice Princess mug, and then at Monu and his wide-eyed animal dumbness, and a brief wave of panic passes over me. What if I really have failed? What if the tired love I give this child, the feeding and clothing, the bedtime story and the morning hug, are just not enough, and she needs, alongside, a worldview? Where would I produce that from? I'm only a sociologist—my subject does not deal in absolutes, not in this century. Will she grow up without a centre? I can't be sure but I'm not about to let that show.

'She knows the difference very well,' I tell Kalpana. 'That's why she's sore, because she can see she crossed a line.'

But she's busy with her boy, twisting his chin towards herself and forcing milk down his throat.

I have two pissed-off people on my hands now. That leaves Monu so I try chatting with him.

'Little boy, tell me what you did in the park today?'

Monu ignores me, lost in the dream he's always dreaming. Then he slowly lifts a finger to point, opens his mouth and lets out the first sentence I have ever heard him speak.

'Is a crow.'

We're all stunned. The crow plants itself at the edge of the banana leaf, like a guest at a table, and pecks at the food. It eats a bit of the rice, some of the greens and even the sambar. Unusually, no other crows come swooping down, so our crow can eat leisurely, thinking its black crow thoughts. When it's done, it lifts the vada in its pointed beak, flaps its wings a few times in thanks and takes off.

I find myself clapping, so unexpectedly glad.

'Is a crow,' repeats Monu, following its flight to the terrace.

Kalpana is on her knees, planting ecstatic kisses all over her son's face.

And then Alu can't hold out any longer. 'Is a *croooow*,' she squeals. 'There . . . is . . . a crow.'

I clap again, marvelling at the sentence, at language itself, and how exactly it can correspond to the world.

'Ma,' says Alu, extending her pudgy little hands, trying to reach mine. I bend down to look her in the eye. 'What is it, Alu?'

She takes the mug out my hands and drains the last of the milk, then sets it down carefully on a corner of the balcony. 'Alu can drink,' she explains calmly.

My daughter is saying she doesn't need me to do this for her any more. Despite the mess she made with the orange juice, she is confident she can feed herself. I tell her she's right. We no longer have to hang out on the balcony four times a day and keep company with Monu. She is going to be sitting at a table now, eating and conversing like a small adult, not flapping about like a chicken.

Kalpana still has her arms around her son's neck, her face squashed against his. She is saying she knew the swami she spent her money on in Tirupati was right about Monu—she always had the fullest faith in the predictive abilities of this seer.

'Monu can talk?' I ask, just to make sure he really can now. He smiles with something like irony and says, after Alu, 'Monu can drink.'

Kalpana and I grin at each other. I look up at the crow, perched on the parapet and enjoying his vada. But what is above him gives me a start. It is a reminder of something else, note to a different self—the thin new moon, the moon of dead souls, pale as a sliver of the skin in my daughter's just-emptied mug of evening milk.

7

THE LADY WITH THE DOG

The phrase that comes to mind is—*bursting into life*. But spring is a gradual unfolding: day by day colour seeps back into the land, expressed in crocuses of lilac and gold. The oaks will fatten with leaves by slow degrees. Will they burst into life? Will the buds on the apple trees?

Everything seems calm and regulated to Karin Gran as she walks her dog on the path by the lake, muddy from last night's rain. It is almost not cold, a whisper of warmth, while yesterday it snowed, shavings of ice issuing from the air, which dissolved on touching the ground, not enough to carpet it but snow, nevertheless. And then rain followed—a suddenly freezing day. And now this: the sunlight nestling on the lake and the seagulls' joyous shrieks. A spring clarity, a newness. On the far side of the water are the birch trees; their bare brown branches create from this distance a reddish fuzz around them—red-headed trees with pale trunks, their bark flaking to reveal that distinctive off-white tone, and between them the island's summer cottages, painted a deeper red, with white window-frames and tiled sloping roofs.

The owners of these houses live in Stockholm and are starting to come down now with the turn in the season. Spend a few days in the country, get the barbecue going every evening. The lake is still too cold to swim in but one can always put out the canoe and paddle. Karin is mildly cynical about Stockholmers. To them this town of five thousand—its cosy town centre and the medieval church decorated with paintings by a marginally famous local artist—is quaint. But to her who lives here, the landscape is not just a diversion. The beauty runs deeper, as does the boredom.

Oskar is nosing about in the grass by a clump of trees where the wood anemones are blooming, the small starry flowers scattered there as if by a human hand. She sets him free, ruffles his neck, and he is surprised—trots a few paces and bounds back to her, so she clicks the leash into place again. That wasn't wise; dogs are not meant to run free in this country. She thinks of the teasing voice in which her son, Örjan, recently said to her: 'Mama, you're happy just to drive out to Clas Ohlson every week and get dog-poop bags that come in a handy pouch you can clip to your waist as you walk Oskar.' He was smiling, leafing through the catalogue on the kitchen table as he waited for dinner. She laughed gamely, didn't ask: *So what's wrong with that?* He didn't say: *I mean, how narrow your world is.* Instead he presented her with a random selection, flipping carelessly through the pages.

'An electrical coffee-measuring device, a robotic vacuum cleaner, a contraption to automatically slice or cube apples, a gumboot dryer, a use-and-throw barbecue, a thermometer to test the temperature of your baking dough, a slow juicer to preserve the fibre in fruit juice, special corks to retain the fizziness of your drink. Anything else? Any human need left unmet by Clas Ohlson?'

'How strange, this variable spring weather,' she'd said to him by way of a response as they ate their spaghetti. 'I don't quite know how much to pile on when I step out.'

Now she pulls loose one of those bags her son finds deplorable and scoops up the shit that Oskar has produced. With the warm excretion still in her hand, she considers the dreamy lapping of the water at the lake's shore and the matching blue openness of the sky. It will not be dark till nine o'clock and even then the light will linger. Languid is the light and the season.

Out of which hidden crevice in this perfect vista did the idea of boredom come to her? And the memory of her son's subtle criticism? She disposes of the bag and they head back into town. At the churchyard, open to the street, spread out on slopes around the red-brick gothic structure with a wooden belfry, she stops by her husband's grave. The yellow of the daffodils has deepened; she placed a pot there the previous week. They appear to be smiling at her, a sunshine smile against the rough grey headstones and the new green of the grass. She imagines her husband in Delhi with her, in their tiny hotel bed, in the many markets where she was jostled and stared at, and then the picture fades. She was in that country only with Örjan and now, two weeks later, she is back in this cold, this tempered cold of spring, and this town where she and David raised the boy who now says he would like to move to India.

She pushes open the door to the church. As usual, no one's there on a weekday evening. She sits down in a front pew and looks at John the Baptist painted on the northern wall. There are octagonal pillars of brick holding up an impressive vault studded with complex flowers of mosaic, but it is the depiction of the saint in the desert her eyes usually find first. He is holding up some water in his right hand—is it to baptize with or drink?—and there's a bush of vivid red desert flowers by his feet. The picture is simple. John the Baptist is alone with the sand and the sun, nothing about him but his shadow. He stands there with his upraised hand, in a loincloth of camel hide, looking out at the viewer, and since the viewer is not there facing him in the desert, the only thing he could be looking at is God. Karin Gran would like to know if John was not bored there, in that desert. Was it the dialogue with God that kept him occupied till he could return to people and preach?

Oskar waits, gently pawing at the wooden floorboards, his ears cocked. Perhaps he can hear mice below. The church was built seven hundred years ago and has been restored many times since. In a cabinet in the vestry is a silver receptacle from the fifteenth century called the Chalice of St Örjan, and it is him she named her son after. Much later she discovered that this lovely gleaming thing was a copy; the real one is in a museum in Stockholm. Sitting there, she runs through what is in her fridge and, feeling the inspiration of spring, decides on a salad. She will open a bag of peas, a can of corn, slice tomatoes and peppers, pluck lovage from her back garden and carefully shred it over her creation. After dinner the TV, and then Örjan may call, he usually does once a week. She will turn later in the night to the rock music of the sixties that she grew up with—those bluesmen and folkwomen still sustain—while she crochets a blanket. A gift, but she is not sure for whom.

Heading home, she lights a cigarette and crosses paths with no one, except, all of a sudden from around a street corner, an enormous African mama completely swallowed by her black burka but for her eyes, which are impassive and show no hint of returning the hello Karin has offered. Contrasting with her traditional costume are the scuffed trainers she wears. Karin imagines something more feminine, statelier, on her feet were she still at home. Or could it be that like John in the desert she had no shoes at all, she was a barefoot traveller, and these trainers are the beginning of her melding, slowly, from the feet up, with the environment of this country?

The lady continues her slow, heaving walk up the street. Karin just read in the papers that many immigrants lie about their age, trying to pass off as children in order to get more benefits. The authorities plan to conduct ultrasound scans on the knees of all newcomers to determine their exact age. Knees don't lie apparently. But this woman would never pretend to be a child. She is a queen or, at least, a matriarch, used to behaving with authority. Now, in this country, only her body and her bearing are intact. Inside she is a mass of silent native words, and even if the Swedish language does come to her eventually, it will not express the whole of her. The experience of being here will distort her. But will it be a good thing too, in some other way? Will she discover a new side of herself, living in this place? Karin stands in her little front lawn, finishing her cigarette, pleased at the efflorescence in her flower beds as a blackbird hops around them, out of Oskar's reach.

Inside, she takes off her denim jacket, pulls out the pin in her hair, setting free the white knot on the crown. She wishes she could have chatted with the African lady instead of that heap of useless, tangled contemplations about her. Was it Karin Gran talking to herself, or was it Örjan's voice again? He has a degree in philosophy and feels compelled to constantly probe the world. Even as a child, his need to analyse things often got in the way of his participating in them. When he first came home with her and David from Delhi, an eighteen-month-old orphan with a thin face and sweet, small teeth, she thought of him as her little Indian boy. But not for long. His intensity did not lend itself to cuddling and endearments—instead, he wanted answers to questions she had never imagined as questions herself. At the age of six it was—*Why*

is the light in your room different from that in mine when we have
the same number and size of windows, facing in the same direction?
At ten—Can I be buried in the churchyard when my ancestors did
not come up the church steps on the lakeshore from the other side in
the days when there was no bridge connecting the island to our town?
At fifteen—Aren't dogs way happier than us because they don't have
countries? They are the true universal humanists, they just want love
and shrink from suffering.

David took recourse to joking; his overall attitude to his son
became an amused one. The boy would rather go to the library
and read up everything at hand on fishing than be on the iced-over
lake in winter with his father, reeling in the pike and perch through
those little drilled holes. He formed intense friendships that often
ended in arguments and tears. As a teenager he started to compile a
history of the town and then of the province, seeking out pensioners
at the local supermarket—shakily wheeling out groceries in their
walkers—for their memories of life in the early years of the welfare
state. The family never returned to India but he made his own way
there as an adult, with a girlfriend whom he eventually lost. Lately
he's been going back more often, attracted, it seems to his mother,
to the thrill of his utter incompatibility with the land of his birth.
Örjan is more Swedish in Sweden than Indian in India, yet he is
pulled back to that country where people might say one thing and
imply another, where the languages are not native to him, where
he is taken for granted for how he looks, rather than respected for
how he feels. He is in love with his own strangeness, determined
to cleave to it, make of it a difficulty worthy of lifelong adherence.

Karin starts on her salad with the radio turned up, hears a
report about a group of masked men attacking, in several separate
incidents over the course of one weekend, women coming out
of bars late at night in a southern town, men who spoke neither

Swedish nor English. She mentions it to David in her head. He no longer replies as he used to. More than a year since he died and the grief has turned . . . to *boredom*. She puts down her chopping knife, struck again by that word. When did it enter her lexicon? She has never spoken it out loud, never said to her neighbours, when she chats with them about how winter turns to spring and then, inevitably, however disappointingly rainy it might turn out some years, summer follows, those particular words—*I am bored*. She always imagined she would go first. David was seven years younger and it was him she'd think of with concern, a widower clumsily folding up the washed laundry, searching hard for a particular cooking pot, a box of tools, a library book, irritable without her. She was always not there in that imagined future when the strands of grey in her husband's hair would crowd out the brown, or when Örjan, awkwardly, without her there to provide reinforcement, tried to explain to his father that he was an intellectual and therefore interested less in bargain groceries at Lidl than in the new archaeological wing being added to the town museum.

Instead, they found David frozen into lifelessness in the office basement, and Karin Gran must now contemplate dying alone. She ought to be thinking of that, David's end and how it will echo her own, but all that comes to her in unguarded moments is a vague emptiness, an awareness of the need to find a way to expend time or life or whatever it is we call the thing we have been given an allotted portion of. Not the end but the distance she must cover to reach it. She had never noticed this space before, the one that can open up between you and that other you who has been insensible all these years to the self-driven tempo of existence. *What an enchanting stranger, that woman*, thinks Karin, as she eats her salad standing up, at the same time filling Oskar's bowl with chopped veal and lamb from one of a stack of tins on the counter. He wags his tail as he eats, perpetually grateful for his daily bread. Örjan is right. He's a true good soul. 'Oh, you darling.' He moves his head in acknowledgement but does not lift it. *Food comes first*, he seems to be saying. 'You are the reason I can still hear my own voice,' Karin tells him, and lets him have another round of tinned meat.

Later, it's not the sound of the phone but of the key turning in the front door that pulls her to her feet from the deep armchair before the TV. Örjan is shrugging his backpack off, then his coat, smiling apologetically at her. 'Surprise,' he says, but there is nothing of a thirty-three-year-old's assurance in his words. He has always been shy of her in some ineffable way, shy of the mother who is both more and less than a mother.

He clears his throat. 'So I got it.'

'The job?' she exclaims. He's been after a teaching post in Delhi, at a college where he has some friends among the faculty. Karin had not believed it would really happen. Even on their recent visit to India, when he first revealed that he was trying to identify a life for himself in that country, not just drawn to it as a tourist, she hadn't thought it possible. She is not ready to accept this undoing of their project of taking him away from there, bringing him up to think of it not as a present but a past.

Örjan is on his knees, embracing the dog with an unspoken ardour he never reveals for humans. 'I needed my books so thought I'd drop by and give you the news. Have to start some reading, classes begin after the summer break.'

When he stands up, Karin takes a firm grip of his arm, as if determined not to let him go that far, and leads him to the kitchen. He's been on the bus for two hours from Stockholm and she knows he's hungry. So he is to go; she will see him once a year, perhaps even less. She is struck by desolation, then realizes she must share in the joy.

'Örjan, this is superb, really . . .'

He concedes to nod at her pride.

'You've always got what you aimed for. You work for it and then you get it.'

'We'll see. I want to teach and I want to be in India, so this is my chance.'

He picks up a newspaper as he asks his mother about her day. Karin makes him a sandwich, takes out the bit of salad she has saved, glad he is here, unexpectedly, to eat it. She could tell him about the evening, that she went for a walk, but how can a walk be news, she does it every day. And to the church? Every three or four days, that too is commonplace. Spring then, the delights of spring? The magnificent colour of the flowers on David's grave? She feels they have not really discussed David, or even begun the habit of remembering him jointly, making him into the dead person who is naturally invoked in conversation time and again, and in this way both memorialized and buried. Örjan wept and then was glum but he did not talk much, never startled her with a sudden need for his father.

As for herself, just recently in Delhi, she felt horrified over the fact that he was not there. 'Have a good day, Mama,' Örjan would say every morning as he was taking off to do his thing—speak at a conference, meet professors, browse in the libraries. She would wave her guidebook at him, nodding hard, frantic to prevent the tears that might ruin her son's trip. They'd have dinner together at the hotel but during the days she was alone, making forays into the city, buying too many gifts, for the neighbours back home, she'd think waveringly—bottles of perfume, bags of dried fruit and spices, clothes printed in a commotion of colours. She was either convinced, resignedly, that she was being swindled over this shopping or sure she'd paid too little, that some misunderstanding had caused her to hand over the wrong notes. It was more than thirty years since she'd last been in Delhi, and the impression she had saved of that hurried weekend was difficult to match with her perception of it now. They'd got Örjan on a slushy, heated July day, and it was his face they were immediately hooked to at the expense of the whole city; now, in milder March weather, she had nothing but time to spend and eyes to see.

Eventually Karin made friends with the couple that ran the hotel—ran it, apparently, by sitting behind the front desk all day and yelling obscenities at the staff, who sang loudly in the corridors as soon as they were out of sight. She was treated politely, however, as were the other guests. The dramatic switch of tone the owners could affect made her curious about which one, if either, was their true face. They chatted with Karin, asked her every evening for an account of her day, even though nothing about Delhi could surprise them, and every experience of hers—the rich lunch she'd eaten off a glittering steel plate, the man who'd tried to slip a hand into her shoulder bag at the Red Fort, the bus driver she had seen almost mowing down a schoolchild—seemed to produce only cheerful affirmation in them.

She was invited to their apartment behind the hotel to see their newborn grandchild. Stiff with politeness, she kept knocking into the furniture, not sure about the etiquette. She placed by the baby's bassinet one of the Swedish wooden horse souvenirs she'd brought over a bunch of, hand-painted red and white, in return for which the child's mother produced a platter of sweets. Karin sat there eating too many sticky sweets and feeling trapped, till the child's father, the hotel owners' son-in-law, stopped by.

'Namaste and welcome to India. How may I help you?' he said as if he were in some kind of permanent advertisement in the presence of foreigners. He was a slick-haired, skinny boy who looked no older than eighteen, told her he drove and offered to take her around. She spent the following week talking with him, in his taxi, being driven to shops and monuments. He accepted without fuss the tips she handed him, and they'd decided in advance on the payment, which had seemed somewhat excessive to her when they discussed it but extremely modest once the week of driving got under way. Manoj's father used to drive a taxi too, as did his father's father. 'I opened my eyes and there was a taxi before me,' he said to emphasize that he had known nothing else since birth. He had a permit to drive all over the country—in winter the foreign tourists went to Rajasthan, in summer Indian tourists did the hills. He explained to her that different places produced different sorts of people. Delhi's people were rubbish, mostly show-offs and gluttons, always intent on the next snack break. South Indians behaved better and showed interest in the sights. He did not say what he thought of foreigners and whether he distinguished between them.

Karin liked him but was also unsettled—watching his quick eyes in the rear-view mirror, the smooth way he swerved in the traffic—imagining Örjan like Manoj, if they hadn't brought him home, or Manoj like Örjan, if they had brought him instead.

One evening, over a dinner of chicken curry and tepid lager, Örjan said, 'I think people are more alike than not.' They started talking about the immigrants to Europe. Karin saw them as tragic, marked by loss. They could neither live in their own places nor embrace their new homes. Örjan thought they pointlessly clung on to what they believed set them apart—headscarves, say—rather than asking what lay inside those headscarf-wearing heads.

'Difference is not of value in itself,' he said.

'No, but we *are* different.' She remembered his observation about dogs and their admirable universalism. Human beings didn't have that homogeneity.

'We have to ask—what is of value in difference,' he answered.

'Why do you keep coming back here?'

'What have I contributed to our great nation? It doesn't run in my veins—the blood of men who worked in the mines or fought in the wars or even just plastered a church wall.' This was one of his favourite themes and his mother had to interrupt.

'But Örjan, you just said it yourself. It's not about blood always. You've had your eyes wide open. Is that not something?'

He looked unconvinced but grinned at her, consoled his mama for his ambivalence with a little boy's winning smile, then coming, eventually, to her question, revealed, to her dismay, that he was thinking of moving to India.

'Why?' she asked open-mouthed. And then, trying to not seem so aghast, 'How?'

'It's only an experiment. To spend time in a place that feels alien to me but which I, in an imperfect sense, belong to. I'm just trying not to end up like all those immigrants back home. They're not asking: "What is the new thing we could be in the circumstances?"'

'True. A new combination. A changed person.'

'Isn't that culture? Always being made and unmade?'

Karin thought of her chats with Manoj, the faint feeling in her that she recognized him, and she decided not to mention this new acquaintance to her son.

'Why do we believe that life is static?' asked Örjan. 'That we *must* die with the very things we were born with?'

His mother ordered a whisky and then, tired of the chillies in everything, a pizza. Instead of Manoj, she told him about one of the hotel guests, Gurov, a tall blond from Vladivostok who spoke broken English and spent his days scouring the city's markets for inexpensive leather goods—handbags, wallets, shoes, belts. Every evening he'd come back loaded with bulging black plastic bin-liners and she'd wonder how he was going to get it all on to the flight.

She had asked him one morning at breakfast. He produced a frayed postcard showing the harbour in Vladivostok and told her that's where he came from. Then it went back into his wallet; he seemed to carry this memento in place of the conventional pictures of wife and children. He said he came to India twice a year to shop and had links with a network of couriers who serviced dealers such as him. These were local guys whose only job it was to fly up and down between Delhi and Moscow with the stuff. He could send all his purchases in one shot and for much less hassle through a shipping container, straight to the port city he lived in, but he worried about customs duties and bribes. He had a quiet manner, he was perhaps used to keeping his head low, but the towering height and blue eyes did not quite suit a smuggler's mien. Karin wondered what, had he been from somewhere other than economically derelict Russia, he would have really liked to do with his life.

Örjan liked the idea of the Russian. 'Gurov,' he intoned, as if he'd met the man himself and already plumbed his depths, 'is on the frontier of culture. And that is because of money. The need for money makes people scale the boundaries, redraw them. He has learnt English, he probably knows some Hindi too. He's figured out the way things work in a new place much faster than any intellectual can.'

Karin had a different feeling about him. She was used to a society where people did what interested them, had personalities that they then fitted to work they enjoyed or at least did not detest. This other idea that you made the best of whatever half-baked opportunities came your way, this evidence of human powerlessness, was a new and sobering discovery for her—people like Gurov, his head hunched under the low-ceilinged dining room of the hotel, eating only boiled eggs and white bread because nothing else in the local cuisine agreed with him, or

Manoj driving even in his sleep because that's all that could make him money. She felt they had potentially richer selves flickering inside them, lives muffled, perhaps even snuffed out, no longer accessible.

Now at the kitchen table, he finishing his meal, she eating a cracker with cheese, they recall their trip to India but in different registers—for her it is a fading dream, for him a new reality.

'What will you miss most?'

'Clas Ohlson,' he says and laughs his rare laugh, which always sounds like it has been bottled up a long time—effervescent, deep-throated. 'I must find a way to get my books there . . .' he says then, worriedly.

Karin imagines herself as him—living with the noise of that city, the noise that has the nature of a constant demand: move out of the way so I can drive my car; come here and buy what I have to sell to you; just look at me, I need your attention. She realizes it's going to be hard for him, that he is doing this very much aware of the challenge. And she is to blame for this—what he calls his experiment—but how exactly? She is responsible in a general sense, in that love does not forestall confusion, painful choices.

'I saw a woman today. She looks newly arrived, all the way from Africa.'

Örjan promptly gives her the break-up of the immigrant population in town—the hundreds from Syria, Afghanistan, Libya, Eritrea and Somalia.

'I said hello but she didn't understand me. Yet she must have got my intention. I was smiling, nodding my head. She could have done the same even if she didn't follow the words.'

Örjan is silent for some moments, washing up at the sink.

'Do you think . . .' he says then, 'you'll be all right?'

Concern in her son's voice. Doubt in his eyes. She wants to say she'll manage, she does believe it, but she'd also like to embrace the moment, wallow in it. Of missing her son and missing her husband will most of the rest of her life be made, and the thought, there is that dreadful word again, *bores* her.

'Have you ever considered working at something new? Volunteering somewhere?'

She wants to say, *Don't patronize me. I've earned my retirement.* 'I could try to find something,' she agrees.

'There are all the immigrant centres that seem to need help . . .'

He comes back to the table, glances at the paper. On the front page is a report of a recent fire in one such centre for children in the adjoining town. The place had to be evacuated. The police suspect arson. Karin knows the unspoken charge: Must you devote your life to Clas Ohlson and American TV dramas? There is so much to do. Go out and engage with the poor and the suffering. *But John the Baptist is by himself in the wild*, she thinks. *That's the stuff of his legend—his aloneness, his desert solitude. How long did he spend there before he felt ready to face the crowds? David would have never suggested that I get back to work. After thirty-five years in that administrative job where I perfected everything I could, made structural changes, led meetings, inspired colleagues* . . . She stops. She can easily work herself into a state of self-glorification over it even now.

'David,' she says, the word out of her mouth before she quite knows what should follow it. But it echoes back to her and sounds right. She stares at her son and repeats, 'David.'

It is so quiet they can hear Oskar's contended post-dinner breathing; he is stretched out like a living rug under the table between their legs. Örjan pushes back his chair. 'Those books.'

'David,' she says again.

Her son looks back at her, no longer with the certainty of a few minutes ago. Instead, that same shyness again. But she has him captive, saying *David* like that. He seems to have nothing quite rational to offer to this and all he has are rational views.

'Mama, stop.' The shyness is giving way to panic.

'David,' she answers.

He comes over to her, puts a tentative hand on her arm.

'Okay, David,' he says.

She cries in absolute silence into the sleeve of her jersey, while he stands there, near enough for her to know that he's concerned but not quite able to comfort her. Oskar rises in alarm and sidles up to her, wagging his tail sympathetically.

'I'll make coffee,' says Örjan. Then, facing away, 'What do you think Papa might have said today—about this, my move?'

'I don't know,' says Karin.

'Maybe we can't know. Because he's dead.'

'I thought he had gone quiet but suddenly he comes back. I mean, his absence is here again, it makes everything feel so . . . divided.'

Örjan is filling the kettle.

'I know. I talk to him too. I think he wouldn't really have cared that much about this particular project of mine,' he says, as if all his other undertakings had his father's passionate support. 'But, still, I'd like to have told him about it. And because it's a big step, he might have said something. Even if he disagreed. I wouldn't have minded that, if he didn't see eye to eye with me about the importance of leaving.'

'It's really a very big step,' says Karin, amazed that she has been thinking of herself when her son is here, on the point of going away. She stands up and embraces him, saying nothing, feeling she has exhausted her language.

The next afternoon she is out again, and the day is warmer than the previous one. She walks past the church without going in, and sits by the lakeside after they have done a few rounds of it, watching a pair of swans. She closes her eyes to the breeze and the seagulls. *Stay, spring, stay*, she coaxes and then wonders: *What form would thoughts take if we didn't allow them words?*

She is heading back, grateful for the weather, for legs that can walk without tiring and for her faithful Oskar, and there is the African woman again, from Somalia or Eritrea, thinks Karin, now that her son has identified the countries for her. With her is a boy of about seven, in a knitted cap, a rubber ball in his hand which he does not bounce or throw up, as if cautious about Karin's presence.

She is not sure whether to greet them but then the boy says in Swedish as they near each other, 'The lady with the dog.'

'Yes, that's who I am,' she replies, smiling, at which his mother or grandmother, it is hard to determine just by those eyes, nods at her, the briefest of nods, a delicate, regal gesture.

Reaching home, Karin wonders whom the boy was addressing. Not the woman, who doesn't know the language, and not Karin, who is aware of being that lady. He was talking to himself perhaps. He was testing his acquired vocabulary, naming the things he sees in the world, giving shape to experience anew.

Karin is impressed and then curious. It could be that someday she will follow him and find out how it is done, regenerating the world, like spring, giving life to familiar things all over again. For now she is content just smoking down a cigarette in her garden while Oskar watches the blackbird, and she wonders if he is, like her, wondering, *Is it the very same one as yesterday?*

8

BIRD LOVE

If asked to name the most unexpected thing about her marriage, she'd have said: the rain. Half a year in and she woke up every day to the reek of damp clothes, wondering whether the capsicum plants and vines of Malabar spinach she was trying to tend would survive yet another day of battering. Was it something else she'd pictured when she went through that blur of rituals with Parthasarathy, dressed in a brilliant sari—pink and beige, or was it, instead, an elusive shade of gold? Was marriage meant to be a different way of life from this: the windows lambasted with slanting torrents all morning and in the afternoons the valley blinded by a mist so thick she felt lost in her own home. *Where am I?* Only a lone coconut palm loomed in the whiteness. The vapour would slowly dissolve away like smoke drifts, and then, for a moment, she'd see a bird or two shaking itself dry on the dripping wires. Her husband was teaching her the names of birds.

'Such a rainy town. We'll have to get you gumboots,' he'd told her, smiling, when they met. She understood the words but not their import. Or she had given them another meaning, as she had all of his remarks. There was a lightness to his tone which had immediately infected her too, an irony in the face of the awkwardness—two people meeting for a predetermined end. It was a bit of a joke, he seemed to suggest. Everything he said, all the small talk, seemed to her actually a comment on marriage. *We are going to get together*—that was the implication running through those two short conversations over coffee and too many snacks being passed around in her parents' living room with its large portrait of Ramana Maharshi looking down at them, along with the stiff studio photos in the cabinet and the handful of trophies she and her sister had won at school. His parents and hers, everyone speaking at the same time.

Then they'd started to call each other in the feverish weeks that followed but he hadn't brought up the weather again. Instead they were occupied with themes such as whether their position in society implied two desserts or three for the wedding lunch, where a friend of hers coming all the way from Delhi was to stay, the gifts, neither lavish nor cheap, to be chosen for aunts and uncles travelling from the village for the occasion, the question of whether she was nervous, the question of whether he was serious. They had begun to tease each other. She was going to set up house with this stranger in a town she didn't know. The thought was wildly exhilarating but, she cautioned herself, in a general sense it was not new. This could not be the first time in the history of the world that a woman was to marry. Her sister was one instance close at hand; she now lived with her doctor husband and toddler in Sharjah. At no point during *her* wedding, or after, had she seemed taken aback by the unprecedentedness of what she was doing.

But to Punitha everything was surprising, and remained so. Partha had a job at the post office, and each evening she presented to him something delectable she had just made because that feel of the novelty of married life was still with her—a sponge cake steamed in a pressure cooker, bhel puri with grated carrot and freshly roasted peanuts mixed into it, thick juice squeezed out of the season's last raspuri or mallika mangoes, squares of chewy barfi pressed together from dried fruit and coconut. Later in the evening, once he'd been diverted by the TV or was on the phone with his hospital-receptionist friend in Bangalore, she would start, on a more sedate note, on dinner. But for that single hour there was a sundown intimacy between them, and her pleasure—held in abeyance during the day—would make her talky again. She'd have redone her plait in anticipation of this evening tête-à-tête, glossed her lips, considered things she'd like to say to him such as: *The woman in the novel I'm reading is unhappy in love*, or *I drew water from the well and scrubbed out the steps today*. But when they were actually sitting down together, she'd wait for her husband to speak. If he admired her cookery, Punitha described the innovations to which she'd subjected recipes picked up online. If Partha had an inspiring day at work, that is, if he'd discoursed with a customer on something of larger interest than that person's postal business, they would chat about this and his dream—to get a transfer to Bangalore so their lives could properly commence.

Till May they'd been on their little balcony every evening, he pointing out the birds hovering in the air, calling from the trees of silver oak and jackfruit. Swallows filled the air as the sun went down. Pure-white egrets flying home. She would confuse their names but one bird remained in her memory. It was at the bedroom window every sunny afternoon, knocking inquiringly at the glass, taking off and then flying right back, captivated by its reflection in the mirror-filmed pane. 'Yellow wagtail,' Partha had said. It was the most delicate thing she'd ever seen—marvellously tiny feet, a grey, almost charcoal, body, pale-yellow breast and long, pointy tail. That such an exquisite creature took up so little space in the world, that this bird was so birdlike, this wagtail, delighted Punitha. It was all still new to her then—Partha's view on the world, her own search for a job, their domestic routines.

But now her surprise is starting to take a different orientation. She hasn't been able to find work at the only college in town; her postgraduate degree does not, it is clear, single her out. The rain has been crashing down for weeks. Most of the day she is by herself and thinking, *So this is marriage*, while trying to recall the avian names her husband has taught her. Her happiness is an inward knot now, held tight against the monsoon chill; it loosens when she sees Partha's face at the door every evening. At night they huddle together under the blanket, driven as much by cold as passion, and the elements of sex that he shares with her she ascribes to impressive prior knowledge that he never reveals the source of—just as he knows but does not say how he knows the names of the birds.

Today she has made little, round guliappas, which Partha dips into the mint-and-coconut chutney and declares excellent. 'In Bangalore I'll take you to Dakshina Bhavan in Rajajinagar,' he says. 'People are out in the evenings, eating everywhere, going for movies. In this place, what? We can't step into the theatre here, it's only for rickshaw drivers and rowdies.' The living-room floor is wet with the water that dripped off the cuffs of Partha's trousers when he came in. The electricity, which was out all day, returns and then abruptly goes off again two minutes later. She is thinking of breakfast. It can't be upittu; mould, she discovered this afternoon, has got to the semolina. This is their little home. Two rooms, a small passageway leading to the kitchen, the precious balcony for her plants and his birds. The landlady lives downstairs and keeps a stern eye on how much water Punitha draws from the well and whether or not Partha double-latches the gate after him when he wheels in his scooter every evening.

'What do I know? This feels big to me,' says Punitha. She grew up in a taluk town and is now in the much busier district headquarters. Bangalore swims out of her grasp. What will its enormity imply? Will it be tougher or simpler to land a job when there are a dozen colleges she can apply to instead of one? Will they still sit like this every evening, sketching the future while they eat her laboriously made, food-blog-inspired snacks, or will the future be upon them then? She is twenty-three and open to everything her husband suggests, but she's a little wary of dreaming. Getting what you want—the double income, the bigger house—might mean giving up something you have.

He says, 'The world, Puni, is a very big place. When you read, talk to those who have travelled, you will see. Don't imagine for a moment that your life is going to be just cooking all the time. And this.' He gestures at the living room which has very little in it other than the TV, the two sofa-chairs of ribbed brown velvet they're sitting in, and a calendar on the wall from the hospital in the Gulf where her brother-in-law works. She knows what Partha's going to say next; he'll inquire into whether she's given any time to the book he bought her—an illustrated history of the Western world, weighty with glossy pages and reams of text. Her English falters before the English in that book. She opens it and then returns to her romantic novels, stories of working women trying to both maintain their dignity and find love, written in a Kannada that is transparent to her.

So she asks him his favourite question instead: 'What about the transfer?' He pops guliappas into his mouth, one after the other, and she watches him as if he's performing a feat directed by her wizardry. 'Told you, *kanna*, have to reapply. I'm going to ask for it on medical grounds now. Say I'm sick and need treatment in Bangalore. Get a doctor's certificate.' He's counting, this time around, on Arvind, the hospital receptionist. She worries he might be found out. But Partha has put his mind to the end and will not be sidelined by any talk about the means employed. He wants to get there and once they do he will join a birdwatching society, write earnest articles for the newspapers, send his wife to a spoken-English tutorial to improve her job prospects.

'If our children grow up there, they will know something. They will get the real perspective,' he says. Punitha would just like the rain to stop, the landlady to loosen up, the semolina to stay fresh, her husband to love the new salwar-kameez she has on, printed with a surfeit of paisleys. She wants things to be as they more or less are. *I am a bird*, she realizes, and just at that moment Partha calls from the balcony where he has gone to smoke a cigarette. 'Puni, come and see, a pair of dusky crag-martins.'

They are circling around each other and then swoop down on the balcony, within touching distance except that they are flying so fast, so excitedly, one could never actually catch them or ever feel their small, plump black bodies, the tails sprinkled with white spots. *Such a naive joy in these two! Their very flight is a song*, thinks Punitha. The wind blows a pointy drizzle towards them, and it's hard to say whether this is a prelude to a stronger shower or the thinning out of the previous one. Partha wants to know if Puni has ever seen ostriches. He's heard of a man across the valley who is rearing ostriches and selling their eggs. 'We could get some ostrich eggs. Ostrich eggs are good for health,' he says. 'Are they different from the usual ones?' asks Punitha. 'Probably bigger,' he says, and she wonders how best to cook them and whether she'll enjoy them. She grew up a sambar-palya-eating vegetarian, and strictly eggless, though in college she took to eggy snacks in the canteen with her friends. Her sister boils eggs for her child when she visits and their parents let this taboo object into the kitchen for the sake of their daughters, or as a concession to the times, or simply because they are somewhat weakened by the modern charge that to only eat vegetables is to miss out on some vital nutrition. Partha studied in Bangalore and is addicted to omelettes. He may have gone even further than eggs but they don't really discuss all the foods he has experimented with. Puni is not sure she wants to know. She makes a shopping list. They are in dire need of those conical, holey cane baskets on sale in this season—one lights a brazier under them and piles damp clothes on top.

The two walk into mist, the road before them all but a fiction. Women in waterproof cloaks appear out of the rain, their arms hidden, waddling like penguins. They pass the corner grocery shop and espy, lit garishly by a hanging battery-powered lantern, the uncle who runs it. The standard evening greeting—*Had your coffee?*—is, in this season, replaced with the observation: *What rain!* Or, *The electricity's gone*—to which the usual, placid response is: *It will come.* Up the road, a gatepost has fallen on its side in the mud, but other than that life goes on. Puni recalls the stab of loneliness she felt during the day, the rain-drenched solitude of the wife at home who has no awareness of herself except as someone waiting for her husband, and she moves closer to him. He takes her hand, and the rain starts up again. Nearing town, they notice the village women on their haunches who have set up shop on the pavements, selling heaps of raw, sliced bamboo shoots, wild mushrooms, small, speckled mangoes—the offerings of the season. To the gutters lining roof edges are attached flapping pipes made of colourful polythene to drain the overflow. When they pass a man dressed in plastic rainwear from head to toe, selling, on a dirty square of sackcloth spread out before him, tied bunches of live, mud-brown crabs, their claws waving, Punitha averts her eyes in immediate alarm while Partha seems to be on the point of asking, just to establish his manliness, how much they cost.

At the ostrich keeper's house they are greeted by two enormous turkeys with livid, wet wattles. In a ring of cement filled with rainwater, a swan floats about forlornly. There are ducks too, one with a head of bottle green, pecking at invisible grain—or insects—in the grass of the muddy yard. A man in jeans and sneakers, looking comfortably dry unlike his visitors, walks out smiling. They ask for the ostrich eggs and he shows them inside the garden shed where the enormous birds are—one apparently in a sulk and cowering, the other flapping its wings at them.

'Useless wings,' says Partha, 'They cannot fly. Flightless birds. Did you get them from Africa?' he asks the man. 'I got them from Hunsur,' he replies. The shed smells of their excrement. They are too big, too weird to be contained by this man-made enclosure. *The ducks and the turkeys are all right but the ostriches*, thinks Punitha, *they have no business being here.* It turns out that the eggs were a rumour. These mighty birds are still too young to produce eggs—not yet a year old. 'I did have duck eggs,' says the man, 'but they're sold out.' He says if they call him later, he will keep a supply for them. He introduces himself as Vihaga, gives them his phone number. Punitha is so relieved to have escaped the eggs that she becomes inquisitive about the ostriches. What do they eat, how much, how often? She is amazed that anyone would want to keep these giant things in such close proximity, a species whose language we do not share, whose needs are inscrutable to us. She thinks of her summer visitor, the wagtail. She would have liked to reduce his pained puzzlement, explain that it was not another bird staring back from the window. But then if it understood the significance of such human things—glass, reflection, the laws of light—how would it retain its simple, infantile bird beauty?

'Are those mallards you have?' Partha asks, pointing to the ducks. Vihaga doesn't know the English name of the species but says their eggs have a strong taste and their meat is good. 'What if you were trying to make an omelette and a baby bird came out?' asks Punitha quite unexpectedly and the two men look at her, both amused, already in fifteen minutes bonded by bird love. She is suddenly nauseated, tasting blood in her mouth. The smell of ostrich shit, the damp she has been inhaling for weeks, the idea of eating something alive, produces in her a wave of sickness. Partha is explaining to her, 'Eggs have to be incubated, in warmth, for babies to be born. If you take them away from their mothers before that can happen, they remain eggs. But they're tested against the light before they're sold, to make sure.'

And Punitha is shocked. She remembers going with her sister to the open-air market back home, standing before the egg seller as he held up each egg against a naked light bulb, twirled it expertly in his hand. She imagined he did it to make sure there were no cracks. She, in her vegetarian ignorance, did not know he was looking for that speck of blood, that dot which signals the start of life. On their honeymoon in the Nilgiris, Parth had explained to her with diagrams and everything how mammals reproduce. She felt she ought to have already known but the biology in her head was blurry and the little she remembered from school seemed to have nothing to do with love. And now, digesting this new information about birdlife, she is pukey and hoping not to do it before the birdman, in his yard. She backs out and is speeding down the lane, trying to find some bit of hedge to bury her disgust in. She turns her back to the bungalows and vomits explosively. Tears flow alongside. She lets go of her umbrella when a gale tugs hard at it. She is a crying, vomiting mess with wet hair, in a no-longer-new salwar-kameez, and she cannot understand how the subject of eggs could have brought on this desperateness. Partha is running after her umbrella, which dances like a bird in the wind.

'I don't want them,' she tells him after he has conquered it and returned to her.

'Have you eaten something bad?' he asks.

'I don't want the eggs!' she shouts. 'Why did you bring me here?'

'Puni, you like eggs. Who made us masala omelettes day before yesterday?'

'No, no,' she cries, and twists her face towards the hedge again to retch.

'Okay, let's go home then.'

She pulls her arm away from his grasp and wonders if she married the wrong man. The person she spent that hour in fleeting conversation with in her parents' living room could well be just a vague lookalike of the one she eventually wore her gold-but-not-quite-gold sari to wed. The first was a gently jokey soul, this one wants to foist duck eggs on her and looks with interest at crawling crabs. *Oh God*, she thinks, *is this what I left my parents for?* The stench and horror of the non-vegetarian world and the sickening insistence of the rain?

She is looking at Partha through a nauseous, anguished blur, while he explains that she is probably sick from excessive snacking even though it was he who ate most of the guliappas.

'I don't want to go home.'

'Puni, we'll go to a doctor?'

'Just promise to stop eating all that.'

'What am I eating? I eat what you give me.'

'How do I know what you order when you go out for lunch with your post-office friends?'

'What?' asks Partha, and Puni realizes this is her first experience of marital discord, of looking into his familiar eyes and feeling she doesn't really know him.

'Say we won't cook eggs any more. From today.'

He shakes his head and says she is being so stupid and maybe that's just what she is—stupid. He is no longer looking at her as they walk down the lane to an empty rickshaw. They return the way they came but the streets of the wet town are not visible to them through the heavy tarpaulin hanging from the rickshaw's sides. Puni cries all the way home, imagining herself in Bangalore and having to face live crabs at every street corner, dead goats hanging from hooks in the market, chicken feathers in open drains, the smell of fish frying in the neighbour's house. She cannot say this to her husband—that Bangalore frightens her. *It's a small thing*, she thinks to herself in consolation, trying to swallow a new wave of nausea, keeping her face firmly turned away from her annoyed husband. *This is only because I've never seen ostriches before.* And again she is struck by dismay, as if someone, an aunt or a girlfriend, when talking about marriage, ought to have mentioned the ostriches.

———

The following day a doctor pronounced her five weeks pregnant, and she no longer cries when she pukes now, or feels like. *It is natural*, she thinks, and has come to love that word: natural. She no longer minds the rain either, it will abate in time and the sun return. That is natural too.

She is woken early every morning by a bird's voice, a three-note call so insistently loud it seems to contain a message for her. 'I'm quite sure I've never heard that bird before,' she tells Partha and he laughs softly at her innocence, tells her it's just the koel. In the evenings she makes snacks—chikoo ice-cream, potato wafers, a gelatinous yellow halwa. Food fills her mind and shapes the day.

After lunch she lies on the sofa. Things do seasonally blow about in her home town too—they call it *ashaada gadi*, the monsoon wind. But this mad creature, which knocks sharply on the panes with almost human fingers, needs another name. What could she call it?

'Why is it so windy?' she'd asked her landlady the other day, wanting to draw her out. To which the elderly widow tartly replied, 'There's no why to the wind.' The words return to Punitha like a melody as she lies looking at the sky through the window, trying to sense the infant inside her, so glad that this is natural, a story that has unfolded a billion times before. Everything is all right, the cuckoo will call tomorrow morning from the treetops as it has always done, and there's no why to the wind. *There's no why to the wind.*

9

I AM VERY ANGRY

It was in February—just as the city's modest flirtation with winter ended and the weather, aided by the exhalations of more than five million assorted vehicles, turned hot again—that T.S. Murthy's neighbours first began their impassioned shouting. They were a new family in a new house on the lane perpendicular to his. In the manner of a creature intimately familiar with the arrangements of his habitat, Murthy had sensed their arrival before he saw them. Walking past it, he noticed no obvious signs of life around the house, but the leftover mound of rubble by the gatepost, which had lain there, irritating him, for months, was gone. He looked up at the three protruding balconies, done up the fancy way, in steel-cinched glass. A sudden breeze shook down the lilac blossoms of the jacaranda tree nearby and brought with it the smell of new paint and raw concrete. *People*, thought Murthy, and there followed that mix of anticipation and worry. He just could not wholeheartedly like his fellow humans in the old way any more. More and more people, it seemed, were less and less like him, and he tended to think of himself as a pretty decent instance of the species.

T.S. Murthy was a retired gent in ancient glasses and a series of serviceable shirt-pants left over from his working days. Four decades he had kept the books as assistant and then senior accounts officer at the Bangalore Electricity Supply Company, never once feeling that life was elsewhere. He'd understood that the times had changed when they did, passing on to his son the values that equipped the boy for the twenty-first century— namely, to be a single-minded earner of money, following it to its sources even if that meant going very far from home. But lately, after his wife's passing and his own crossing over to the far side of seventy, contentment seemed to be slipping away from Murthy. Reviewing his years, he'd find them strangely insignificant. At times the whole city—its massive confusion of souls pressed cheek to jowl—was an unbearable blight and he would prolong his afternoon nap and then wake up aghast at having missed his appointment with himself for his five-o'-clock stroll.

Yet Murthy's curiosity, his outgoingness, remained. He still engaged with young men on bikes who might have stopped to casually chuck plastic bags festering with garbage on to street corners, flower vendors liable to overcharge, the municipal officials when there was no water supply three days in a row. He monitored the habits of his only two friends, both elderly men in the colony, neither apparently as disciplined as him. He took his breakfast at eight o'clock sharp and neither would he brook any delays for lunch, even if, more and more, all he felt like was just a small heap of curd-rice.

The day after he'd stood outside the new apartment building with the jacaranda drifting down on to his head and felt the pressure against his temples of the city's millions, the first set of occupants were there, standing outside as if not quite prepared to move in—a middle-aged couple with their bespectacled daughter, the Krishnaraos. Engineer, civil engineer and housewife, they said, when he introduced himself, and their girl was studying medicine, first year. In fact, they had shifted to the neighbourhood because it was near her college, just a short bus-ride away. She, Sonia, had greeted him effusively but the lenses of her glasses were speckled with stains so Murthy couldn't tell exactly what her gaze was like. She was dressed in a skirt that ended above her knees, a child's dress, felt the old man, yet the glasses and the voice were a woman's. The contrast confused him and he did not say very much to her.

Later he would see her going past the house, to the bus stop. She dressed strangely, in flapping salwars and army boots, or that tiny skirt, taking giant strides, her heavy plait swinging behind her, always on the phone, always apparently in some place other than the one her body was restlessly moving through. The family spoke Kannada with him but their shouting, when it commenced, was in their native Telugu, which he knew a little of, not enough to make proper sense of their battles. The house that had once stood there, a small, neat, flat-roofed home with veranda, garden, mosaic floors and stucco patterns on the outer walls, had given way to something bulkier and pricier but sans these older things. 'They don't know what it was like before,' Murthy would repeat to himself, distressed by the noise. His friend Viraj had lived there, and when he died his children let the whole thing go to a developer. Murthy was no nostalgist, but the ugly starkness of the new construction and the daily unhappiness of its recent inmates seemed to grow from the same source, though he could not say what exactly it was.

That month he felt the turn in the season. Since December he had, with unnecessary carefulness, wrapped a frayed muffler around his throat as he walked, starting at six thirty—several times around the block and then to the main road to pick up the milk and newspapers. He'd got into this custom when his wife died— going out to get the things that would otherwise come home to them. To endow his evenings with purpose, he had searched out the farthest store with the cheapest groceries, a difference of a rupee or two here and there, but enough for him to feel he was not being foolish in going all the way. There was a little kiosk near it where he sometimes smoked a cigarette and had a thimble-sized plastic cup of coffee, listening to the chat around him, workmen talk, often in languages of the north that he didn't follow, and with it, sweaty, workmen smells.

If he was going to the temple, there would be no giving in to roadside coffee and the stolen cigarette. He'd listen to the chanting at the Raghavendra Swamy Temple, or join the singing at the Siddhivinayak Temple. These experiences did not seize on his emotions; he did not lock eyes with the elephant god's slanting ones or makes entreaties of the Swamy. It was just part of his hygiene—the daily five-minute invocation before the pictures in his puja room at home, the giving of leftover food or a few coins every week to the gypsy women who came begging in Shiva's name, the regular rounds of the temples. Evenings he reread the morning papers and listlessly watched the TV soaps his wife used to. He cooked for himself. He'd always known how to cook; it was he who put the sambar to simmer and got the palya frying when his wife had her periods. Women in Brahmin households such as his didn't cook when they were menstruating—though he wondered if his daughter-in-law followed that principle in Toronto. Or, indeed, if the shouting engineer family, who were clearly Brahmins too, did.

The morning he first heard their noise, in the middle of February, he'd just read in the papers about a nineteen-year-old boy who had stepped on a drunk man's toes while dancing during a temple procession in Adugodi. The man and his friends had retaliated by stabbing the boy to death. The police had ruled out rivalry as a motive; the two parties didn't appear to have known each other. He was just pondering this piece of news when a scream made him look out of his window. The Krishnarao girl, Sonia, was sobbing loudly, standing pressed against the railing of their first-floor balcony as if she would rather spend her life there than with the people haranguing her from within. There was some English mixed with her father's Telugu but not her mother's. 'Do you want to make a laughing stock of yourself?' he shouted, to which Sonia, crying, said, 'You have no respect for me.' Murthy wondered if it was about the girl's eccentric dress sense. He winced at how she addressed her father—in cold English. 'You' she'd called him, and no 'Appa' to soften it. She strode back into the house and banged the door shut after her. Through their open windows the quarrel could be heard to continue for a good hour before it was time for the girl to head out.

A few days later Sonia came to his house to borrow a griddle because they had relatives visiting and needed an extra one for the dosas. She seemed blithe though jumpy, her glasses foggy and her speech hurried. 'Uncle, do you live alone? You could come sometimes to our house and eat with us. My mother is a very good cook. That's all she does, you know. When did Aunty pass away? Oh, I can't imagine what you do the whole day alone. You don't even have Wi-Fi in here? My father said to tell you that he is on the lookout for a tutor for me, and if you have any suggestions, to please pass them on. But I myself am not interested. I spend hours slogging in class and then this nonsense.' Murthy was flustered at everything she said and could not immediately recall if he had a griddle to spare.

From day to day, the weather turned hotter; he let the fan run all night and put away his muffler. He missed his wife, noticing her old cotton saris in their wardrobe, and wondered whether he would miss her less or more if he gave her clothes away to the alms-seeking women. It was a matter he had not been able to resolve in the two years since she'd died. February was almost over and he read in the papers about a couple of college students who had been beaten up the previous night in Sanjay Nagar, apparently because they'd parked their bikes the wrong way outside a grocery store. Some toughs picked a fight with the boys over the parking issue and later that night went to where they stayed and beat them so bad one boy needed nine stitches on his head. It turned out they resented the students because they were from Kerala and, said one of the injured boys, because they 'knew that we did not have local support'. Murthy didn't like it. He didn't like it that there were too many people in Bangalore either, pouring in from everywhere. But murderous violence? People needed words, to talk with each other and bring out their difficulties.

He saw the Krishnaraos again on the day of the by-election in early March. As sales of watermelons and ice cream rose, and winter became first a memory and then a dream, the people of the area queued up at a high school to vote for a new legislator in place of their local one who had died of a heart attack some months previously. The candidates were all young and inexperienced in Murthy's view, though he voted, of course, for the right-wing party. They had promised to clean up the country, and no political goal seemed more vital to him. He thought of the machetes flashing, the bicycle chains whipped out, and he wanted someone to put an end to it. Mrs Krishnarao thanked Murthy for his help and, now that their house guests were gone, said that he must please drop in. 'For the first time in a long time, I feel like voting,' boomed

Mr Krishnarao. 'Finally a leader I can support.' He meant the prime minister. They discussed the many good things their chosen party had pulled off at the national level, such as getting into power in the first place. 'Do you have novels in your house, anything other than books to be studied? I need some timepass. These people are anti-WhatsApp, they would even take away my phone if I should let it leave my hand,' said Sonia, and Murthy promised to see what could be found on his son's shelves. She did not seem immersed in her medical studies. Murthy wondered what kind of doctor she would make—one who prodded her patients aggressively with her stethoscope and wrote out hasty prescriptions. All the same, he was sorry for her; he felt himself on her side even though, aside from the hysteria involved, he couldn't see any obvious faults with her parents' disciplining attitude.

Sonia had laughed contemptuously at her parents yet the three seemed all right together; the quarrel must have just been that wrinkle that can momentarily appear on the face of even the most harmonious family. The same evening, Murthy spotted in the paper an item he had missed in the morning. 'Silly Facebook Tiff Claims Youth's Life'. A twenty-one-year-old boy who worked in a cargo company at the airport had messaged a senior of his on Facebook with the salutation *Hey buddy*. This older friend considered the familiar tone an insult so he went across to the boy's house in Vidyanagar with a gang of friends and killed him. *There must be more*, thought Murthy, disbelieving. *This is not a story! There must be more.* People were dying like swatted flies, and with even less cause, if these two-inch-long reports were to be believed.

'What will you do here? Exactly what you do there,' his son said to him over the phone during one of his biweekly calls. He wanted his father to visit Canada, had been persistent for some time now, but Murthy, having gone and returned, was reluctant to repeat the experience. His wife had spent more time there—several months each year till the grandchildren started junior school. She stayed in most of the time, while Murthy, on that one visit, would zip up his borrowed jacket and walk in the neighbourhood, or take two buses to the library. He had formed grand opinions of the country and the culture but couldn't bring them to mind just then. Instead, only minor images: how the bicycle paths were coloured differently from the motorable roads, the cheery text on a carton of cereal, the mystifying sculptures of steel blocks set up in a park.

'Yes, yes, all right. We will make a plan next summer,' he said to his son. 'This year I might go to the hills with Tilak's family. They are heading to the north for some pilgrimage or the other.' But he did not really want to take in Canada all over again. Lying in bed in the afternoon, struggling out of his nap, he would try to face the worst things possible, and they always took the form of acute helplessness, a sense of being cowed down by realities beyond his grasp. The rest of the world followed its own logic, why should he be obliged to make sense of it?

And now even his own city was changing its face. He had settled down in Bangalore, taken the measure of it through his job, his friends and colleagues, his domestic satisfactions—getting married, raising a child—but the lessons of that life could no longer be applied to the things he read in the papers. He dreamt of politics, a heroic force that could restore order. What would that be like—order? He had not missed it in his younger days. Then, too, he read the papers, but those dowry deaths and gang wars of long ago, those occasional conflagrations over who owned Bangalore, were reassurances that the city was large and full of life, brimming with the expectations of its many people. Now those people had grown into an infestation and their outlook had turned sour. They no longer seemed to need a reason to bring out the knives.

He thought he would speak out during the next phone call, explain his tiredness, his worries, to his son. Then he went out into the warm March night. 'Bhakti can help us remove our ignorance, our mistaken knowledge, but for the true devotee there is no goal to his bhakti. His adoration of Vishnu is more important than the release that ensues from it.' There was a sermon under way at the Raghavendra Swamy Temple, being delivered sonorously by a representative from the head monastery in Andhra Pradesh. *Bhakti as an end in itself.* It appealed to Murthy. And he had no trouble reconciling this Vedic philosophy of self-realization with a belief in Ganapati—who presided over the other temple—as an intercessor in the affairs of men, a remover of obstacles. After the lecture, Murthy bumped into Tilak, a squint-eyed man made tragic by his and his wife's lack of children, a man with whom Murthy had spent his career working the numbers in the electricity supply company. They went over to the fellow selling coconuts from a pushcart under a gulmohar tree, and started to discuss Muslims, one of Tilak's abiding annoyances. 'Nobody is saying they should leave but if they want to go, and there is a country that was created for them, why are they here?' he said. He had disarmingly contradictory views; he felt, both, that Muslims should conduct themselves more like ordinary people such as him and that they could not expect to be treated at par because they were in fact not like him at all. Gulping down his sweet coconut-water, Murthy vaguely agreed. It was wonderful to escape the stuffy indoors and be out at night in this season, watch the families clustered around the snack stalls, check out the season's first mangoes, dodge the groups of boys on bikes, cruising. There seemed to be no ill will in the air. Murthy had another coconut, strolled with Tilak in the back lanes, bought some loops of jasmine for his home shrine, noted happily that the street corner near his home was free for the moment from surreptitiously thrown garbage bags, then declared it was time to go and look into the matter of dinner. Tilak had no interest in dinner as yet; he took his at 10 p.m., or even later, for which he received his regular scolding from Murthy. The latter believed that waking early, taking meals in good time and walking a couple of kilometres every day were the cornerstones of a good life.

A good life. The swami had said that the highest devotion was the unmotivated one, but the next morning, woken by the Krishnaraos shouting, this no longer seemed such a reliable principle to Murthy. He longed fiercely for another kind of devotion—one that would lead not just to individual salvation but inflect a common fate, improve everyone's lot. He drew back his curtains and listened. This time it was the lady arrayed against the man and the girl. She cried and spoke voluminously in Telugu, which the other two kept cutting into, apparently unfazed by her grief. From what Murthy could tell, it was something about Mr Krishnarao's interest in another woman, his having spoken inappropriately to her or looked at her in a particular way. 'Amma, control your imagination!' Sonia yelled at one point, while her father did not appear at all like the genial man Murthy had seen on election day. He barked at his wife in a manner that suggested it was not new to him. They moved out into the balcony, then back into the house, shouting all the while. The following day they were, shockingly, still at it, and then for a whole day after. Murthy would be returning from his morning rounds, or tidying up in the kitchen, and it would come to him yet again—the intolerable sound of people fighting with what seemed like relish. When he phoned Tilak, who lived on the far side of the new apartment, to ask what he thought of it, Tilak said he hadn't heard a thing.

The Krishnaraos eventually returned to peace, whatever tattered sort of peace obtains in the aftermath of such bloodletting. Murthy had never before witnessed wholly respectable people, people like him, indulge in naked savagery, and he wasn't quite sure how he would face them, but Sonia rang on the doorbell a few days later. She seemed unembarrassed. He let her in and she looked around, finding a couple of James Hadley Chases and one book of spiritual guidance by a Tibetan monk. 'I have no friends in this colony and none in college either,' she declared, and Murthy wondered if it was appropriate to offer her a cup of coffee. His wife would have pressed something on a guest for sure, so he decided to do likewise. She followed him to the kitchen.

'Are you liking the course?' he asked her.

'It's just study. Like any other study. Where are your children? Canada? I want to go there too.' She sat down and sipped rapidly on her coffee, ate all the kodubale he'd laid out and told him of her ambitions. 'Whatever I do in life, I don't want to be like them.' He wondered what she meant and also how she could tell *him* this, a man who was older than her parents. 'I don't want to have a child like me, get some well-paid coolie job like my Appa's, or stay at home like my mother. I don't want to study all the time either. Though I have first-year exams next week, you know. Suppose I fail? But I'm okay, I mostly get things quick. So I might pass.'

It struck Murthy that she could turn out to be one of those Bangalore kids who kill themselves in this season—for March was not just new mangoes and the pleasures of night breezes. It was also the time when a child might come out of an examination hall, go home and hang herself. These suicides were in anticipation; the next spate would take place in June, when the results were announced. Sonia's jittery movements, the way things dropped from her hands constantly, the unsuitable man's trousers she was wearing, all worried Murthy. He ought to do something—warn her parents, try to counsel her. Instead he just let her chatter on, then told her to drop in whenever she wanted to.

The following day, the eighteenth of March, was Murthy's wife's death anniversary. He dusted the garland of sandalwood shavings around her photo on the living-room wall and said the necessary prayers at the home shrine. It was something of a shortcut; he ought to have gone back to their village for the proper anniversary rituals, as he had done the previous year, but the idea of travelling in this temperature frightened him. He wondered if he was weakening; he did not feel reduced in body but the strange heat around his ears and the anguished beating of his heart when faced with the anger and cruelty of people was, perhaps, as much a sign. *Whatever happens, I must not let go of my daily routines*, he thought, as he took up the papers and there discovered that the city had suffered yet another meaningless act of outrage. The thirty-five-year-old owner of a roadside eatery in the Wilson Garden police-station limits had been stabbed to near death by an irate customer to whom he'd refused a third helping of chutney to go with his breakfast idlis. The man had asked for more chutney 'despite being served twice' and, when the owner displayed some impatience towards this chutney fiend, had pulled a knife on the man. It was twenty-four hours since the incident and the injured man was either dead by now or better, but Murthy knew that there was no chance the following day's papers would have any news of him. One man's life was not significant enough to make the news twice. Murthy fretted about it; he imagined intervening, stopping the knife wielder, not heroically but simply, by chatting with him like he had with Sonia. And yet Sonia might jump off the balcony regardless. Or kick out a chair from under her and swing lifelessly, ridiculously, from a ceiling fan.

Because they were at it again. Murthy heard them later that day as he was making his wife's favourite jackfruit payasam, cooking the pulped fruit with coconut milk, nuts and jaggery. He planned to take some over to the Krishnaraos as a neighbourly gesture, and give a portion to Tilak and his wife as well. He was stirring a large pot of payasam, the aroma inevitably reminding him of a festive occasion when there was none. *Yet does not the making of this dish, the fragrance of it in the house, the sharing and eating of it, itself mean something?* Murthy asked himself. *We create the occasions and this is mine today, making this sweet for Amma's sake, because she liked it and liked making it. Later I will go to the temple, on the way back.* The Krishnaraos' shouting cut into his thoughts. At first it seemed they were just talking loudly, not being angry. They were discussing something about which each had strong views. It was merely their way—to debate things to death. He should not make this his business at all. But soon she was out there, in tears on the balcony—Sonia. When his boy was her age, he never, as far as Murthy could recall, displayed such tumultuous emotion. He could be obstinate, and Murthy's wife equally so, but the family never came close to raising their voices. And then there was Sonia; he could make her out clearly through the netted screen on his windows. She was on her knees in the balcony, crying for all the world to see. Her mother appeared and wagged a finger at her. Father said something from within that seemed to be in support of the girl. Soon mother and father were fighting and the girl rushed back in, and then Mr Krishnarao came out and declared in English, 'I have had enough of both of you.' But there was no going forward from the balcony. He had to return inside and face what he possibly hated.

Murthy raised the volume of the TV, ate a little of the payasam himself and put the rest in the fridge when it cooled. He tried to avoid rereading the report on the chutney murderer, instead scanning the paper for pleasant things—his party at the centre had completed two years in office, unchallenged, for instance. Then his thoughts drifted to Toronto. Impossible in apartments such as the one his son lived in to hear what your neighbours were saying in their own homes. There is a necessary distance between the houses, wide streets intervene, and through the thick glass of the windows, the city is at a remove. You might open your apartment door at the same time your neighbour does, and thereby catch a glimpse of his first-world existence behind him, but all you do is say hello and move on. The next time that door opens it could be someone else; the man you'd greeted is gone.

Murthy has been in this colony for a very long time and never before contemplated shutting his windows on it. He changed out of his home shirt into a better one for his evening walk and left home. March was winding down; the jacaranda had shed its blossoms, the gentle pink cassia flowering now. He walked aimlessly for a good hour, then stopped and wondered where he ought to be instead—at the grocery store, the temple, the pushcart with the coconuts?

The next time his neighbours screamed, Murthy could not tell who was ranged against whom. Nor did he care any longer to impose a narrative on their insanity. He tore out the netted screens, drew his windows shut and lay breathing hoarsely in the middle of the day in a house he could not remember ever having been so inhospitably hot. At midnight he let himself out and paced the lane bare-chested, in his *veshti*, delighting in the short-lived freedom the way a prisoner would.

On the third-last morning of March, T.S. Murthy read that a group of neighbours had gathered in S.K. Garden to watch an India vs Australia cricket match on a big screen erected in a playfield and that one of them brought a dog along. Some youths objected to the dog's barking and roughed up its owner. He went home and returned with a bunch of friends. Pro- and anti-dog factions clashed in the street, and one boy, who was attacked with a broken beer bottle, died on the way to hospital. Murthy folded the paper away. He waited, but the lane was eerily silent. The crows and vendors and children seemed to be holding their breath. Perhaps it was the heat, at 7 a.m. already offensive. He finished his breakfast and prayed to his gods. Still nothing. He looked out through the windows and paced his rooms. Silence all around. Finally, he stepped out and walked across to the corner of the lane. He could hear a sentence repeating itself in his head, the very same one that young men on the boil across the city had shrilly articulated of late. I am *very* angry. I am very *angry*.

As he approached the apartment building he was struck by a very vivid sense of having been there before. The feeling intensified as he came nearer. *I know this place, I know this place.* He was in a dream, certain and uncertain simultaneously, disoriented by déjà vu. Something was expected of him, an act of recognition that he could not define. He climbed the stairs to the first floor and pressed the bell. Sonia opened the door, talking on her phone. 'I am very, I am very . . .' he whispered, while she carried on about something someone had said to someone, which someone else altogether had, scandalously, overheard. She gestured for him to come in, didn't seem to notice his trembling hands, the incoherence. He sat down and waited to remember what he wanted to say. When Sonia ended her call, she explained that her parents were out of town for a couple of days. She was alone and watching TV indiscriminately. That seemed to be the extent of her rebellion.

'I am very angry,' said Murthy finally.

That gave her pause.

He repeated it with as much affront as he could, trying to bring something of the emotion on to his face.

'I am very angry.' But he didn't feel sufficiently so.

'I know,' said Sonia cheerfully. 'This water scarcity is driving us all mad.'

Murthy breathed and nodded, thankful she had chosen her own explanation. Then he grew self-conscious.

'My friend Viraj used to live here. His house stood on this plot. I just wanted to see what it looked like. This new place. Nothing left of the old but still. Things were different then. He was a peaceful man.'

Sonia seemed to have no idea he had dropped a hint. She grinned at him and said, 'I don't know how to cook, so after I finished the leftovers yesterday, I've just been eating chocolate biscuits and peanuts. I can't make you coffee, so sorry. But do you want to watch TV here?' She gestured at the enormous screen mounted on the wall on which there was the usual breaking news. He nodded in the negative but kept his eyes on the streaming headlines, unsure of why he was there, trying to find a way out of his sudden awkwardness.

Why fight? he wanted to ask Sonia, while she chattered on about how she had aced her exams despite studying very little, and how her parents had gone to their home town to consult the family guru over a personal problem.

She seemed cheerful but he knew she could easily break into wails or pull fiercely at her long hair. If she were his daughter, and he had never had a daughter, he would educate her better, tell her a thing or two regarding the right conduct, and never raise his voice at her. She would dress better too and never be so solitary as to have to befriend an old man. He looked again at the horrors being enumerated on the screen and realized it was not anger he was feeling any more but something akin to a muted melancholy he hadn't known he possessed.

'Why fight?' he asked softly.

But Sonia hadn't heard; she was telling him she'd finished the books he'd lent her and wanted more.

'I can cook you lunch,' he said, sitting up, happy at the sudden inspiration. 'You have nothing to eat. Come over and we will eat together.'

Sonia jumped at the idea.

'What would you like?' he asked, and found he could chat comfortably with her, at last, about her preferences among rice dishes and varieties of rasam and seasonal vegetables.

Back home, chopping tondekayi, he heard the itinerants calling from the street. He brought out the box of payasam from the fridge and the saris from the cupboard and handed both over to them. The two women with babies on their hips took the gifts, mumbled Shiva's name a few times and went away.

And after that all was wonderfully peaceful for some time.

10

ELITE

Each of us, the guiltily innocent, has his own means of getting away from the news.

It's Wednesday and not early in the night but I anyway stop by after work at Elite, on the main road two streets away from my apartment, and head to the rooftop. If you stand by the parapet you can see, over the pots of desiccated cacti fenced in with bamboo splits, shoals of winking cars gliding by and shoppers picking discounted vegetables out of the plastic crates outside the supermarket. There's nothing to see, really, this place is only three floors up from the road, but it makes the drinkers feel liberated— the enclosed patch of fuzzy Bangalore sky and the freedom to fill the ashtrays at your table. The laughter is always more strident here, on the roof of Elite, pronounced, for some reason, 'E-Light'.

I order my whisky and wafers and resist scrolling through my playlist. I'm meaning to meditate today. While waiting for the alcohol to hit home and help me deliver some kind of verdict on the news, I think of Elite and why I always end up here once a week, sometimes more. I consider my co-drinkers—there is one gang already pretty deep into their cups of Khodays XXX Rum— and cannot believe they're in love with the place either. But there are so many Elites all over this city of easy-drinking, semi-plausible watering holes such as these for those who like a little space for conversation, waiters in shoes not chappals, and clean forks with which to polish off plates of chicken-fry and greasy fish. By itself, Elite can even depress me—how to see myself as sophisticated, someone prone to subtlety, sitting at this listing table ringed with beer and masala stains? But thinking of Elites collectively, I start to feel a certain affection for this gigantic, sweaty, toilsome city, only held together by half-decent bars such as these where men can stretch out their legs and let loose. Perhaps we all know we're not living our best lives, and these interludes between the cacti and the fogged-out stars is what we have while biding our time.

There's a girl in the corner, waiting for her boyfriend obviously. The girls don't come here in groups and they don't come alone either. I try not to stare, since everyone else is; she is cool, already a drink before her. She has cropped hair and is in a T-shirt, jeans, sandals, nothing eye-catching. She looks like she could be thinking, and I remember why I'm here. I eat one wafer after another, crunching them down slowly, and recall once reading about a man who, after the Gujarat riots, stopped taking salt in his food. Why salt? Perhaps because every time he ate, every single meal, three times a day, he would remember what he had no direct part in but could not forgive or forget. But I'm not looking to make any gestures, just sort things out for myself. Sudama calls me a nihilist. I don't believe in much and neither does he, except that he wants to make acres of money, while I can't be bothered. I'm not for career success, for the patronage of the gods or the politics of men—screw all that. None of it seems essential and all of it is messed up. And I'm not responsible for the chaos either, it was there before I got here. So what gets me out of bed in the morning? I look in the direction of the beer-drinking girl and wonder, on her behalf, where her boyfriend is. *Metal*, I tell her mentally. As long as there is the music coming out of my earphones, I have my armour, my ironic glaze, my thunderous, wondrous nullifier.

Yet I'm struck by the news and trying, like some conscience-stricken wimp, to work out what to do about it. I go to the loo. The graffiti is honest and tacky, like this bar. *Dipali I love you chinna. Call this mobile number for ladies massage.* On the way back I think of asking the girl for one of her smokes—she has a whole packet on the table—but only manage a weak smile. She actually smiles back.

'Would you like some company while you wait?' I ask her.

I'm no good at suggestive. I end up saying things straight-up and it usually fails. But turns out she's straight-up too.

'I'm not waiting.'

I'm stumped. This is too easy. And if it's easy for me, whose glances never seem to find their mark, who hasn't figured out, even at twenty-six, the secret lingo that the most callow boys and giggliest girls seem to have been born with, then this chick must be up to something. Maybe she's desperate, but she's too pretty to be desperate. Carefully avoiding the looks of the rum drinkers, I pick up my glass, go across and ask her, 'May I?'

She shrugs and pulls her beer mug closer towards her.

I'm sitting by an attractive, mysterious woman within half an hour of entering Elite. Maybe it *is* the direct, manly approach that will get me there in the end.

'Have you heard the news?' I ask her.

'Yeah,' she says. 'Serious stuff.'

'Coming from work?'

'Not working right now, I'm taking a break. Was in corporate communications. Five whole years devoted to that shit. Shit!' she exclaims, as if suddenly realizing she's lost something, forgotten her phone or handbag somewhere. 'You?'

'Oh, I never talk about work. Can't bear to bring it up. I come here often, live nearby. And it's with just this one idea—to kill all thought of my current employment. I turn on the music high . . .' I indicate the earphones strung around my neck, 'and try to think of other things.'

'Nobler concerns?' She smiles.

I nod. 'I'm a nihilist though, so nothing's too precious.'

'Why that?'

'Ah,' I say and order another whisky. She puts her fist under her chin and looks at me. I noticed it earlier too, from my table: her steady gaze and the thin silver ring on the forefinger of her left hand. Like she was utterly comfortable here, in this bar full of men. Amused even. I want to ask what brings her here. But I'm enjoying this enigma. A woman in a bar, sharing her table and her cigarettes, not self-conscious, not waiting. This town is easy with a lot of things but this is still weird. Not that I mind. I'm okay with weird. Weird I can enjoy.

When the drink arrives, I try to explain my nihilism. How it's not just about not believing in anything, but a test of conviction. Hold things up to the strongest light and see if they can withstand the scrutiny.

'It's an attempt at purity, you could say. Who's that European novelist, Drakune or Drakund, you know him? I'm thinking of this one novel, it's the only one by him I've read. There's a man, a minor character. He works in a factory, labours with his hands all day and spends his evenings at home in the bathtub, reading. That guy is my hero. He has no truck with anything. He has no philosophies or opinions. No family or obligations. He earns an honest living for himself, eats his bread and meat, spends his own time his way. Has sex now and then.'

She looks at my drink and smiles again. I realize I don't yet know her name.

'So this is your "bathtub"?' She's pointing to the whisky. We laugh and I take a big gulp.

'You might have thrown out the baby with the bathwater,' she adds. She's drinking slowly, so slowly it almost seems like a ploy, like she's a spy in disguise, an infiltrator. She's not smoking either. It's a new pack.

'Won't there come a time when you really must have a point of view?'

'No,' I declare. 'Let them take me down but I won't take sides.'

'But you did ask me about the news?'

'That's the rub.'

'You're bothered.'

'I ought not to care. But my friend Sudama is involved. His uncle is among the people who've been shot. He wants me to write a letter of protest to the authorities. He can't write, he's not into grammar and stuff. As for me, I could do it with my eyes closed. But Sudama is . . . Well, he knows me. I can't fake things when he's involved. And neither can I wriggle out of this. It's his uncle and all.'

'Existential dilemma,' says my mystery woman, then extends her hand and adds, 'I'm Vidya.'

'So who's the baby, really?'

There's a tiny flutter in her equipoise, then she remembers and says, 'Oh yes, yours. The poor, discarded baby. I don't know. But I'm too young to give up. There's got to be something to keep us going, beyond the distractions we surround ourselves with, never mind how numerous and enticing they are. When I was a kid I was sure it was physics.'

'Physics? You mean you were into gravity and stuff? Seriously?'

'I loved physics, I didn't need anything else—just this fascination with how things behave. I was reading encyclopedias on the Greeks, Spanish Muslims, Arabs, Galileo, Newton, then I grew up and read whole books on the same guys. I loved the past especially. The big adventure was over, but one could still get excited by the history of discoveries.'

I try, and fail, to imagine myself, at ten or thirteen, being seized by an equivalent passion. I dipped into comics and then, with reluctance, dipped into my homework, but my major preoccupation was playing the fool. My dad would never give up trying to rein me in. Looking back now I wonder which came first—his pig-headedness or mine.

'I remember being mildly amazed by Archimedes's claim that he could lift the earth if he had a long enough lever, but other than that . . .'

'I was obsessed,' says Vidya. 'Everyone around me knew I was big on science. They were quite bored by my certainty. But I didn't do well in college, almost flunked out. I'd fallen ill in the second year, like really ill. Spent six months in bed. And somehow in that time I didn't feel much like physics, all I read were kids' books. I was twenty years old and reading my battered copies of *The Bobbsey Twins* and *The Enchanted Wood* over and over again.'

She hasn't said if she knows Drakune but she would probably recognize him if she read him. And she speaks well. I speak well. We all speak well. That's what we have in the final reckoning. But it won't save our necks. It didn't help Sudama's uncle, whatever his name was. He spoke well all his life. He pretty much died speaking well. Sudama doesn't get it. I could write a great letter—excellent English, persuasive and entirely without feeling. And no one would notice the difference.

'So what happened then?' I ask Vidya, intrigued by her story, ordinary, and yet not. 'Corporate communications?'

She nods sadly. 'I'm considering my options now,' she says. 'Further study could be one. I still have my dreams of really getting into something.'

'You want to go abroad, I suppose.'

She shrugs. 'I could but not as a career thing. It's the idea of scholarship. That still fires me up.'

I feel old, like I've lived a very long time. Vidya must be about my age but she's looking forward. Me, I have the distinct sensation of already staring at the end. And I still don't know what to say to Sudama. Meanwhile, Elite has emptied out and starts to fill again but the boisterous group is still around, ordering their second bottle of Khodays. I am reckless suddenly. I want to get drunk and try flirting with this girl.

'I can't be bothered usually but this time I'm really pissed off about the news,' I tell her. 'What are we to do?'

'My father,' she says, tasting a drop of her beer, 'is convinced that we have lost touch with the people.'

I want to match this with a platitude from my own father but nothing comes to mind. He's not a moralist. You could say that, or you could say he's pitiless. His thing has been to make a living and, in the name of providing for the family, take a few cuts on the side. We've had our bitter fights about it and now we have our bitter silences. He's risen slowly through the ranks in the state audit-and-accounts department, sharing the shabbiest room in the building with the other flunkeys and, now, two decades and many deputations later is, as audit officer, the proud occupant of a carpeted room of his own with a nameplate on his door. His specialization is the system and how to work it. And to him, the news is just politics, not apocalypse.

'Your father's right,' I say. 'We've been too busy blubbering among ourselves. And now the chickens have come home to roost.'

I'm trying to catch Bhaskar's eye. *Come to me, my friend, bring me my salvation.* All the waiters in Elite look alike—teenaged, skinny, enthusiastic yet somehow distracted, dressed in cut-price white shirts and black pants. But Bhaskar's my man. I signal to him and he's at the table pronto with the 60-ml shot glass of whisky, the ice bucket, the new plate of wafers. Vidya looks on in silence.

'Listen, do you want to go somewhere nicer?' I ask. 'It's only ten o'clock. I have my bike.'

'No, I'm fine. Weren't we having a conversation?'

'Oh, come on. You really are the sincerest person I've met in a while.' I regret at once the sardonic tone this comes out in. I'd meant to be flattering.

'And you're the least,' she shoots back at once.

'I'm not surprised. I've been dying to ask what's a girl like you doing in a place like this, et cetera, et cetera.'

She raises her eyebrows at me and doesn't smile.

'Does it bother you? A woman just hanging out?'

No, it's sexy, I think. I wonder if I've already exhausted my repertoire of nice, socially acceptable things to say to women.

'Oh, I get it. You're here to connect with the people.' I laugh out loud.

She turns expressionless.

'Seriously, is that it? Fieldwork?'

I'm laughing harder now and she's starting to look hurt, but it's hilarious. This girl, a well-brought-up creature without the least interest even in drinking, sitting here in earnestness, trying to get close to the real world. Taking the measure of Elite, which is pronounced 'E-light', a place that has nothing—just the random, insistent talk and the men drinking. Over on one wall is a muted TV playing the same news clips over and over again. Images of suspects and no one apprehended yet for the murders. In another corner is a sad little cloudy aquarium with fishes the colour of rangoli powders.

'This is not the place. Perhaps you should go do social work in a slum or something.'

'Fuck off. Leave me alone. What gives you the right?'

I look at her and think, *I'm being an asshole and she's so pretty.*

'Sorry,' I say. 'Would you like another drink? Ever so sorry. I thought I'd dispensed with the world but this thing about Sudama's uncle and the letter, it's getting to me.'

She doesn't reply.

At the next table, the conversation is in morose Tamil and the drink is the most ridiculous in my book: vodka with Sprite. Meanwhile, more men have joined the Khodays party, and they're bragging about their business pursuits, comparing notes. They seem to be into hospitality, running hotels or something, and chat about how much they pay their staff. 'These fellows all come from Assam,' one guy declares. Another says, 'They say they're from Assam but they're actually Bangladeshis. Check out their papers, they'll be forged.'

'Vidya, we could talk.'

She clears her throat, takes several sips of her beer and finally looks at me.

'So why was he killed, what had he done?'

'He gave a public speech recently asking if fellow feeling was not morally superior to idol worship. So he had to be fixed. We're in the Middle Ages after all.'

'No, we're in the second decade of the twenty-first century.'

'Why does it all seem like it's happened before? Think of the futility. People crying themselves hoarse over the same things through the ages. It makes my position the only tenable one.'

'Let them take me down but I won't take sides.' She's quoting me back to me but not entirely with derision. There is a reflective note in her voice for sure.

'What would you do?'

'Wrong question, no?'

'But this needs conviction, passion. Which, you, remarkably, have. I came here to drink some and obsess about the damn thing, and I run into you. I'm sure you were meant to be involved.'

'What would you lose if you lost your nihilism and did put real hurt into that letter?'

Before I can answer, we hear something break out at the other end of the terrace and turn to see one of the burly rum-drinkers hitting Bhaskar, yelling at him.

'What the . . .' exclaims Vidya.

Before I can rise from my chair, Bhaskar is on the floor and the fatso is kicking him as he lies there, shielding his face with his hands. There's a second guy—tall, thin, one gold earring—aiding in the kicking and shouting.

I rush across, try to push them away.

'Guys,' I say. 'Stop it.'

'Too late,' says fatso.

'Bhaskar, get up!'

He's on his feet very quickly and the other waiters who've gathered around add their voices to the clamour, demanding to know what happened, trying to find out if he's badly hurt. Bhaskar looks dusty and diminished, dazed. Meanwhile the fat man and his friend want to get to him again. They're pulling at his neck, twisting his arm. And the fool does nothing to resist.

'Go downstairs,' I tell Bhaskar. His colleagues take him away, and the pair, who hasn't looked me in the eye so far, makes as if to follow them. Their formerly animated drinking companions continue to sit at the table, not saying a thing.

I face off the bullies. The last time I was in a brawl was in junior school, when a snide remark I made about a fellow cricketer's batting skills led him to smash the handle of his otherwise ineffective bat right into my forehead. It wasn't much of a fight, more a murderous attack, and I lacked the means to retaliate, except with more sarcasm. Already then, all I could do was talk. I went home grim-faced and bleeding and didn't cry till my mum opened the door.

I don't want to fight these men but I can't just stand by either.

'Leave him alone. Enough! What really happened?'

'What business is it of yours?'

Aggressive, of course, spraying spittle into my face as they talk, but they're not going to touch me, I determine that. They've seen my chinos and my fitted linen jacket, they've heard my accent, so they're keeping their hands off me, at least for now.

'Boss,' I say to the overweight bully. 'My friend and I are sitting there quietly having a drink. You're disturbing the peace.'

'He insulted me.'

Fat Man is drunk, pockmarked and speaks like a caveman. Thin Guy, equally drunk, says nothing, just weaves a little on his feet, shaking his head. The perversity of the situation—these two hooligans and their gang of silently supportive friends against one poor serf—seems not to have struck them, nor, indeed, to be bothering anyone else in the bar. Half the tables are taken but no one moved when the fracas started, and now they're pretending that all is well, that not a whimper came between them and their oil-fry kebabs. Some of the waiters have drifted back up and are taking fresh orders.

'Look, I know this waiter. He's a good guy. Very decent,' I say.

'I told him, get me some food, and you know what the motherfucker replied? He said, "I will clear that other table, then take your order."'

'He said that to our face. Which good waiter treats people like that?' chips in Thin Guy. The stooge, obviously, which is strange because he looks like the stud. Taller, better-looking, more sharply dressed.

'Fine,' I say. 'Why don't you put in a complaint with the manager?'

'I'm not used to taking insults lying down. You're asking me to take an insult just like that?'

But the edge is going out of his voice and he pulls out his chair angrily and slumps back into it. A Bhaskar lookalike comes up to the table and apologizes on his behalf.

Fat Man repeats the story of the insult, and why he was entirely justified in hitting Bhaskar and why he wants to go down to the kitchen where Bhaskar is hiding and hit him some more. Thin Guy reiterates what his friend said.

I go back to Vidya and outline the scenario. She seems shaken but is trying not to show it.

'Just an ordinary Wednesday night at Elite,' I say, grinning and mock-dusting my hands.

'Brutes,' she says, then shrugs with some effort. 'Thank you,' she adds.

I assay heroism, and some of the more macho songs on my playlist do begin to stir in me, but mostly I feel paltry. I'm a man who patronizes dives where the servers are stomped on and those who try to intervene spat on. I rearrange my chair so I have a clearer view of the vile Khodays. A new guy has just joined the group, some kind of a bossman, judging from the welcome he receives. All the handshaking and high fives raise their collective spirits and, apparently forgetting dinner, they call for yet another bottle of rum.

'I've been giving it thought, your letter,' says Vidya.

'Fantastic, I knew I could depend on you.'

'It looks like you've tried hard to kill your instincts but what if there's some life in them yet?'

'How about if you decided to help a friend and write it instead of me? I'll tell Sudama. It'll be hard but I'll speak to him.'

'It's not about Sudama. Or me. The thing is we're all brats. You know that, no? We're spoilt stupid. And only some of us get a chance to break out of it. This is it for you, a real opportunity.'

I say nothing, think nothing, except what I'll have to tell Sudama in office tomorrow. *I share your grief but please don't entrust this sacred duty to a brat like me.*

Vidya is getting her things together, abandoning her beer.

'I could drop you somewhere.'

'Thanks, but I'll call a cab.'

Fat Man has now collared the manager. He's on his feet again, Thin Guy there to pitch in as usual, and the manager is trying to reason with them in a soft, conciliatory tone. Fat Man puts a hand on the man's chest and pushes him, but not too hard. A manager-level shove as against the waiter-level shove he gave Bhaskar, the one that sent him down. What was the boy thinking as he lay there? That he's not going to make it back up? He looked shamefaced, crouched on the floor, rather than upset. I have to talk to him about it the next time. But it will only embarrass him even though it wasn't his fault.

The manager's shirt is rose-coloured and a nicer texture than Bhaskar's; he looks better-fed too. And he's standing his ground, not raising his voice to match Fat Man's, but not getting browbeaten either. Thin Guy is bellowing threats, along the lines of, from what I can tell—Do you know who we are? Or, don't you know who we are?

The crowd has swelled, waiters rush about, the bill arrives. Vidya is saying that she's fine with Elite, despite everything.

'I might come back here. Bring a book.'

'Break up fights.'

'It's part of the milieu.'

'Oh, yes, I forgot. These are the people, after all.'

We're almost at the door when I hear someone yelling, 'Sir, please wait, sir.'

That awful pair are waving from their table. *Sir?* Why the sudden deference?

I turn away and follow Vidya.

'Boss,' I hear behind me in the stairwell.

They're coming after us. It makes me uneasy. Maybe they remembered they have a score to settle with me too. For interfering.

Vidya notices, and I say, 'Let's just ignore them.'

But they catch up with us outside. The lane with my bike runs on the far side of the building and we are by the main road with its milder traffic at this hour and the shops shuttered. The air smells of what the air smells of every evening when the city is done with it. The sorry, wrung-out Bangalore night. The two men have their drinks in their hands and say they just want to talk.

'I wanted to apologize for the disturbance,' begins Fat Man and I'm flabbergasted. 'You were with your girlfriend, hanging out.'

I don't know if he's being ironical, they probably saw me go over to Vidya's table earlier in the night. What is clear is that he's beyond drunk and yet still able to stand here, continue drinking, frame largely coherent sentences. What could it be? Monstrous vanity or a marvellous liver? Thin Guy is almost smiling at us.

'You shouldn't have hit that waiter,' says Vidya, emboldened.

'Madam, let me tell you. I run six hotels in this town. I have dozens and dozens of staff working for me. If any of them answered back to a guest the way this boy did tonight, I wouldn't stand for it. I've taught them respect.'

'Respect,' I repeat. I'm still amazed but have realized now that they don't care about having upset us, they just want to justify themselves.

'These people should know how to talk to their customers. They're running an establishment,' says Thin Guy.

'You honour people, they might honour you back,' says Vidya. 'It's a mutual thing.'

'Never would any of my staff behave that way—with me or anyone else. And you know why?' Fat Man's on his own trip. 'Because I feed them. They have food on their plates thanks to me. And they know that.'

You feudal bastard, I think. *So you're their mother and father, you're their God-sent provider.*

'When a man is misbehaving . . .' says Thin Guy. 'Can you hold my glass?'

He hands it to Vidya and lights a cigarette. Then he extends the pack to me. I take one.

'Are you saying that we should just sit back and keep quiet when something really bad is happening before our eyes?' asks Fat Man. 'Suppose that waiter was troubling a girl, suppose he did something to your girlfriend here. Would you keep quiet? Should I keep quiet, even though I don't know you?'

The tone is conversational but the words are threatening. To an observer we're just some people standing around smoking and chatting. Late-night bonhomie. But in truth I'm quite sure this fucker is off his rocker. He's the kind of citizen who throws his garbage on the street, plays Honey Singh loud enough to wake the dead, prays vociferously to all the deities but will happily run his four-wheel-drive over a beggar. And has a best friend whose singular role is to always swear he's right.

Fat Man is eyeing Vidya in the dark.

'What's your name?'

He introduces himself and so does the sidekick. Hands are shaken all around. They've inched very close to us as they're speaking so that Vidya and I are compelled to retreat till we're backed up at the steps of Elite.

'Actually, we're Kshatriyas,' says Fat Man. 'You know, the warrior caste?'

'You could say it's in the blood, fighting,' adds Thin Guy.

Again I try and fail to respond. Their logic is all the sicker for the sureness with which it's belted out.

'There are ways to be honourable and express displeasure at the same time,' Vidya says. 'You might have withheld paying for your drinks till the matter was sorted.'

Fat Man launches into a speech on how no one in India can be expected to rely on the rulebook or the law. 'My father,' he tells us, 'was involved in a property dispute for fifteen years. He's dead now. And still the thing's unresolved. I'm the one who has to land up every time for the court hearings. That's the justice system in this country.'

He looks sad for a moment. Then he says, 'I know one of the chaps who runs Elite. I could have called him and got that boy fired. But I didn't do it, why?'

'Because he wouldn't have anything to eat then,' says his echo. 'He'd be out of a job.'

I feel, with this revelation concerning their hearts of gold, that the conversation is at an end. But they're still hanging around.

'I don't quite understand the problem. He said he would clear the table and then serve you, how is that an insult?' asks Vidya. She's a scientist. And I sense that her lucidity makes her vulnerable. She's probably the kind of girl who, if attacked, will try to get her attacker to first submit a concise account of his motives.

'Madam,' says Fat Man and sighs. 'You got distressed. For that I've tendered my apologies.'

'Still, you shouldn't have hit the boy,' insists Vidya. 'You were wrong to do that.'

'I didn't know what else to do at that moment, I was so angry.'

Vidya says, 'Whatever problems you have, violence is not the answer.'

'I was born on 2 October,' says Fat Man. 'I can be non-violent too.'

'What I'm saying is, you've achieved nothing by this. He will not become a better waiter, if that was your aim.' Her face is tight with emotion.

Fat Man thinks for a moment, then declares, 'I own a gun but I wouldn't shoot to kill straight off. If someone provokes me very badly, I'll aim at his legs to begin with.'

'He was weaker than you. A young boy.'

'Okay,' says Fat Man. 'All right.'

His friend is swaying, on the point of but not saying anything. I notice for the first time that he looks a bit like Eddie Van Halen.

'Fine, I shouldn't have done it. Sorry.'

We're all silent now, us talkers. Us brats. The few passing cars pick out our vacant faces, before Vidya turns away and I follow.

'Goodnight,' she says to the two men still standing there, holding their empty glasses, their half-smoked cigarettes. Above us the lights of Elite go out all at once.

11

NUR

After an exasperating week, Nur heads out to look for her husband. He disappeared once before; pilfered all her money from the cupboard where she keeps it hidden in a bundle of her underwear and took off to Delhi to attend a spiritual conference—the annual congregation of the Tablighi Jamaat. He came back after four or five days, bored with their teachings, all the cash gone, of course. They'd wanted serious souls, boys who would dress themselves in beards and kurta-pyjamas, and go into the Muslim colonies to tell the women to stay at home in purdah and the men to desist from drinking and follow the pieties. They want to improve the state of the nation of Islam. 'It's not for me,' Salim had said. He'd been taken by the idea of Delhi and a new career, but he only prayed on Fridays. He had dropped out of the madrasa when he was ten, and couldn't follow the Koran very well. So he went back to his electrician's job without saying sorry to Nur for wasting all her money on nothing.

Nur has been in a burka since she was twelve. But she goes out to work and so does her mother and all the women in the community, all of them covered. As for drinking, her father died from it and one of her brothers is on the same path. Salim doesn't drink but he's restless and gets into fights. Or loses interest in the electrician's life and stays at home for days, watching TV—her home, the house she shares with her mother and two nieces. She couldn't move into his parents' house, there is no place to lay down a head in that two-room dump off Shampura Main Road, shared by seven people. Her mother, Sultana, is happy to let them stay with her; she is alone now after Nur's five siblings moved out and got married and had children. Later, Sultana took in two of her grandchildren after their mother, her middle daughter, set herself on fire and died following a minor argument with her husband. Her husband was unrepentant after the tragedy and he didn't want the girls, so Sultana said that even if she had to slave in the tannery, she would do it to feed them. 'Some people have no shame but Allah is watching everything,' she said. As for Nur, she keeps a sharp eye on her. 'I won't let go of you,' Sultana tells her. 'You're the youngest. You stay right here with me.'

So Nur is married but also a child in her mother's home, still longing for Sultana's beef curry and anda mussalam, still listening to her stories about the Sufi she-saint Mastani Amma who died sixty years ago and whose grave is now a dargah on Tannery Road. Their house is just two rooms too, but larger, and Nur likes it that they have space for a sofa on which Salim can sleep if they have fought, and a cupboard where they keep an assortment of things—a couple of their nice cups and plates, packets of spices and biscuits, a photo album of Nur and Salim's wedding, the Koran Sharif on the top shelf, Salim's Class Eight passing certificate, a furry fez her father put on every Eid, her grandfather's rosaries and *tabize*s, a picture of the dargah in Ajmer, the nieces' schoolbooks, the boxes of incense sticks that Nur has nicked from the factory where she works and the saris her mother used to wear before she took to the burka. And the money, now missing.

Nur has woken up on a Friday feeling both desperate about Salim and glad that she can buy slices of raw mango with chilli powder that afternoon if she feels like, or pani puri from the Bihari man who makes them best. She has fifty rupees to spend, the last of the money in her purse, and a day off from the factory. In the morning she is meant to be in Khayoom Garden at her part-time maid's job, but instead calls out to her neighbour and best friend, Rebeka, who lives with her parents in the rooms downstairs, and tells her they have to go look for Salim. 'Make up something,' she says to Rebeka, who is also a maid and at it most of the day in a bungalow in Fraser Town. 'I'll tell her I have back pain,' says Rebeka. 'She'll say, take a tablet and come. Think of something better,' replies Nur. 'I'll tell her I have a really bad stomach,' says Rebeka, always ready to go along with Nur's plans. She is diminutive and dark, with big teeth. Nur is tall and skinny with hollowed eyes made deeper with kohl. 'Tell her your mother is sick and you have to take her to hospital.' Rebeka giggles, her teeth flash in her small face. 'What kind of sick?' 'Bad, deathly. The kind that comes from eating nothing but raw mango,' replies Nur. 'Where is Salim?' asks Rebeka. Nur gets a box of incense from the cupboard and shoves it into her handbag. 'He's hiding somewhere, the *khabees*. He must have spent all my money and is now scared to come home.' 'He's not scared of you,' says Rebeka. 'What if he's been killed in an accident?' asks Nur. 'I don't have cash for a headstone.' She did not want to say this; she has managed to dispel the thought even from her dreams. But now she must sit down for a moment and try to force the words back down her throat. If she is able to summon her annoyance again at his taking off like this, she can squash the idea that he might be in trouble, even dead.

Nur breathes out a plea to God, washes her face, puts on her black gown, pins a bead-lined hijab into place over her head, slips into her nice sandals and skips breakfast. All the rotis her mother made that morning have been eaten by the two little girls before they went to school.

Rebeka accompanies Nur as she is—in bathroom slippers and a worn-out salwar-kurta, her hair in a thin plait. Modi Road is alive at ten in the morning. The leisurely men in skullcaps are already sitting in the tea centres, eating biscuits from the glass jars on the counter. The working boys sandpaper the wooden frames of sofas in the furniture shops or make dough for parathas in the small, open-faced eateries or haul marquees and plastic chairs into tempo trucks to rent for weddings. The schools are buzzing behind their closed doors but the madrasas attached to the mosques are silent—the children go there early in the mornings to learn the *qaida*, or after school in the evenings.

Rebeka and Nur walk very fast. Slow-walking women are considered wanton, they have learnt. They also know, at twenty, how to filch a piece of fruit from a pushcart whose owner is weighing oranges and apples for someone else, which shops will give them a loaf of bread or a kilo of sugar on credit and how to tell the bus routes from the numbers on them since neither of them can read either the Kannada or the English alphabet.

'Let's pray first, Rebeka,' says Nur. She wants to ask for a baby. She has been married for two years and it's in God's hands now. Everything will light up with a baby. She'll quit that dirty factory job and stay at home, Salim can work harder at his electricianing. But where is Salim? She feels light-headed with fear again, then certain that he can't be far. 'What should we do?' her mother had asked that morning. 'Put in a complaint at the police station, go to the hospitals?' 'His phone is switched off,' said Nur. 'After he's spent all my money he'll come back.'

She won't go to the police. It was after his run-in with the police the previous year that Salim became edgier, lounging in front of the TV often, neglecting work. They had taken him in following a bomb explosion outside a shopping mall in some fancy part of town. Someone had put the bomb in a dustbin and it went off, hurting two girls standing at the nearby bus-stop. The police came to Modi Road. 'They were looking for some other Salim,' said Salim. An engineer who'd worked in Mumbai and come back recently. A man with a degree. 'I don't know how they thought it was me, I've never even seen this mall,' he said. The man they were looking for had started out doing electrical repairs but then moved up in life, and someone had told the police to hunt down electrician Salim from Modi Road. He spent three days in the lock-up and when he came back he wouldn't tell Nur what those three days had been like. He spoke less than before and got angry quicker.

When they get to the dargah, Rebeka bows her head, touches the grass-green satin in which the humped mazar of Mastani Amma is draped and then brings her fingers to each of her closed eyes. She does the same when she goes to church, reaching out for the feet of the crucifix and the Madonna, the way her mother does. Nur doesn't go to church with her but Rebeka has been coming to this place for years. They sit on the floor for a while, praying and whispering along with the other women there, who read from their prayer books or just pass the time with their toddlers. One old woman in a corner, the long, grey hairs on her chin testifying to her age, is always there, muttering and dozing. She could be Mastani Amma herself; she looks a bit like the wizened woman in the black-and-white photo on the wall, the mystic mother who became a saint because she could, according to Nur's mother, make people abandon all desires except the one to get close to

God. Before she saw the light, the saint was a tannery worker too—salting the hides of animals and then sending them to the leather-making factories up the road. Now the factories have moved to Tamil Nadu and only a few of the tanneries remain.

The keeper of the shrine sits before a wooden desk on the floor, doodling in the margins of an Urdu newspaper, guarding the locked metal canister with a slitted top to put donations in. The girls go up the green-painted stairs to the upper floor—everything in the dargah is green—and Nur pulls out a couple of the incense sticks, lights them and sticks them into the candelabra of burning oil-lamps. They settle down before a filigree-edged flag propped on a stand in one corner, topped with a replica in brass of a human hand inscribed with dense Arabic calligraphy, which is taken out only once a year during the Muharram procession. 'Ya Allah, send Salim back so I can have a baby,' says Nur out loud because there is no one there to listen and then, giggling, the two girls rush down the stairs and into the traffic-fuelled chaos of Tannery Road.

A drove of burka-clad girls is crossing the road, heading for the open gates of the Eidgah grounds. Even from a distance, and despite no obvious difference between her get-up and theirs, Nur can tell that these women are not like her, that they have each had a good breakfast, have money in their purses, fathers secure in businesses or jobs and husbands who don't go missing. She quickens her stride as she goes past the gates, recalling the Shadab Fashion Designing and Tailoring Institute near the Eidgah where she had once wanted to enrol, before she was told that as someone who had dropped out of the Quwathul Islam Higher Primary School without having learnt to read or write, she was ineligible.

'Tamarind!' exclaims Rebeka. 'Do you want to get whacked?' asks Nur. 'The guard will be right there.' 'Join the girls, quick!'

says Rebeka. So they run back and fall in with the students just as they are going past the guard who has a short, thin stick with which he does his guarding. Rebeka veers off and heads to the copse of tamarind on the right of the field that is also strewn with mango, pomegranate and guava trees, with open grass at the far end for men to pray on during Eid. Nur pretends to waver in case the guard is still watching. She moves slowly out of his line of vision, taken in by the heavenly scene before her. She would like to lie down on the soft-looking grass, hum a song or two. *Stupid Nur*, she tells herself. *Are you imagining yourself a film star? You're not even a student of Shadab Fashion Designing.*

She closes her eyes and the world swims in the dark. A couple of years ago she had fainted while walking home from work, fallen on the corner where her lane met Modi Road. The doctor said she had a vitamin D deficiency. 'You didn't let her play outdoors when she was a child,' she said accusingly to Sultana. This doctor, an overweight Tamil woman with an impressively thick gold chain around her neck and massive arms dimpled at the elbows, was someone all in the neighbourhood were afraid of and all went to when they were sick. 'You kept her covered since puberty,' said the doctor. 'Get her out of this burka, she needs sunlight.' Sultana reported the matter to Nur's father who said 'Thoo!' in response to the doctor woman's blasphemy and declared that what Nur needed was more meat and eggs. Then nothing happened—father kept drinking and driving his rickshaw, meat and eggs continued to be eaten no more than once a week and sunlight didn't get a chance to come anywhere near Nur. She took the doctor's pills and didn't faint again but sometimes, walking about, felt quite ready to.

Rebeka has a way of secreting the tamarind pods in her dupatta that makes her look completely innocent of any theft. They hurry past the guard, pretending to be busy, and he is talking to himself as he sits on his chair and beats the ground with his short stick. *It is a couplet perhaps*, thinks Nur. *'Nur-e-haq shamme ilahi ko bhujha sakta hai kaun.'* Despite herself she slows down near the gate to catch the second line. *'Jiska haami ho khuda usko mita sakta hai kaun.'* She likes this without understanding it completely; she approves of the guard thus declaring his full trust in God.

As they eat the tamarind, sucking it voluptuously and then swiftly flicking out the seeds with their tongues, they discuss their employers and how each, respectively, treats them—Rebeka's boss is kinder than Nur's and gives her hand-me-downs and daily lunch—inevitably, the women they're talking about call, one after another, to ask why they're late. Nur addresses her employer as 'Chachi' because this lady could have been her own aunt except that she married a well-to-do butcher and they can afford a small flat and servant for a couple of hours a day. Rebeka calls hers 'Aunty' because she lives in a grand house and speaks a lot of English. 'I am on my way,' she tells her. 'The bus broke down, can't get another one going in my direction. I'm walking.' Nur's impromptu explanation to Chachi is not that her husband is missing—somehow, she is convinced this will give a bad impression of her—but that she's been delayed because she had to go to her nieces' school to pay their fees. Just before Tannery Road diverges into two, with one of the fathers of the nation standing on a plinth at the junction in his polished metal suit as usual, there is a photo studio called F.K. Pictures with a painting of a demure, red-lipped woman on the wall outside, lopsided images of still and video cameras, and Fairoz Khan, the proprietor's, two mobile numbers.

Fairoz is Salim's best friend and is sitting behind the counter, working at a computer—lightening the cheeks on the face of a lovely child. Nur considers Fairoz's thin, bearded profile for a moment and wishes she had married him instead: someone with a shop and a steady income, someone who could be tracked down at all hours of the day. Fairoz says he doesn't know where Salim is. He tries his friend's number while Rebeka asks if he wants some tamarind and Nur tells her what a good job he did with their wedding photos. 'He made us look much shinier than we actually are. He'll do you when you get married,' says Nur, to which Rebeka says, 'But my parents will want the Christian photographer.'

Fairoz reveals that Salim has lately been bent on trying something new. 'I told him to think of mobile-phone repair, there are courses you can do in five days and he's already familiar with electrical stuff,' says Fairoz. 'He didn't tell me anything about it,' murmurs Nur. 'He trusts you more.' She hopes Fairoz can help, give her a lead. She knows of no one else she can turn to, and feels that buried panic again—*Where is my husband, really?* 'It's been one week, Fairoz bhai . . .' she says, and the sentence concludes with a muffled sob she hadn't wanted to let out. Fairoz and Rebeka look at her in pained sympathy. 'There are no men in my house to turn to,' explains Nur, all calm again though still wet-eyed. 'My elder brother is too busy, he doesn't even answer when his wife calls him. My younger brother . . .' But she leaves it unsaid, that he is usually lying in a drunken stupor somewhere.

Fairoz goes out and bellows across the road for tea. 'I think we should ask Mushtaq bhai,' he comes back in and says. 'He is a man in control of everything that's going on in the area. Just in case anything out of the ordinary has happened to Salim, he'll be the first to know.' Rebeka asks, 'Mushtaq bhai? The one who helped when Salim was in the lock-up?' Fairoz nods and says, 'I went to him straight. He said he couldn't promise anything but then two days later Salim was out. I'm sure he had a hand in it. Nur, remember?'

Nur wipes her eyes carefully so the kohl doesn't run and says he must be an angel from heaven, this Mushtaq bhai, but won't he require a payment of some kind? 'Forget about that for now. He's one of the richest men in Bangalore. He's made his fortune getting people from here jobs in the Gulf,' says Fairoz. 'Will you take us to him, then?' asks Nur. 'I would have, but I can't leave the shop today. I'll see what I can do from here.' They sip from the thin plastic cups of tea and Nur says, 'I would have asked the boys with whom he ran away to Delhi that one time but I don't remember who they are. My people don't go to their mosque, the Tablighi Jamaat mosque.'

Fairoz promises to talk to them. Rebeka says, 'Maybe we could do one of those posters with the faces of missing people on them? In case anyone has seen him?' Nur feels that would be the last straw—to have her Salim's face all over the neighbourhood. But what if someone could actually help? She has no ideas of her own in any case—only a certainty that he could not have abandoned her (but then why hasn't he gotten in touch yet?), or a dread that he might be hurt (which would explain the silence).

'Let's do that. I can put my phone number on it. Just WhatsApp me a recent photo,' says Fairoz. Nur appears doubtful, so he immediately adds, 'Never mind, I'll use one of the wedding pictures, though Salim looks too happy in all of those.' 'Of course,' says Nur, smiling now. 'He was happy because he was coming to stay in my house where you don't have to queue up outside the communal toilet every morning,' and Fairoz looks sheepish, then grows serious. 'Let us wait to hear what Mushtaq bhai says before we put out the poster. The first person you will meet is Mushtaq bhai's bodyguard, Bilal. He's a hefty guy with curly hair who decides whom to let into his boss's presence. Most people he turns away. You head to the house. I'll call Bilal and tell him to expect you. I would have gone myself but there's no one else to manage things right now.'

Rebeka is better with directions than Nur, so it is to her that Fairoz explains where exactly in relation to the prominent Arabic College the don's house is. She wants to take an autorickshaw but Nur is already marching ahead, asking why God gave them feet if they can't walk, warning Rebeka from having evil designs on her last fifty rupees and declaring that there is no way this day will end without her having her fill of raw mango and pani puri. But even as she says it, she feels the deeper, resounding hollow of her hunger. She needs breakfast though it is almost time for lunch. Her eyelashes are still damp with tears over Salim, yet part of her really wants to veer off from this quest for him to some place where a substantial meal is assured. She is not sure where that is. 'What did you eat for breakfast, Rebeka?' but Rebeka is too far behind to hear the question. They pass the Bismillah Mosque, a collection of sad-faced old women sitting on their haunches outside, and Nur realizes it's Friday. She wonders how it is that all mosques have old women outside, where they come from and where they would go a-begging if there were no mosques. She might end up there too when she's past a certain age and Salim is gone, but Salim may already be gone, in which case what is to be her fate? A young woman can't be outside a mosque, scrabbling in the dust with these grandmothers.

Rebeka catches up with her. Outside the Islami Nikah Centre, where Salim's sister's wedding was fixed, the henna-bearded proprietor stands in a creamy kurta and fixes his eyes on them. Nur is about to say something to him, just a hearty 'Salaam ailekum, chacha,' if nothing else, to break his stare when her phone rings.

It's not Chachi again but her boss from the incense factory, the slightly shifty, toweringly handsome Zafar. 'Nur . . .' he says, and that pause makes her pause too. He rarely calls her, and when he does it is always about how her pay is going to be delayed that week, business is slow. He never says this to her face when she comes to work, always on the phone. He has found Salim's corpse somewhere. Or her mother is in trouble. Her nieces. They've been thrown out of school. Or the house. It's been burgled. Something terrible, at any rate. Or has he just been told by one of her back-stabbing colleagues that Nur occasionally carries home a box or two of incense. 'What is it?' she blurts. 'We're done, I can't go on any more,' says Zafar. He explains that the women who used to work for him have been moving to the garment factories in Govindpura, it's just her and another girl left and he can't keep the factory running without labour, all the other units packed up long ago and incense-making has shifted to Tamil Nadu.

'So does this mean I don't have a job? How will I cover the rent next week? My husband has taken all my money. I already have two loans from Chachi. You tell me how I'm going to manage,' she shouts, while Rebeka murmurs, 'Let's find Salim first. I have a feeling this Mushtaq bhai will help,' and the nikah fixer, whose business seems slow too, continues to study the girls. 'Anyway it was a dirty job. You call that a factory—sitting on the floor in that suffocating little room and ruining our hands with your work. Thoo!' Nur shouts and puts away her phone. She glares at the staring man and the two take off at great speed. Soon they are turning into the lane before the imposing, minareted Arabic College.

The house they're looking for is a brand-new three-storeyed place, rising above the low concrete huts surrounding it, with stairs running on the outside, their steel banisters gleaming, balconies on each floor, well-fed potted plants, large windows to which air conditioners have been affixed, and some words in English on a plaque on the wall by the high wooden picket gate. They enter somewhat fearfully, noting the two giant cars parked nose to nose in the basement, and climb the stairs. A ring on the doorbell produces the man Fairoz had described—dark, big mop of hair, fancy shoes. He doesn't say a word, waiting for them to speak. 'Did Fairoz call you about us?' asks Nur, and only then does he deign to open his mouth. 'Yes,' he admits. 'Fairoz did say something about a missing boy.' 'He's been gone for a week.' Tears threaten again. 'Mushtaq bhai helped the last time too,' says Rebeka. 'When Salim was in jail.' The man looks sceptical but allows them in.

They are shown to the largest sofas they have ever seen in their lives and settle, awkwardly squeaking, into the plush black leather; a girl who could be a servant but has cleaner feet than theirs and long, painted fingernails brings them glasses of the iciest water they have ever drunk. On the wall is a TV so large that Nur cannot focus on the picture, her eyes keep darting all over the screen trying to find it. 'This must be paradise, Rebeka,' she says in high-pitched awe without caring that she might be heard by the man who is making a call about their case to someone, and whose name she now remembers is Bilal. 'Mushtaq bhai is on his way,' he says and vanishes, leaving Nur to ask Rebeka loudly if she thinks they will be served lunch, considering the hour, and Rebeka to say in a whisper that she's not to tell Mushtaq that Salim vanished once before, or he might think him a good-for-nothing. 'Say he's a reliable boy,' she advises. They sit there sipping on the too-cold water, stealing glances at the girl in the kitchen who is talking to someone on her phone about the superbness of the pulao her mother is going to cook for her birthday.

They rise to their feet without being told to when Mushtaq bhai enters the room. He is followed by Bilal and two other Bilal lookalikes. The don is shorter than his hangers-on and dressed unlike these jean-clad youth in a simple kurta-pyjama but he has an array of rings on his fingers, mobile phones in each hand and a piercing gaze above the bruised pouches below his eyes. He looks like someone whom it would take a great deal to agitate, and this realization is agitating. He glances at the girls, then heads to an inner room as if they aren't there, studying one phone and then the other. Nur expects him to sit, ask the girls if they'd like some tea, wonder what he can do for them. But perhaps that's a sign of his importance— the busyness or the appearance of it. He's almost inside when Bilal says, 'Sahib, two minutes, these sisters . . .' Nur knows she has to be quick. She rushes towards him, raising her hand in an *adaab*, and says breathlessly, 'You are the only one who can save him.' And then, seeing him close up, her suspicion is confirmed that no words could melt the heart of this man, and she starts either by accident or design to cry again. Rebeka has to explain it all. How Mushtaq bhai had got the blameless boy out of jail the previous year, how he has vanished now and they're not sure where to look. Could he be in jail again? Mushtaq says, 'I'll make some inquiries. Give Bilal your number. He hasn't called at all? No news whatsoever? Hmm. I keep an eye on those from this area who are inside. I have a contact there. I'll inform you. Hmm. Keep praying. You'll hear from him. It's all God's will in the end.' And he's gone.

The girls leave and rush down Nagvara Main Road, back the way they came, then slow down when they think of the distance still left to walk. 'What makes him so big, Rebeka?' asks Nur, and Rebeka echoes what she heard Fairoz say—he sends people to the Gulf. 'He must be taking a commission for that,' she says. 'There's so much work to be done there, so many dying to go. All that construction business, all the servants needed for rich people's homes, and then plumbers and electricians and drivers and cleaners.'

'If only people like us—me and you and Salim—had the brains to think up a business opportunity like that,' says Nur. 'Don't imagine that was his only house,' says Rebeka, suddenly an authority on Mushtaq bhai. 'He must be having dozens all across the city.' 'He will find Salim, who can if he can't?' A beggar on the pavement thrusts the rounded, blackened stump of his missing arm at them; they walk past him and then Nur gasps, 'I took Salim's name just as that beggar cursed me in his heart. Quick, find him some change.' They manage three one-rupee coins between them and go back to drop them in his bowl. 'Pray for me,' Nur tells him warningly. The beggar rattles his bowl with his good hand and nods ambivalently.

'I am coming, Aunty,' says Rebeka into her phone when it rings. 'Still walking. Okay, I'll get a rickshaw. Thank you, Aunty.' They flag down the first one; it has a cut-out on the windshield of a very young Salman Khan holding up his biceps, and below that the word *BABA* spelt out in orange flames. 'Are you sure she said she'll pay you for it?' asks Nur. 'Yes,' says Rebeka. 'And you can share my lunch too.' *The queue was too long at the school,* says Nur in her mind to her own chachi as they speed to Fraser Town. *I wanted to call you but my battery died. I have to take care of these girls, there is no one for them. Yes, they're doing well at school, maybe they'll go on to study at Shadab Fashion Designing and never have to hide money from their husbands in their underwear or be fired from their two-bit jobs over the phone by gutless bosses.*

After they have paid off the rickshaw with Nur's money because Rebeka has none yet, they find Aunty in the living room of the old-fashioned bungalow, in conversation with a saintly looking man in a long beard. 'What, Rebeka, so late?' she says in mild rebuke, while the man keeps up his dialogue. 'It is all in the Koran,' he says. 'Much before this science of the Western world there was a science in the Koran. How a child is formed in its mother's womb, how the earth revolves around the sun, the ways of wind and fire and water—everything can be gleaned from there if only one knows how to read. One surah is worth the knowledge in a hundred books.'

'This summer when the children are back, I will bring them to you,' says Aunty. 'They need this education too.'

Rebeka heads straight to the kitchen sink and starts to run a gushing tap over the pile of dirty dishes while Nur walks around inspecting the microwave oven, the ceramic spice jars, the pictures stuck on the fridge door of Aunty's shorts- and T-shirt-clad foreigner children. 'What does her husband do?' she asks. 'Shush,' says Rebeka, her manner suddenly meek, her eyes not rising from the vigorous scrubbing she's doing. 'He has a sari shop on Commercial Street,' she whispers.

The maulana in the living room continues his lecture. 'I was a student of Western science,' he says. 'I could have got scholarships, gone abroad for further research . . .'

'My girl is studying biotech. Just one year left and then she can join a firm.'

'We don't approve of women earning their own living,' says the maulana.

'*Accha*,' says Aunty. 'But . . .'

'The Koran is very clear on this. For a woman to earn and for her husband or parents or in-laws to be in any way dependent on her is against Allah's wishes.'

'Aren't these somewhat old-fashioned views? In this day and age . . .'

'It's Allah Mian's word. What does it have to do with us mortals?' says the man, sounding almost puzzled.

'So true,' says Aunty hurriedly. 'Please, your tea is getting cold.'

Rebeka clashes the crockery in the sink and whispers to Nur, 'It's time for her afternoon TV serial, she wants to be rid of him.'

Nur, walking restlessly about the kitchen, inspecting the coffee maker, the kitchen towels, the shelf full of cookbooks, wonders what's for lunch and knows that the old man is right. God's word is timeless. Aunty isn't the least bit convinced, she can sense, but Nur herself can feel it sometimes when she's woken by the dawn azan and lies in bed thinking of a God she is too tired to get up and worship—human concerns don't count for that much when one thinks of the almighty, world-bending strength of His will. It's another matter that she cannot abide by that will always—must head to work every morning and provide for Salim too, when he's in one of his moods. Her mother gets just a few rupees on the days she's not too hobbled by arthritis to work. Nur stops pacing about the kitchen and slumps down on to the sparkling tiled floor. She likes the sound of the old man's voice. 'You can read it on the Internet,' he is telling Aunty. 'No other religious scripture has as much science as the Koran.' *Ya Allah*, thinks Nur and starts to not so much pray as float away to God, feel time become puny and her own worries microscopic. She knows Salim is somewhere or the other, well within the sight of God, and the thought comforts her. She tries to recall the line in the God-affirming verse the watchman at the Eidgah was reciting to himself. *'Nur-e-haq shamme ilahi . . .'*

Her phone rings. 'Aren't you coming at all?' Chachi asks her, breaking into her religious reverie. 'No,' says Nur, not caring to lie any more. 'Not coming today.' Chachi cuts her dead before she can say more, Rebeka is drying the dishes, the maulana declines more tea and says his goodbyes and Aunty's phone rings. 'I had an unexpected guest,' she says to the person at the other end, 'from the eighth century.' She sweeps into the kitchen, pulling her dupatta farther up on her head, ignores Nur, instructs Rebeka to leave the house key with the neighbour when she's done.

'The cash,' hisses Nur. Rebeka rushes out but Aunty is already getting into her car.

'The payment for the rickshaw, Aunty?' calls out Rebeka politely.

'Tomorrow,' shouts Aunty.

'I thought you said she's going to settle down to her serial now,' complains Nur, still on the floor. She no longer has the stamina to throw a tantrum over the money due to her.

Rebeka, exploring the fridge, finds it empty of leftovers. 'She must have thought I'm not coming today and given them all to the gardener,' she says stoically and makes them both tea. Nur swallows down a couple of biscuits with hers. 'Let's go to the Jayamahal Road dargah,' she suggests. 'They sometimes hand out food there.'

'Where's the money?' asks Rebeka. 'We don't even have enough for a bus.'

'It's just half an hour's walk.'

Rebeka mops the floors, dusts the living-room furniture and irons a pile of clothes while Nur, in her new, sombre mood, sings a hymn her mother used to when Nur was little— *'Mere ghar aana pyaare nabi, mera ghar chamkana pyaare nabi . . .'* Then they walk past the glossy, glass-walled restaurants and well-endowed grocery stores of Coles Road, turning into Netaji Road banked with sooty apartments on one side and the rubbish-filled embankment of the railway line on the other. On the stretch of viaduct running parallel to the line, a man is selling unripe tomatoes from the back of a tempo truck for five rupees a kilo. Nur says she'll spend her last coins on a few of these for her mother but then Rebeka happens to look farther up the road leading to the railway station and there is a man on a pushcart with the delights Nur has been waiting for—slices of green March mangoes, the tender, pale-yellow flesh smeared with shockingly red chilli powder. They get a slice each and walk past the hectic front of the station, under the narrow arches of the railway bridge, cursing and giggling as the vehicles whizz too close past them, and then on to Jayamahal Road. 'I love raw mango,' says Nur and reluctantly drops on to the road the peel she has been on the verge of nibbling at as well in her ecstasy.

Unlike the small Mastani Amma dargah with its homely air, the one the girls enter now is a significant landmark with its high, tapering dome, large outer corridor circling the round room in which the mausoleum of the grand old Sufi stands and its bevy of worshippers outside lighting candles and incense. Nur takes Rebeka's hand and they head into the adjoining graveyard first, searching for her father's grave. It is a modest headstone among the tall ones with cusped arches, elaborate lettering and marble crypts strewn with fresh rose petals. She lights a couple of incense sticks for him, puts her head to the bare, cold rectangle and mumbles a prayer. Her sister is around here too, the one who died burnt such a raw pink she looked like one of those plastic dolls with golden hair that rich children play with. But Nur doesn't go to her graveside. Who asked her to set herself on fire and abandon her two girls, lovable as they are, for Nur and her mother to handle?

The sun is dropping behind the dome of the dargah as they head towards it, filtering its brick-coloured light through the brick-coloured leaves of an almond tree. Nur's phone rings. It's a number she doesn't recognize but it's him. 'Salim, Salim,' she screeches, sobbing at once, and then she puts on the speakerphone so Rebeka can hear too. 'It's okay, I'm fine. But I don't like it here much,' he says. 'Where are you?' Nur asks. 'Don't shout but I'm in Dubai. I got a job here so I thought I'd try it out first and then call you.' 'Come back at once.' 'They say I can't.' 'Why? Salim, I'm going to kill you. Are you lying?'

'I'm here but the place we're staying in is no good. Eight people to a room and a bathroom that leaks shit. Above all it's too hot and they're getting us to work fourteen hours a day. I ran away from the construction site today. I can't take it any more.' 'I don't understand anything, explain to Rebeka.' She flings the phone at her friend, and while Rebeka talks to Salim, Nur weeps and laughs, horrified that her husband could land up in another country without telling her, yet forever indebted to God for being able to hear the boy's voice again.

Rebeka listens and listens and then hands back the phone and tells her the story. Mushtaq bhai, it turns out, is the devil himself. Some months after he got Salim out of the lock-up, he called and told him he needed to return the favour, so if Salim wanted, he could set him up with a good job in the Gulf, all he needed was fifty thousand rupees to make the arrangements. Salim said he wouldn't mind a job but he didn't have that kind of money. 'Never mind,' said Mushtaq bhai. 'You go and start working. You can repay me in a couple of months, the salaries there are good.' So Mushtaq bhai's men got Salim a passport and air ticket, he packed a few clothes, took Nur's money and landed in Dubai. Now he wants to come back but the agent who received him there, one of Mushtaq's men, says he has to work for at least two years to fulfil his contract and make good on the loan. He's taken Salim's passport and Salim is stuck. 'Tell Nur to speak to Mushtaq bhai and get me out of here somehow, he says.'

Nur crumples to her knees, finding herself among the leprous men and destitute women who line the entrance to the dargah, who hang around there all day, who must practically live there, only needing some hole to sleep in every night. She is still staring into space when a boy in snowy-white clothes comes up to them and starts handing out small plastic packets of sweet boondi to all supplicants, including Nur and Rebeka. Nur looks at the packet in her hand, looks at Rebeka, sighs softly and faints.

When she wakes up with her head still on the ground she can see the evening star right above her in the diamond-blue sky. And she remembers with sweet relief the second line of that couplet: *'Jiska haami ho khuda . . .'*

12

FATHER, SON

Looking at the mammoth, spotlit ads for chubby babies and running shoes, the poet feels very far from home. When he imagines talking to his son, the voice isn't right. Too stern. Or too soft.

They haven't spoken for three years—after their fight in a room hung with photos of the family younger and rosier. The boy had said, *You have no nerves*, and flung the full plate of his dinner against a wall. The father had said, *You mean I don't have the nerve, you idiot*. But then anger sparked in him too and he said, *Get out of here*. His wife, crying, wiped her nose and laid out more food as if some bird had flown off with her child's dinner. She had ruined him with adoration. They'd been arguing about money— son for, father against, mother inconsolable. And here he is now, where the billboards are aglow with wealth.

He peers out into the night through the large bus-window, trying to read the road signs. The address, which had seemed self-evident to him when he'd noted it down from his son's email, now feels quite irrelevant. He knows the name of the place but it is a sign he's looking for. A large gang, all young men and women with backpacks and earphones and none of his nervousness, get off at the following stop and he does likewise. He senses he is near—and besides, there are rickshaws. The night outside the air-conditioned bus is warm, scented with eucalyptus and the fumes from a biryani restaurant. The driver of the first passing rickshaw he asks looks nonplussed for a moment and then agrees to take him to Gundu Circle.

The poet feels a moment of relief. He hasn't written poems for a while but now contemplates one. He's seeing his son after three years and is not sure he wants to. The invitation to read from his work in Bangalore, the sudden light in his wife's eyes, and the ensuing pleading. *Meet him? I should send him a bill of accounts— that he would appreciate*, said the poet. *You don't understand*, answered his wife. *Who speaks to him on the phone every week? Who can hear the great big hollow in his voice?*

So a reunion was engineered and the boy sent an email saying: *I am alone in a villa, come and stay with me for as long as you like.* The poet replied as tersely. *Coming to read my poems. Can meet you for dinner.* And then he signed—*Love, Baba.*

Less than a minute later he regretted that word. It burned in him like the memory of the curry dripping off the dining-room wall. He consoled himself with Shakespeare. *What's gone and what's past help should be past grief.* He examined his son's note again. *I am alone*, it said. *Come.*

The rickshaw judders under him as he thinks with dissatisfaction of his day. The poetry was mediocre all round. Delivering his own lines, he sensed their lightness and wished he'd put on a finer shirt or had Tagore's beard. *This is literature*, he thought. Poetry's never grander than the life of the poet. He'd felt dazed, as if some treasured thing had turned on close inspection to dust and air. On the podium, a lady weighed down with silk declared: *No one remembers the date of my birth, and that is a good thing. Animals, trees, the earth and the sky don't have a date of birth.*

Literature is bodies and voices, thought the poet. A tall man towers over the rest and a sweet-faced woman's words go a longer way. Over lunch, the poets discussed their health problems and children's careers. He brought up the subject of his unpublished manuscript so he could get advice from the superior ones. They were sympathetic but no one said, *I'll help*. So he focused on his lunch and ate more than necessary.

He is still uncomfortably full and soon there will be dinner, during which he will have little to say to his son. Something like a line of poetry tugs at his tired mind, the feeling that he has no word for his wordlessness. They keep driving—past a hospital looking oddly radiant, like a monument to pain—finally reaching a junction at which the traffic is ranged on every side, straining at its leash. As soon as he alights he is helpless again, the lefts and rights he has painfully transcribed from his son's directions meaningless to him in this brightly lit, howling island of the night.

The poet stares at a glass-walled gym on the second floor of a corner building, people inside running strenuously towards nowhere, and wonders if it is a possible landmark, the talisman that will bring them together finally. Where does he turn from here? He can hear his son, berating him for not possessing a mobile phone, a savings plan or a streak of modern ambition. He appeals to a passer-by who, without breaking his stride, points into the distance and says, *Fifteen kilometres. That side.*

Impossible, says the poet, pressing his fingers to the bridge of his nose. *This is the place, I am here.* He waits, imagining his hotel room. And then the phone on the nightstand and his wife on the other side, not asking a thing, waiting for him to yield. He singles out two elderly men who seem to be taking a leisurely evening walk in some halcyon dimension, unconcerned about the present one filled with car horns and commerce.

One remains silent while the other says, *Good evening*, and scrutinizes the poet's crushed scrap of paper, looking up and down the street in thought. Then he says with great consideration, *You're in the wrong Gundu Circle, sir. There are two in this city.* *Wonderful*, says the poet wearily, trying and failing to remember where he has gone wrong. *The best thing to do*, says the kind man, *is to get on to the Ring Road and take a bus*. The poet wants to say, *But I just took a bus*. He thanks his saviour, pressing his hand. The walking companion remains quietly supportive.

The conductor on the bus tells him it will take forty minutes and suddenly the poet is relieved again and loses himself in the journey. They go into striped-blue underpasses and wide-open overpasses. Outside is his son's world—high-rises that enfold hundreds of homes, huge banks of lit-up office windows, names of international companies in blazing letters crowding the sky. *There is no word for the wordlessness within us*, he thinks. *And there is no love that is not a measure of defeat.*

The conductor nods at him eventually to signal his stop, and he steps out on to a street that feels so uncannily similar to the one he was in an hour ago, he is almost shouting for the bus, afraid to be abandoned there. *Of course, it's not the same place*, he admonishes himself. Carver Street, says a signboard. *And take this lake, I haven't seen it before.* There is something otherworldly about the lake. It is completely overrun with weeds and at its centre is a tiny island on which stands a lone tree, lit up by the artificial glare of the city. He walks with purpose, seeking, as before, an intimation, and comes to a bus stop where a girl stands waiting. She seems to anticipate his questions and tells him he has got off the bus a couple of stops before he should have. It's a bit too far to walk, he needs a rickshaw, she says, and then returns to her silent vigil.

So he is near and there's even an interested rickshaw at hand. He gets in and shuts his eyes. It is late and the boy has perhaps given up on him and gone to sleep. Thinking of the email again, he is enraged. Why did he feel the need to mention his villa? Of course he hasn't changed. There is nothing to him except this lust for more. The unspeaking rickshaw driver has been speeding without awaiting instructions. The poet taps his shoulder and repeats, *Gundu Circle*. He nods and continues driving.

Enough, says the poet suddenly. He is certain they have overshot their mark. His man goes on. *Stop, stop!* he cries. *What?* yells the driver. It strikes the poet that he could be an unsavoury type and this an evil city. *Not reached*, says the driver in English but, just as the poet is contemplating either jumping out or wringing the man's neck, the vehicle hits a red light. The poet pulls out his wallet angrily and there is some argument over the right fare and the question of who is to blame for this unnecessarily long journey.

It is only when he has worked his way through the stalled traffic and is on the pavement that he knows his right trouser-pocket is empty. As soon as he registers this thought, the light turns green and the monster rickshaw shoots off. He had, for a moment, dumped the wallet on the seat while counting his change. The address is in it, as is all his money.

Wonderful, says the poet out loud. He puts his hands into his wide pockets and begins walking in the opposite direction. He walks without tiring, crossing roads and slipping into side lanes without the least care about where he is going, glad that this is a city without end. At the end of a potholed, shadowy road is a small bar; a man stands smoking outside. *Decent place?* asks the poet, gesturing at the door. *No*, says the man. *Lousy.* They both smile. *I'm new here. Exploring Bangalore*, says the poet. *You like it?* asks the man. *Lousy*, says the poet, and they laugh. The man extends a hand. He is a property consultant. The poet tells him he is a poet. *Yes-ah?* says the man. *Then I must buy you a drink.*

They go in and sit down with the other men talking in the humid bar suffused with the aroma of fried fish. The waiter brings them their whiskies and sodas. He slowly drops ice cubes into their glasses. *I was a poet too once*, says the property consultant. *Lousy poems I used to write.* They clink their glasses together. The poet's cheerful companion asks, *And you?*

The poet, smiling, says nothing. *Lousy*, he is thinking, with new-found joy. *Lousy.*

13

LITTLE GRANNY'S SONG

One of my legs is shorter than the other. The doctor told me that. If he hadn't, I wouldn't have known.

I wake Aarti in the night and hobble to the toilet outside, holding her arm, and then hobble back. I either sit on my bed and talk to myself or lie down. I embroider sometimes—little yellow champak flowers and pink roses. I can never tell what the time is; the only clock in the house is in the front room. If my thimble slips to the floor I have to shout for someone. If I want a drink of water I have to swallow spit and wait. Aarti is always doing something—making rotis or washing clothes. Three times a day they bring me food and the bhindi will be underdone or the rice too sticky.

There was a time, after my sahib died, when I'd single-handedly cook for eight people—roast brinjals on the coals, make the softest koftas, thicken milk for kheer. They let me do it all and I didn't have the kind of thoughts I do these days. Now if I think of something I don't want to think about, then I think about it even more. It can keep going through my mind all night like television. I remember how my mother-in-law fainted when my sahib died. The way she lay there with her hand still clutching

mine! I go back to the first time my father let me carry a canister
of oil back from the shop to our home near the Old Delhi Sabzi
Mandi and I dropped it. When do one's thoughts start to curdle
like this? I am at an age when people's jaws slacken and their eyes
go stupidly blank but I haven't forgotten anything. If there were
someone here other than that thick-skulled Aarti to listen, I could
tell them the whole story: how my sahib's father woke up before
anyone else could, every single day of his working life, made a
paste of almonds and poppy seeds which he mixed into a brass
tumbler of warm milk, ate three rotis and three eggs and then put
on his cap and took off on his bicycle.

He had a job on the headworks of the Agra Canal, he'd been
handling the taps and regulators there since 1925. He had grown
up and studied in Ghaziabad and then come up to Okhla and
got this job in the time of the British. They built it long ago, the
canal, to carry off water towards Agra and Mathura. It irrigates
the fields there, my father-in-law would tell us. I used to imagine
that he was the boss of the whole canal, and that if he didn't wake
up in time and head out, people would have no food to harvest in
Uttar Pradesh.

When my sahib joined the new factory that made electric
irons and coil stoves, and the following year when I married him
and moved here, this was still a village—Okhla Gaon. They call
it that even today, though now so much land this side of the river
has become part of Delhi too. They hadn't put up the wire fence
around the Yamuna then, we could walk on the floodplain, I and
Sarita, my brother-in-law's wife, go to the temple downriver and
sit with the other women singing bhajans twice a week.

When you're young, people can see you. Your sister-in-law
shuffles in and out of the kitchen so you don't pop a piece of
shakarpara in your mouth while frying them. Your sahib kneads

your breasts at night. Your nephew laughs at you when you ask him to explain what's happening in the newspaper. All the time, you have your eyes on yourself but from the outside. When you're older, when you're an old woman like me and people forget to take away your empty dinner-thali, forget to give you the mirror when they give you the comb, then your eyes are not on the outside any more. Everything is inside.

They would all say I was prettier than that Sarita, and she had her revenge. Or God made sure she got her own back by giving her first one son, then another, then a third. All those children and me not one! She would pinch the thin flesh on my arms when she talked to me and tear holes into my cotton saris when bringing the dried clothes down from the roof, but after her three beautiful babies started to grow up and the doctors were sure I would have none, we started to tolerate each other. We became sisters, our unequalness made us equal. I used to cry at first and want her dead but not her babies. Especially the middle one, he was mine. He spent much more time in my arms than his mother's; she was too exhausted after the third one came.

Who is left to whom I can ask—Have I been all right? If there is anyone who holds a grudge against me, let them say it now. I ask Hanumanji, I tell him when I can walk I'll come to him, I'll bring him all the clean new rupees I've been saving under my mattress. I'll climb the steps up to him and fall at his feet. But nothing. Silence. I feel as if an important visitor has come and gone and I've forgotten to ask him the most important question—Have I been all right? Did I wrong anyone? Did I cast the evil eye in someone's direction? I used to believe it was Sarita who had cursed me as soon as I stepped into this house. I came and she was standing there. She snatched the veil of my sari from my head—no gentleness in her for the trembling new bride—and said something cruel under her breath that I didn't catch. Who knows if that was the jibe that struck at me. But the way things turned out didn't bother sahib. He would take me to the movies and the fairs that came to Okhla and to temples in the city and all the parks, and even the Taj Mahal and Fatehpur Sikri. He'd say, 'Not having children doesn't make us any less human.' I think he loved me more because of my defect.

When he died in the factory, killed when the assembly line broke and all that heavy machinery fell on his head, just two or three years before his retirement, everyone started saying to me— *Can you winnow this rice, it'll just take five minutes. Can you bathe the boy, he has to go to school.* I did all the work I used to when he was alive and, on top of that, the work of another person. I had become two people—sahib's wife and sahib's widow. Only when the three sons married did I get to put my feet up. And then last year, this happened. Sarita's daughter-in-law, Rupali, had washed clothes by the outside tap one day and the black-face didn't even have the brains to throw down water afterwards and let the soap run. I was carrying a full bucket into the bathroom and I fell so hard, I broke my leg. They took me in a rickshaw to the Holy Family Hospital and the doctor said—*Operation.* After two months the pain was still so bad I used to cry going up the stairs, cry shifting positions in bed. They took me back to the same doctor and again he said—*Operation.* Later he told me that they had to cut away some piece of bone that wasn't healing and my right leg was now shorter. 'Everything will be fine now,' he said. 'You'll just have a limp.' But it isn't. Months have passed and the same pains, the same questions in my head.

Sushil, my younger grand-nephew, comes in and says, 'The Muslims are celebrating. It is Eid today.'

'What's it to me that it's Eid?'

He gives me a warm bowl of sewain from the pot that the neighbours have sent across. I look at the milk-soaked raisins and fat green pistas in it and feel a knife carve my heart thinking of how in this family we haven't been able to afford dried fruits for years. We don't give the Muslims anything for our Diwali and Holi but they still send us sewain and biryani twice a year, for big Eid and small. Last week they parked their car in the lane in a way that made it impossible for anyone to either get into or out of our house. Sushil's elder brother, Aarti's husband, Rana, who drives a rickshaw and is usually in a bad temper, went and shouted at them. Sushil came and reported it to me. 'He told them he'll smash the windows if they don't move it at once.' I smiled. I don't smile any more but that made me smile. 'It's a new car,' Sushil had said. 'They don't have anywhere to park it.'

Sushil is only twelve years old and holds forth on everything like an adult. He has failed his exams twice and yet is clever. He can do all sorts of things on his father's phone, which is in his hands most of the time, read books in English and Hindi and mimic the dialogues of all the films he watches.

'Do you know the story of Abhimanyu?' I ask him. 'I don't know why, but you've always looked like Abhimanyu to me. It could be because your father was my baby Krishna. That curly-haired little fellow was my special one. I brought him up, do you know that? Your grandmother was a queen, she wasn't going to look after all three children and do the housework, the little that she deigned to do: make a chicken curry once in a while . . .'

Sushil shows me a photo of the neighbour's car on the phone.

'They went to Bombay for a holiday and brought back a suitcase full of giant teddy-bears for the child,' he says.

I eat the sewain slowly, trying to chew the nuts with my toothless gums, wishing I could give this child something too—

but stories are all I have apart from those few notes under the mattress. 'So Abhimanyu was born with a gift. He could fight thousands of men at one go, he could work his way into the very centre of the battle on Kurukshetra, but the tragedy is he didn't know the way out.'

'Could he fly a helicopter?'

'This is the Mahabharata I'm narrating. People fought with swords then. On horseback.'

Then he hears the sound of the television, says, 'Wait a minute, Chhoti Dadi,' and runs off. He won't be back unless Rupali or Aarti send him to me again.

I'm so tired and everyone's dead—my sahib the first to go, then my old in-laws, then the brother-in-law, painfully dying of cancer. Sarita was some five or seven years older than me, but she was always healthier, and she went peacefully. Only the middle of her three sons, my Krishna and his wife, Rupali, and their two boys, still live in this house. Rana got married to Aarti and a child is on its way. And then there is the younger one, Sushil, who keeps failing but will never, I know, drive a rickshaw nor do any of the jobs his father does. He will want something fancier but I can't think what that will be.

Sarita's other two boys have done well for themselves, and in Okhla village if a Hindu makes even a little money he moves out. The Muslims have swarmed in, it's their village now. Krishna says we're not natives any more and Rana is always getting into fights with the neighbours; or, if there's nothing else to be heated up about, he will argue with Aarti about her rubbish cooking or berate his mother, Rupali, whenever she wants some of his money to go to the ration shop. 'Where do you want to move?' I ask my Krishna. I know if we sell the house, we'll all scatter apart like grain. The money could disappear anywhere. Krishna has tried different things—he worked in a factory nearby that made packaging, then he had a small grocery store for dal-rice. When that made losses—how many groceries will people buy, after all, the main road is crammed with stores—he bought the rickshaw that his son now drives. These days he's up to something else, he won't say what. The money trickles in somehow but he had to take loans for my two operations.

They used to help us, Sanno's family, who lived next door. She married and came to that house about the same time as me. Her husband ran the packaging factory that Krishna joined for a while. Then this man—he was always a sharp one for business—started another factory to make clothes that go abroad. They extended the house upwards. They were always there—when my sahib died, when the others died, Sanno's husband was always one of the men shouldering the bier. When Krishna needed money for my operations, he turned to them. Then they bought a house in Patparganj and moved to the other side of the river. Sanno cried when she was leaving but she was happy to go, I know. The Muslims moved in after that. I don't talk to them the way I used to with Sanno and her people. Any time I was up there, putting out pickles to sun, drying my hair, letting Krishna run around, I would lean over and call out to Sanno and she'd come to the roof, leave whatever she was doing, and we'd relate everything to each other as if our lives were running dramas, Mahabharatas, unfolding day by day just for the other person's pleasure. Now she might well be dead in Patparganj and I wouldn't know. Every day I tell Krishna to phone Sanno's husband so I can speak to her, and every day he says he forgets. I don't think he's repaid the loans either.

The Muslims came to visit us the day they moved in but I refused to go see them, stayed in my room and worked on my roses. I was angry that day and I cursed them in my mind, hearing their loud, excited voices. I said: *May they be unhappy. May they go back to wherever they came from and Sanno return.* Yet they stayed and the son married, like our Rana did, and they had a baby girl. Ever since they arrived, there have been relatives visiting and the smell of rich food, laughter and scolding, cars coming and cars going. At first I thought it a celebration because of the new home or the son's marriage or the baby but now it appears that this is how they live their lives. A tamasha day and night while our house is mostly silent unless Rana flares up over something. The rest of us seem to have forgotten how to talk for more than five minutes at a time. The house of the dead this is—only I am left, Chhoti Dadi, little granny, who should really be on the other side, one-legged and full of memories.

Maybe it was because I cursed the Muslims, they cursed me right back and I slipped that day. They know these things, they have their fakirs and pirs to help them. And then even Hanumanji with all his powers is helpless. If I sleep I sleep but once I wake up in the night it's hell. The pain feels like it'll take the leg off. I plead with the person across the wall, whoever they are, the man or the woman who is blighting me in their dreams. *I'm a poor woman*, I plead. *I'll give you all the money I have.* At other times, I say, *All right: take me away. Why have you stopped at the leg? Eat up all of me.*

I've gone through this before. I will never forget that one litchi season in Sabzi Mandi, my sister and I sitting with a basket between us, litchis so juicy the flies wouldn't leave them. Our neighbour Kanno came in to ask for a few bulbs of garlic, her mother had run out. We could have offered her some litchis. There was no good reason not to but it was as if we had lost our reason. We just sat there giddy with sweetness, our hands sticky, laughter making our already sweaty faces sweatier. The next day Kanno's evil eye came for me. My stomach cramped so badly and I vomited so much I thought I would die like that, before I had a chance to clean myself up. I only ate watery dal for ten days. But this leg is something else. This is not some slip of a girl cursing me over a basket of fruit. This is Yamraj himself that someone has set upon me.

I start thinking of that Kanno, I remember her small, big-eyed face well. Her name was Kaneez so everyone called her Kanno. She and her brothers and sisters, children of Basharat Mian next door and his cross-eyed wife, would be in and out of our house all the time, and we theirs. On Eid there was no question of them sending across anything, we had to put on our nice clothes and go to their place for a big lunch on a *dastarkhwan* laid out on the floor. I still remember the richness of the blues and reds embossed on that satin spread.

'Do you want tea, Chhoti Dadi?' asks Aarti. She's come in to sweep the room. The girl is five months pregnant and needs to rest her swollen feet but Rupali won't let her. I feel sorry for her, pull her towards me with her long plait and say, 'Aarti, whatever happens I must go to the roof today. I am tired of sitting here in the cold, waiting for someone to come and thread my needle for me. It's dark in here once the sun leaves the room.'

'You can't put your foot down without moaning, how will you climb all those stairs?'

'Sit here for a moment.'

She flings her broom aside and says, 'I don't have time. I still have the sabzi left to cook.' But she sits down anyway and lifts my sari to look at my leg.

'How long has it been since you broke it?'

She hasn't known me any other way. When she came to this house I was already a cripple. I ask her to get me one of the pills the doctor gave for when the pain is bad. It doesn't really cure me, just numbs the suffering for a while. I swallow it and ask her what Rupali is doing, where Sushil went, what day of the week it is, what the time might be, what she's cooking for lunch. She tells me that she wants to have the baby at her parents' place in Badarpur, but Rana and his parents are adamant she have it here.

'I won't poke my nose in that quarrel,' I say. 'Bring me the bottle of mustard oil and let's go.'

Each high step of the two flights of stairs to the accursed roof is a small death and I don't know if I will ever come down again. Tears blind me but how can I cry before this child who hasn't seen anything yet—not the pain of childbirth, not the loss of a husband, not the wrinkling of skin or the shrinking of the heart. But she has some strength, this Aarti. She doesn't let go of me all the way up, despite the weight in her own womb. I never got close to Rupali, she was always a tight-lipped, somewhat grim one, but Aarti came to me the very day she moved in, laughing and talking as if she already knew me, and now she sleeps on the floor next to my bed and comes in once in a while during the day to say a few words.

As soon as I sit down the winter sun starts to soothe my bones. Or it could be the medicine finally taking effect. Aarti sits by me and I open out her plait and slowly start redoing it. She is the same age that I was when I married. When her baby comes, she'll throw it at me, of course, and go off to do the cooking. And what can I do—I'll take care of it. Women who've never had children have that itch in their hands. They want to oil a small boy's limbs. They want to teach a little girl to sing. I spent so many winter mornings here, keeping an eye on Krishna. Krishna was not his name really, his parents gave him another, but when I took him up—and didn't let him go, not till he was big enough to run off

and play in the lane with the other boys—I called him Krishna.
And it stuck.

'The baby will be a year old next week,' says Aarti. She's
talking about Nida, the neighbour's daughter.

'They are having a big party. Her grandfather has come back
with the family from Bombay and they will put up a shamiana on
the roof and get the food from a restaurant. We could go. If they
call us.'

I give Aarti a sharp rap on her skull, then knot a scrap of
ribbon at the end of her braid.

'Don't go on about what the Muslims are saying and what
the Muslims are doing. Sushil has started singing the same tune,
listening to you.'

This makes no difference to her jabbering. She is besotted
with Nida; if she has a minute between her chores she'll run up
to the roof to see if she can glimpse the infant, exchange a few
words with her mother. It's not like how Sanno and I were—
sisters for life. Aarti gets gossip from their servant, stopping her
when she espies her passing in the lane. The rest she imagines.
I imagine them too, the fair baby girl with kohl in her eyes, the
mother whose skin the sun has never touched, whose hands are
tender because the family can pay servants to do the housework.
And then I think—*How can someone you've never seen, and who
has never seen you, put the evil eye on you?* The Muslims visited us
that first time but never after that. I don't even know what they
look like! How has this come to be? Yet, didn't I just lick up the
sewain they sent? I can hear them very close at night too, through
the walls. And then all those smells—the mutton simmering and
the puris frying and the rose water and saffron they put in their
pulaos.

Aarti helps me to the parapet to look out a little. I can see the water and on the other side the city they call Noida. I can see the tamarind trees on the banks of the river, and swarming all over one of the sturdier ones at least a dozen small boys in white kurta-pyjamas and white caps. How do these little Muslim boys keep their clothes so immaculate? My heart feels light looking at them and at the sun sparkling on the water. I have been all right. I didn't harm anyone, I gave all the help I could. When I cursed someone, I had to suffer through the nightmares. The following day, it would be myself I took to task. I can look into Hanumanji's face with a clear conscience. Aarti sits me down, pours mustard oil into her palm and rubs it gently over my bad leg.

'Take me to the Shiv Shakti Hanuman Temple one of these days,' I say.

'What will you ask for?'

'That I live long enough to see your child.'

Aarti sighs and says, 'If I bring the peas up here, will you shell them? I have to wash some of Rana's clothes and put them out before afternoon.'

So I sit there with the sun on my back, working on the peas, and later ask Aarti to bring my plate of food up there. I think of the trips taken across town with my sahib in buses and *tangas*, how I have not seen the Sabzi Mandi after it shifted to Azadpur, and how looking at the river can make your thoughts swell to match its size.

It's late in the afternoon when we go down and I am glad all evening but that night the pain is worse than ever. I don't sleep at all. Next door the baby is crying and I start to cry with it. What is the worst thing about pain? That you don't know when it'll end. If someone told me, your leg is going to hurt for the next one week, I could sing through that week. If someone said, one month, I could live through that month without cursing. But the gods, the demons, whoever created pain, haven't made it that way. There's no point asking what time it is because in the land of pain there are no clocks.

I'm too tired to even pray. I lie there with an empty mind, no words left to fight with. And then, suddenly, without my even asking for it, a voice comes to comfort me. *Golu, oh Golu.* A voice that's muffled and far off, yet closer to me than the beating of my own heart. *Golu, oh Golu.*

A gentle voice, no urgency in it. It's the voice of my sahib. No one else in the world would call me by that name, it was the nickname he gave me for my moon-face. This is my sahib telling me that no one's to blame. *Golu, oh Golu.* Pain is not the fault of the person suffering it.

I feel such relief and joy that I get out of bed without caring about the leg. I drag myself slowly to the front room. I haven't been here since my fall. It looks small to me and that makes everything that has happened here seem so unimportant, trivial—all the Shah Rukh Khan films I have watched on television and all the scoldings that Krishna used to get, and now Sushil gets, over his undone homework, and all the visitors who have sat cross-legged on the sofa eating the perfect malpuas I made. The clock is in the same place, above the TV. Sushil's schoolbooks are scattered all over the centre table. I take a pencil, tear a blank page from one of his notebooks, snatch the clock, go back to my room and wrap a blanket around myself. After I have written down what I have to say, I hold on to the clock tightly under my blanket. My steps are slow and heavy and the voice of my sahib is still calling to me. I go to the kitchen, unlatch the door and am soon out in the alley. In the old days it used to take twenty minutes to walk to the river. Now it will probably take me all night but I'm determined.

The cold is like a wall I have to break through at every step but I am at the river sooner than I expected. The moonlight in the smelly water is very still. I drop the blanket and fling the clock into the Yamuna, as far out as my weak arm will allow. Then, smiling and stumbling and praying to my sahib to keep his arms outstretched for me on the other side, I jump.

———

Aarti stirs in her sleep, hearing voices from the neighbour's house. Nida's crying. She listens without breaking the filament of her dream. *Golu, oh Golu*, calls her visiting grandfather, trying to get her to go back to sleep. But Nida cries even louder. It must be a new name that this new relative has given her but she's too small to know it belongs to her. Aarti's head sinks deeper into her pillow at the thought of the birthday party, snuggling with the lovely child, and her dream becomes a question about her own child, about whether she or he will produce in her an equal joy.

In the morning she will find it—the note on Chhoti Dadi's bed saying to Rana and Rupali that they must let Aarti go back home to have her baby, and that the new handkerchief she has embroidered is for Krishna. Attached to the note with a frayed rubber-band is a wad of money that she has left for Aarti. They will not have to wander very far to look for her. She will be found stuck in the water, the rubbish and weeds and clogged sewage of the Agra Canal, though it will be a few days before they notice the missing clock.

14

A SHORT HISTORY OF EATING

At seven, I read about hunger in the story of 'The Barmecide's Feast' from *The Arabian Nights*. A poor man is invited to dinner in the house of the rich Barmecide. When it's time to eat, Barmecide mimes eating and enjoying his food. The visitor, puzzled at first, plays along so as not to offend his host. After they have finished their imaginary meal, the poor, and by now very hungry, man gets a lavish real one—as a reward for having put art over hunger.

I ate breakfast, two lunches and dinner, and was always hungry. There didn't seem to be much food out in the world either. The Chinese restaurant opposite the house seemed to stand more for intrigue than cuisine—only beautiful couples or disreputable men went in there. The pakori-wallah next door used a black-as-sin vat and ancient oil for his frying. The red and yellow lollies sold from wooden iceboxes by roving men in grungy clothes were rumoured to be made from drain water. The rice cooked in pig's blood always on offer in Shillong's tea shops was off limits. And flies dipped their trembling limbs in the basins of syrup with floating rosogullas on display in the greasy windows of the sweet shops.

Alice in Wonderland became an obsession, a novel in which there is no pretend food but neither is hunger properly satisfied. At the Mad Hatter's tea party, Alice is offered wine when there isn't any, discovers that butter is used to keep a watch running and tea to keep the Dormouse awake. She gives away the comfits she has in her pocket as prizes after the caucus race. Subsequently, there is the matter of the tarts at the trial. *I wish they'd get the trial done and hand round the refreshments*, thinks Alice. But of course they won't.

I re-engineered recipes for my siblings' birthdays—peppermint creams with vanilla essence and pizza with ketchup smeared on it. I made sponge cakes that sank. I ate things that no one seems to any more, that have vanished with the Palaeolithic eighties—macaroni rice and poppy-seed-flecked thekua and red-tipped Phantom Sweet Cigarettes. Yet food was a fantasy—not this that existed around me, but that which the magazines sometimes illustrated, that adults described from another lifetime, that children ate in rosy Blyton land.

I was sad for Alice but sadder for David Copperfield, ejected from his family, on his way to the dreaded boarding-school. He stops at an inn to have a meal. David is immediately beguiled away from his chops and vegetables by an affable waiter who eats them, he says, to neutralize the bad effects of a mug of beer that he's just drunk—David's beer, as a matter of fact, which David is prevented from drinking because a man who drank similar ale the previous day apparently fell down dead. Then there is dessert. 'Batter-pudding,' says the waiter, taking up a tablespoon, 'is my favourite pudding! Ain't that lucky? Come on, little 'un, and let's see who'll get most.' Obviously, 'with his tablespoon to my teaspoon, his dispatch to my dispatch, and his appetite to my appetite', David barely manages to capture a spoonful. The child imagines he is being provided with succour—in the form of friendship, when it is actually being taken away—in the form of his dinner.

But it was really Little Women I wanted to be when I was older—poor themselves, yet giving away their breakfast on Christmas morning to the impoverished mites begging at the door. When I grew up, I could go to the restaurants sometimes and drink pale coffee with my college friends, which I never drank at home, eat crusted cutlets with fork and knife. My sister and I saved to gorge on greasy noodles till we felt sick and disinterested in them; then the weeks would pass and chicken chow would come to seem the highlight of life again. I ate and ate Uncle Chipps and Maggi noodles when they first announced themselves in every grocery store in the country, excited by the glamour of their Western names, mistaking them for liberty. Later I spooned rice and meat off enamel plates in the tea shops, on break from philosophy classes at university, thinking of the gaunt Wittgenstein alone in his Norwegian fjord, eating a loaf of bread or nothing, and I read R.K. Narayan's *The Guide*, wondering what bondas tasted of, like the fasting Raju does before he becomes indifferent to food—ennobled and unhungry.

I was still hungry. I lived in Bangalore now and was married to a man who was hungry too. We cut out newspaper notices about new restaurants and changed buses to get to them. Food was our food of love; we talked about what we ate and ate everything we talked about. We dwelt on remembered meals with the tenderness of starving jailbirds and the eagerness of gluttons. We shared the memories of foodlessness that swam in our genes— his grandmother had ground wood bark into flour during the war, my grandfather had got tuberculosis from malnourishment. And now it was as if the world had ended and the only excitement left for us was eating. I had never encountered such a profusion of food—spaghetti and meatballs with a sprig of green pepper on top, whole pomfrets, dosas larger than the plates they were sitting on, medieval-looking pots of biryani, good for four, eaten by two. We were children tasting indulgence with our crab masala fry, not gourmands making sniffy mental notes. We would eat pizza because of those delicious syllables in our mouths even if the crust was doughy, and not mind the cockroaches on the walls of the little fish place because the thalis were filled to spilling. I, small-town rustic, ravenous gamine, learnt a new word every week—mulligatawny, tournedos, bangda, shawarma, sashimi, John Dory, chow-chow bath. At every turn in the road, we tasted a new country, surprised it had taken India so long to awake to life and liberty—Tex-Mex, Naga, Nawabi, Colonial, Chettinad, Mediterranean.

It wasn't just us, all our compatriots had fat and greedy hearts in that innocent turn-of-the-century time, that softly-spotlit-restaurant time when people had to learn to make conversation as they waited for their order to arrive. Of course, some ate oil-fry kebabs with their beer in dingy bars and didn't gush in admiration, some just slurped up the ruddy slop pretending to be sambar and rushed to office, some ate evening-pushcart snacks such as gobi manchurian the orange of the national flag with equanimity rather than awe. But some were ecstatic about their eating, they were decadent before their time, wallowing in the supposed era of plenty, eating each marvellous foreign thing in the name of food, even as food was still foreign—those legendary, phantasmagorical three square meals a day—to so many of their bony countrymen.

Instead of caring, they just ordered dessert. I read Allan Sealy's *The Trotter-Nama* about then, and how one of Justin Aloysius Trotter's last wishes before he dies is the desire for something sweet. He can no longer be bothered about his staple of tandoori partridges and curried doves—what afflicts him now is the lure of the elemental. Sugar held 'the promise of a sensation intensely pleasurable—sinfully, maddeningly, cripplingly, suffocatingly pleasurable; it was a siren song calling one to endless debauch . . .' I watched the endless debauch in Peter Greenaway's *The Cook, the Thief, His Wife & Her Lover*, much of it set in a restaurant. Where there is food there is necessarily both depravity and refinement, Greenaway seemed to be saying. The manifold hungers of the flesh cannot really be distinguished from each other: eating, sex, physical violence and cannibalism form one messy whole.

I wrote verse about food and longed to both stuff myself and become thinner. T.S. Eliot advised the poet to look further than the heart, to also consider 'the cerebral cortex, the nervous system, and the digestive tracts'. I crammed my mouth with chips every evening to erase the boredom of work, and read recipe books lying down in order to dream. The Urdu one had an account for biryani the length of a short story and instructions to use one's own judgement for proportions and cooking time—that is, '*hisaab zaroorat*'. The Scandinavian one had a picture of a very clean fish, with a ruler held next to it and the caption reading, 'It is the thickness of the fish, not its weight, which decides how long it should be cooked. Lay the fish on its side and measure it where it is the thickest.' An article in the *New Yorker* informed me that American women have been buying and reading cookbooks voraciously since the eighteenth century because they left their mothers behind in Europe and had no one to give them 'the wisdom that is said to be passed spontaneously from generation to generation, like the gift of prophecy, in the family kitchen'.

I used to tinker with all my mother's recipes but now started to realize the originals were better. My husband and I loved the baingan mirchi ka salan in Nagarjuna Savoy and the fish and chips in Victoria, but Victoria was torn down and Nagarjuna Savoy went down. Slowly it started to seem that every place we'd collected memories from had gone or deteriorated. That upstairs restaurant with the best momos in north Bangalore. That unhurried cafe with white leatherette sofas and hot chocolate. That Mangalore seafood place with water dosas and fiery squid. That old-time chain that really knew their Wiener schnitzel. That bar with the great music and the kokum in the fish curry and the tapioca mash. That other bar with the cane furniture and the brain fry. All fading out before our eyes that could still see flavours, hearts that still hungered, stomachs that still cherished.

The world was trying to tell us something. Maybe that one ought to eat to forget rather than remember. I wrote a story about my grand-aunt who took to her bed and stopped eating when she received news about the passing of her beloved younger brother. What was she thinking of as day passed into night, became another day, and still she resisted food? What did she fill her thoughts with, she who had cooked all her life? She fasted to death, like Gandhi might have done. He was quite clear that a person who is scrupulous in his diet but feels nothing for the principle of ahimsa is 'a pitiful wretch' compared to one who may eat more than he really needs to but is yet in other matters 'a personification of Ahimsa'. Grand-aunt ate less than she needed to and put herself on the altar of ahimsa.

We had long stopped saving restaurant reviews and opening announcements. The lighting in these places had become fancier and the prices climbed high. There was still the food but something else as well audible in the tinkle of the fork and knife, the music on the loop—the hunger for sophistication, the absolute need to look good. There was, in any case, far too much traffic blocking the way to go out into the city merely to eat. I stayed home and read J.M. Coetzee's *Life & Times of Michael K*. Michael K is a kind of Robinson Crusoe in reverse who, when he has to fend for himself on an abandoned farm in a country racked by war, does not tame the wild to meet his needs but is able to whittle down his needs to match his environment, living on the occasional raw pumpkin. Later, he is rescued. The doctor who tries to get this skeleton of a man to eat is puzzled by his obstinacy—Why does he want to die? The answer, the doctor realizes, lies far beyond commonplace wisdom about why we eat. 'Suicide, I had understood, is an act not of the body against itself but of the will against the body. Yet here I beheld a body that was going to die rather than change its nature . . . You did not want to die, but you were dying.' Michael K's long siege at the farm has changed his very constitution—his body is no longer receptive to food. He is subverting the seemingly axiomatic principle that we are by nature meant to consume.

I started working harder and eating less. I crashed so many times, too feverish to finish dinner, too insomniac to face breakfast. I read books on mindfulness: how to taste a single raisin slowly as if it were the food of the gods. I learnt to cook broken rice gruel, eat yoghurt, drink green tea. The newspapers talked of healthy eating now and diabetes, and the neighbourhood was crammed with faddish restaurants that shut down before you could walk twice through their doors. I ate boiled carrots every morning and no longer ate meat. So many years of all that living flesh passing through my own! 'Odd that we eat birds and animals, growing like us,' I read in a poem by Jeet Thayil. I had a dream about cutting open a fish that spilt out my own menstrual blood into my hands.

The other day, walking down Church Street, a little past seven on a Saturday night, I felt slightly alienated by all the new restobars and gastropubs and the girls in stilettos stepping over the broken pavements to get to them, places with names like 'Smallys' and 'Russshh'. Time was running out, there was too little of it now to make memories or feel regret for wasted, overfed youth, no time to hanker, compare this with that—barely enough time to eat.

My husband and I often make salted porridge for dinner. We don't eat French fries more than once in four weeks. We still speak of food—remember that risotto in Verona, that bag of smoked prawns in Waxholmen, that dumpling soup in the old quarter of Beijing, remember that . . . ? We go out for a meal now and then. We order a plate of something and a drink or two. We share a main course, we skip the sweet. And after we have finished, paid the bill, are walking home through the drizzle, it occurs to us that we are full. That is, we realize we are no longer hungry.

ACKNOWLEDGEMENTS

Versions of some of these stories previously appeared in *Granta*, *Indian Quarterly*, *Verve*, *Moving Worlds*, *Mint Lounge*, *Griffith Review* and *Asia Literary Review*. The lines of poetry quoted on pages 90 and 92 are from Adil Jussawalla's *Gulestan*. Reproduced with the kind permission of the author.

The Cosmopolitans

Shortlisted for the Crossword Book Award

Qayenaat is a drifting, solitary, sensitive figure at the edge of the Bangalore art scene. When world-famous artist Baban Reddy, once a young man who hung on her every word, returns to the city to show his latest artwork, all her old longings rise to the surface. Baban's arrival accompanies other momentous events and sets Qayenaat off on the most unexpected journey of her life—to the heart of rural, war-torn India, and into a relationship with the unlikeliest of men.

The Cosmopolitans is a novel of ideas and emotions—one that questions the place of art in modern life, and draws a vivid portrait of a woman at odds with the world. Tender and wry in equal measure, and rich in thought and insight, it confirms Anjum Hasan as one of our most exciting novelists today.

'Anjum Hasan brings an ironic and subtle intelligence to a great novelistic theme'—Pankaj Mishra

'Perspicacious, funny, and at times profound'—Amit Chaudhuri

'A writer of worth, and worth reading'—*The Hindu*

Difficult Pleasures

Shortlisted for the Hindu Literary Prize

A solitary economist drives from France to Sweden to try and redeem a tragedy; a boy fervently hopes his father will not miss his appearance in a school play; a painter on the way to Europe is about to board the wrong flight; a village boy leaves school for the bright lights of Bangalore; a man tries to stop time.

Wry, tender, borderline surreal, *Difficult Pleasures* is a collection of stories about the need to escape and the longing to belong. Accomplished, ambitious and full of surprises, this is a masterful collection from one of India's most gifted young writers.

'The thirteen stories in *Difficult Pleasures* are a good indicator why Anjum Hasan is widely regarded as a rising star on the literary horizon, as fluid in prose as poetry'—*Hindu Literary Review*

'You will get hooked'—*Express Buzz*

Lunatic in My Head

Shortlisted for the Crossword Book Award

It's raining in Shillong. Eight-year-old Sophie Das has just realized she is adopted, but there is also the baby kicking inside her mother's stomach whom she is dying to meet. IAS aspirant Aman Moondy is planning a first-of-its-kind Happening and praying the lovely Concordella will come. College lecturer Firdaus Ansari is going to finish her thesis, have a hard talk with her boyfriend, and then get the hell out. Poetic, funny, tender, *Lunatic in My Head* is an unforgettable portrait of a small town and of three people joined to each other in an intricate web, determined to break out of their destinies.

'Haunting, lyrical and daring, bringing fresh air into the stale confines of Indian writing'—Siddhartha Deb

'The delicacy and pungency of her portraits . . . is very striking'
—*Mint*